THE CHILDREN OF THE LIGHTNING

JUDAS THE HERO

MARTIN DAVEY

This is a work of fiction. Names, characters, places, and incidents either are the product of the author's imagination or are used fictitiously. Any resemblance to actual persons, living or dead, events, or locales is entirely coincidental.

Copyright © 2020 by Martin Davey

All rights reserved. No part of this book may be reproduced or used in any manner without written permission of the copyright owner except for the use of quotations in a book review. For more information, address:
adam@strangemediagroup.com

This paperback edition September 2020

Cover design by Jem Butcher Design
Published by SMG

www.strangemediagroup.com

ISBN: 9798681779278

For Natalie,
the angel that helps me battle my demons every day

CONTENTS

1	Soldiers of the Lightning	1
2	A Ghost Knows Another Ghost from Afar	8
3	Ice in the Eye	39
4	Iron Wings	56
5	Evenor	66
6	The Graveyard Grapevine	76
7	Silver Spears of Death	83
8	Destiny Calls from the Dark	97
9	Black Fire in the Sky	104
10	The Turning	109
11	The Wave Killer	129
12	Standing and Delivering	145
13	Your Money or Your Life	152
14	Silver Swords in the Sky	162
15	The Ghost Fleet	170

16	The Badge of Betrayal	195
17	Jung and Kessel	197
18	The Doors of Death	204
19	Two Grey Ghosts	217
20	The Hidden Doorway	225
21	A Fool Rushes In	230
22	Fight and Flight	236
23	Above and Beyond	241
24	All Hands	248
25	The Sea Calls	259
26	Fire and Water	263
27	The New Blitz	266
28	A Ghost Dies	276
29	Calleva	286
30	The Ley Line Express	294

1 SOLDIERS OF THE LIGHTNING

Millennium Eve, 1999, London.

The silence was deafening.
 The whole city seemed to be holding its breath. The cars, normally so loud and aggressive, were mute, impotent and stationary. Their bright, yellow eyes were shut tight, and their engines were dead to the world. London's low-level hum and sky roar had been turned down. Fewer planes criss-crossed the sky above, and the all-day chorus of alarms and horns had been paused, just for tonight.

The only road users out in number were the delivery cyclists with their big green boxes packed with hot Indian takeaways and rapidly-cooling pizzas. Keeping the riders company were horny tomcats looking for love, and urban foxes looking for half-eaten hamburgers.

The pubs were packed to the rafters with people

desperate to see the new century in. Inside, sweat dribbled down the windows like reversed rain, and air-conditioning units struggled to cope. Loud music was playing, but hardly anyone was listening.

Images of the world's other big cities were being looped on giant flat-screen televisions on walls. Hopeful punters strained every sinew in their necks in order to try to catch the eyes of the bar-folk. Everyone was desperate to get a round in before Big Ben started to welcome in another year with its booming chimes and spiky coat of fireworks.

Behind the bar in every single one of these smelly public houses, the glass-washing machines were doing overtime, belching small clouds of hot steam into the faces of the harassed barmen and women that fed them again and again and again. Tall glasses, shot glasses, cocktail glasses and pint pots went in dirty and came out clean and hot, turning ice-cold lager into warm yellow stuff within seconds.

The floors were already starting to get sticky with spilt beer and warm wine, and chewing gum and squashed cherries from rubbish mocktails were rapidly multiplying under-foot. Five-pound notes, and sad, never to be used condoms peppered the spaces underneath the small, round wooden tables that heaved under the weight of drinks that would never be drunk and the elbows of boys and girls that would regret everything the following morning.

Forget the carpet cleaning cost, the plasma screen repair bill, and the ticking off from the local police force for public order offences in your pub. And you can stuff Christmas Eve, Christmas Day and any other public holiday for that matter. New Year's Eve is where a publican's real money is made.

Customers had already started making best friends with complete strangers. Any other night of the year they'd have been giving each other the 'London look'. The 'don't talk to me, I don't want to know you' look.

But tonight, they were giving it a rest, because tonight was a special night. It was nearly time to join hands and celebrate. This was the big one. This wasn't just the end of the year, this was the end of an era. In 23 minutes precisely, the skyline would turn red, white and blue with fireworks, and the city would erupt with hollow, forced cheers, and plastic goodwill.

Policemen had been told to turn two blind eyes to the punchy little boys who couldn't handle their ale and were busy creating hot steamy rivers of urine in the alleyways and on street corners. They had also been advised to pose for as many 'selfies' as they could. It had not been a great year for public relations, so the Superintendent's instruction to "Be Nice" was being followed to the letter, although the cells would fill up at exactly the same rate regardless. But in the heavens at least, the skyline was still undisturbed, and with 15 minutes to go no premature ejaculations of light could be seen, while the great river beneath it looked like it was full of submerged pearls.

At the heart of the city stands St. Paul's Cathedral, no longer the tallest building in the city of London itself, but by far the most iconic.

At the top of this architectural homage to St. Peter

by Sir Christopher Wren, is a small *tempietto*.

It's an odd little room, or rather structure, being square rather than circular, and sitting incongruously on top of the 'Golden Gallery' right at the very top of the main dome.

The tempietto doesn't get many visitors at all, because it is practically impossible to gain entry to it. One of the official guides that takes the tourists around the building tells the same joke every day.

"We had a guest from Tibet, last week – one of those Sherpa fellas. He needed to be airlifted down, that's how high it is. Anyone feel like a challenge today? No? Don't blame you; the view's better from the London Eye, and it does all the work!

"Moving on, ladies and gentlemen, let me show you the rest of the cathedral…"

Tonight, though, it has visitors that have made the climb easily. These men have not come to see the architecture, or to view the fireworks. Their intentions are far more sinister.

The two figures that stand at the centre of the small, dark room have a different series of explosions in mind. Both men are wearing black robes that swish on the floor as they move around. Short puffs of breath escape from their hoods at regular intervals as they prepare the room; this vantage point may have views, but it lacks heating, or double-glazed windows. Strange symbols are embroidered on the arms of their robes, and when the symbols catch the moonlight, the silver thread strobes for a second.

There are now 10 minutes to go.

One of the men checks his watch and begins to write four names on the floor, in chalk. Then he takes out four black and white photographs, each of which shows a child wearing the uniform of the Hitler Youth movement. He places each one on top of the corresponding chalked name.

The other man, who is considerably shorter, takes a metal rod from within the folds of his robe. The rod is approximately one metre in length and 30 millimetres in diameter. When the rod catches the light, it gives off a cold, cruel, silver glow.

Etched into the metal are four names, repeating over and over again up and down its length in a spiral of mathematical precision. The man lays the rod down on the floor at his feet and steps away from it, carefully. The rod twitches uncontrollably, like a patient in a psychiatric ward waiting for the squeak of the medication trolley.

Both of the men then throw back the hoods of their robes, and take up position on opposite sides of the room, facing each other. They are careful not to move the photographs, or touch the silver rod. The spell that they begin to cast is not welcome in this holy place, and the building fights back. The air crackles ominously, and the taller man looks nervously down at the rod and the photographs on the floor.

"Something is missing," he says.

"You are right. This is missing," says the small man.

He produces a shiny, well-oiled, silver, Luger pistol, and calmly shoots the other man in the face. Blood sprays out of the hole that's left behind, and what remains of the man crumples to the floor. A tiny droplet flies across the room and spatters onto the handle of the pistol. The red spot disrupts the symmetry of the red, black and white flag with the swastika on it. The little man lifts the weapon to his mouth and licks the blood off with relish.

"Powerful magic needs complete faith and a powerful show of force to give it life. That, my friend, was why you were brought along. Your power was needed to break the defences of the building. You have earned your place now, may your passing be swift."

The silver rod on the ground begins to hum and glow even brighter; the human sacrifice has given it life.

The little man passes his hand over the rod, then points upwards toward the ceiling.

The rod begins to float, then turn in the air. It moves through 180 degrees, giving the impression of the minute hand on an invisible clock, rotating its way to 12.

Then, it starts to glide upwards. It touches the ceiling, then passes slowly through the plaster like a hot needle through a slab of butter before disappearing entirely. It comes to rest one metre later, having found its resting place inside the golden cross that points straight up at the heavens, atop the dome of St. Paul's. Then, like a living missile, it goes to sleep, ready to play its part in a magical blitz.

There are now two minutes to go.

Then there are two seconds.

And then the sky burns with millions of pounds of pyrotechnic fire and light, and all the people cheer.

They are unaware that a magical lightning conductor has been hidden in the city they love, just waiting to channel the hellfire and hatred of a beaten race of self-proclaimed super-humans.

The tempietto inside St. Paul's is empty now; all of the photographs have been collected, the chalk has been brushed away, and the body of the man has disappeared. The little man has left the Golden Gallery and taken a seat opposite the Apse and High Altar on the ground floor.

The bells of London start to clash, and their collective boom makes the world shake.

Stranghold – for that is the small man's real name – crosses one leg over the other, and sits back. A smile creeps onto his face; it looks unnatural there. He has hidden his robe where no one will ever find it, and has changed back into his favourite suit.

A fleck of dust floats down from the ceiling and rests on his thigh; it spoils the symmetry of his pressed woollen trousers, so he flicks at it and watches approvingly as it floats away.

The Millennium is here at last, and all of the magical rods are in place. When we have the book and the children are finally ready, we will light up the sky once more with such power that this city will be scratched from the pages of history like the scab it is. The death toll will make the Blitz seem like the pop of a champagne cork!

High above in the dome, a bell sounded again. Before the sound had faded, the little man was gone.

2 A GHOST KNOWS ANOTHER GHOST FROM AFAR

15th June 2018, Jersey.

The jagged trident of lightning tore across the deep indigo of the night sky, turning the world into a vivid black and white negative. Mother Nature was having a hissy fit. Her second destructive white flash of atmospheric anger caused the island of Jersey to jump out of the darkness for a split second, then disappear twice as quickly.

The angry little storm passed on into the dark of the night, drifting away into the distance diminishing slowly, and shifting from side to side like a drunken man's ravings as the bell sounded for closing time. Then, all was quiet once again.

The ocean heaved and frothed stubbornly. It was surly and argumentative, ancient and deep, and it would not be talked down to by a mere storm. It gave as good as it got, crashing and shouting back at the sky above.

The sky had already turned a deaf ear, though, so the sea lashed out at the nearest thing it could find, sending wave after wave to attack the nearby land. With great energy and enthusiasm the waves crashed up against the small island, surging up the vertical surface of the cliffs, metre by metre, climbing higher and higher until, like a pole-vaulter at the extent of his pole's flex, they faltered, falling back down to the ever-moving, liquid surface below.

High up in the cliff face was a big hole that the waves would never be able to reach, however hard they tried.

It was a dark eye that never blinked, and in its iris stood a strange little boy.

The boy should have been at home, tucked up in bed and dreaming of daredevil pilots, muscular sportsmen, warm motherly embraces and bright, sunshine-filled mornings full of youthful mayhem. But he wasn't.

Instead, he looked down at the waves that crashed onto the pebble beach far below; as they struck the shore the cliff-face shivered, and it seemed as if all the sounds of the world were being turned off, just for a second or two.

This gap in the rock was just one of many similar fissures. If you knew the island's defences well, you could have picked out a handful on this stretch of the cliffs alone. The local fishermen knew most of them, and used them just like road signs. If you passed the point, and were level with the 'Gun Hole', then it was only 25 minutes back to port, as the seagull flies.

Whole colonies of screeching birds and clicking bats made their homes in some, while in others you'd find only the spiked barrels of impotent howitzers and countless spent brass bullet cases. Many of them occurred naturally, having been formed and shaped by the wind and the rain. The deepest and darkest, however, were all man-made.

The particular hole that the boy, whose name was Joachim Weiss, stood in now, was his favourite; it was the highest, hardest to reach, and most importantly – the emptiest. He had removed the signs that led to this place years ago. He was the only visitor, and he liked it that way.

Joachim cocked his head to one side and smiled. He liked the slow hiss of the black, shiny pebbles as they surged back down the beach, chasing the waves back into the sea. Having spent the last three months below ground in relative silence, all of the sounds that surrounded him here were stimulating. He liked the little round stones most of all though; they would fight to keep the waves at bay until they were reduced to grains of sand, or until time itself ran out. Hiss followed boom again and again on the beach below, as each side gave no quarter to the other. It was, by his reckoning, the first thing that had made him feel happy that year.

He was wearing his Hitler Youth uniform, the same one he'd been wearing for over 70 years. It was still spotlessly clean, and pressed with such vigour that the creases looked razor-sharp in the moonlight. In the lapel of his starched white shirt was a small, red, circular metal badge. There were deep, violent scratches etched into the enamel surface, while the swastika that once sat proudly at its centre was riven in two and barely recognisable now. The boy hated the badge very much. He despised what it stood for now, and he hated the fact that he could not take the damn thing off. It hadn't always been that way, though.

Joachim Weiss had loved his uniform in the beginning. He remembered the special, sunny afternoon when his mother and father had summoned him into the parlour and presented it to him, watching from the comfort of the chaise longues on the other side of the room as he tried it on for the first time.

There was such pride in their eyes when he stood to attention and gave both of them a hearty "Heil Hitler!" He had made his salute with such force that when his arm came up his hand had knocked his father's cap straight off the sideboard. Luckily for him, it had missed the opening to the fireplace by inches.

His father, a stern man of few words and even fewer smiles and hugs, managed to give him a pat on the shoulder, and ruffled his hair. There was almost a hint of love in the gesture. But that was then. That was 1945.

Everything about Joachim, from the centre parting in his perfectly blonde hair to the folds in his troop leader scarf, was ridiculously neat and tidy. He was impeccable. Not one single, solitary hair on his head moved, even though there was a gale blowing down the tunnel. The fabric of his clothes didn't display a solitary ripple either. Because Joachim Weiss was dead. He was one of the ghost children of Jersey, and he was waiting for the world to end.

The tunnel went dark for a second because the clouds overhead had joined hands in an attempt to block out the moon. Then the squalls arrived. The air filled with water, and the wind increased in strength, pushing the waves even harder and whipping their tips into a white froth that blew into the air. Joachim looked out, enjoying the sudden change in the weather. It would have sent the people up top running for shelter or searching for an umbrella, but he was a ghost, and ghosts like things that make them feel more alive than the living.

He stayed at the entrance of the tunnel for a long time and was thinking about remaining there to watch the sun come up, when the nasty little badge in his lapel began to glow red in the darkness like an angry, blinking, bloodshot eye. He quickly took two paces back into the darkness and turned away from the outside world; if the red light was seen by a passing fishing vessel the coastguard would have been informed, and that would not have been good for him or the rest of the ghost children living in the tunnels below. There were enough rumours of strange and eerie things happening on these cliffs as it was, and Joachim didn't want to be responsible for adding another to the list.

He shuffled forward again and took up his position

at the edge of the tunnel, looking out at the dark sea. He scanned the horizon once again. There was nothing out there tonight, apart from a seagull battling valiantly against a spiteful headwind. He watched as the bird banked and coasted back and forth, exploring the channels in the air and looking for a hole in the wind to fly through; none presented itself, and the bird screeched angrily as it was forced back again and again. Finally, the bird gave up. It had given everything, and now looked spent and weary. The wind would not let it pass, so it retreated back into the calm of the dark night sky in the sheltered cove on the other side of the point.

Joachim smiled, recognising the sense of futility and despair that the two of them shared; neither of them could get away from the island or find rest whilst they were still on it.

The badge glowed again. He was being summoned from down below. The priests of the Black Sun were gearing up for war and their foot soldiers had better be ready.

Earlier that morning Joachim had been told that Stranghold, one of the most powerful magicians in the order, was returning to the island after completing a secret mission. The rest of the ghost children were wary of the little man; he had a reputation for being short-tempered. Some of the older boys who were much taller than Stranghold were fond of saying that his height was in perfect relation to his temper threshold, but they only whispered this behind his back, or when he was deep down in the lower tunnels.

At precisely 21.00hrs they were to be ready, all present and correct, in neat, regimented lines, wearing their best uniforms and their most hopeful smiles.

"If only Riefenstahl could see us now," muttered Joachim.

The island evidently did not like its secrets told to the world; a sharp gust of wind censored his words, blowing them away into the silence of the night sky.

The waves continued to come and go, and if Joachim could have thrown himself down into their cold, rolling embrace he would have done so, but he could not get off the island by any means. He'd tried to leave the black city and the deep tunnels many times before. He'd even thrown himself into the sea, hoping that the waves would help him escape. But there was an invisible barrier all around the island that could not be breached or scaled. It was a wall built with bricks made from the souls of the innocent. Its foundations were strong, and they were anchored deep down in the seabed, while up above it reached into the sky forever; the only things that could ever get over it were the clouds.

Joachim sat down and leaned back against the granite wall, closing his eyes and listening to the sounds of the real world going on around him. Ghosts can sit and lay down on the ground if they choose, although they have to concentrate in order to fix themselves to the earth. It takes an even greater degree of energy and willpower for a ghost to go further, interacting with physical objects and becoming a Poltergeist, and it is a skill that only few can master. But all the energy and willpower in the world are not enough if the ghost has lost all hope. Hope is the battery that gives them form. This is why most appear as faded smudges; they are just faint echoes of the spirit they once were, having died twice and become one with the mist in the air after their cries and wailing went unheard for too long. Joachim had clung to as much hope as he could muster, and it enabled him to anchor himself to the present, going to places that some of the others could not. He knew the rock was there but couldn't exactly feel it; it should have been cold and wet for one thing, but it wasn't.

There were some benefits to being dead, he thought to himself.

Today was the anniversary of Joachim's death, and the reason for his trip to the surface. Yesterday, the grey sadness had come to visit again. He noticed its heavy tread behind him, its parasitic hunger for his warmth and the ever-diminishing sands of joy that remained inside him. Today, it wanted to sap his strength even more by wrapping its long, cold arms around him to settle on his shoulders like a heavy, wet cloak. He defied the feeling, though, and cast it off.

It always came at this time of year, so he'd been ready for it. He would not give into it. He would not be like some of the other weaker children who had allowed themselves to drift into the fading mist, disappearing into nothingness. No way. Not after all this. He was a fighter, and if he was the last ghost child left on the island then so be it.

He opened his eyes and stood up again. Now was not the time for inward reflection or tears. The chin tremble could get lost, too. He attempted to spit, as young boys always do when they are perched high up in a tree or leaning out and over the edge of a tall building. He would dearly love to see a small wet cloud of phlegm shoot out and down into the sea below, but there was nothing inside him to cough up.

Instead, he turned away from the surface world again and headed down into the city of black tunnels and dark waterways. To the place where all of the rest of the remaining ghost children lived, and still dreamed of the mothers and fathers that had murdered them and then run away.

Joachim stepped over a small pool of rainwater that collected the moonlight at the entrance to the hole, descending into the gloom and the deep darkness of his cold world. Soon he was alone again, with only the deep hum of the wind ranging around in the tunnels for company. He didn't need to count the turnings or leave a trail of breadcrumbs because he knew this maze like the back of his opaque hand, and a short time later, after taking the right amount of right turns and the right amount of lefts, he found the tunnel he was looking for.

The main tunnel was like a stone spine that reached deep down into the bowels of the island. You travelled up or down the spine by walking along a series of angled walkways. It was spirit-level straight, with smooth, rendered walls and chequered flagstones on the floor. A perfect German tunnel, it was ridiculously clean and neat, and looked like the paint had been applied with a set square. There were lights on the ceiling, too, but they had not been turned on in over a decade. Only the moths mourned their passing. It was not quite pitch black in these tunnels; there was some light here, down in the depths. A light that clung to the dead stone and would never let go. It was a weak, dying torch battery sort of light, flickering and pulsing with the faintest blue tinge. In the swamps and the forests of Europe where this eerie light could also be seen, locals gave the glow a name. They called it a Will-o-the-Wisp, and advised travellers never to follow it because those that did were never seen again. In these tunnels the light was supernatural, and it did not come on with the flick of a switch.

Joachim spotted a marble on the floor; it must have been dropped by one of the living children that had accompanied their living parents on a trip to see the spooky tunnels of Jersey many years ago. He picked it up, and rolled it away. He saw it disappear around one of the bends in the corridor that sloped away from him, and expected to see it waiting at the bottom. It had gone by the time he got there, though; it had either reached terminal velocity and shattered against one of the walls, or one of the other ghost children had stolen it.

He was thinking about the marble when he felt a bat flying straight towards him. He stopped walking and stood perfectly still.

He hoped that the bat would fly past him, but it was

not to be.

Bats could not see the ghosts with their echolocation. It was almost as if they knew something was there, but couldn't see what it was until the last second, panicking, and swerving or pulling up sharply, usually into the nearest wall.

The bat came straight at him as he knew it would, giving out a high-pitched squeak of alarm just before it crashed into the tunnel wall and thudded to the ground with a sickening plop. Joachim looked down at the poor little quivering body and shook his head.

The bats were just like everything else on this cursed island, he thought. We ghosts are invisible, even to creatures that can see in the dark.

He heard the slap-slap of a broken, leathery wing against the tiled floor as he walked on, before all fell silent again. Joachim felt sorry for the bat, but there was nothing he could do; he carried on down the tunnel, thinking of black pebbles and the soothing hiss they made.

Joachim was halfway down the spine when his badge gave two more quick bursts of red light. These indicated that it was nearly time to receive Herr Stranghold at Landing Pier 9, so he hurried, half-heartedly, down the tunnel. Whatever else they may or may not be, German ghosts are never late.

At the end of the Second World War, the German forces had evacuated from the island of Jersey in a really big hurry. If their arrival on the island had been swift, then their departure set a new record in running away. Their race was run, their war was lost, and in their blind panic to escape the approaching warships of the victorious British Navy they panicked, doing something that would haunt the island forever more.

In the small town of St. Helier, the German Commandant stationed on the island had followed protocol and burned all of his most sensitive papers in a bonfire in the courtyard of his HQ building. The smoke from the fire turned the walls of the courtyard black, and the men whose job it was to feed the flames took the swastikas from the walls and tied them around their mouths in order to breathe. In the fierce heat and the dancing orange light they looked like demonic imps shovelling coals into the pits of some unholy landscape.

The Commandant was very close to fulfilling his orders and fleeing with the rest of his general staff when he received a last-minute communiqué from Berlin. He read it three times to make sure that what he was reading made actual sense and was not the result of a typing mistake, or a fault with the deciphering machine along the hall. As each evil word landed on his conscience with a thud, his heart tightened and shrivelled inside his chest. He had heard from friends serving on other fronts that atrocities were being committed to order by certain sections of the Army. But he treated them with scepticism; they were unspeakable acts, and surely no serving German officer would really countenance carrying them out.

Now he knew that the stories were all true.

He had the proof in his very hands; hands that

shook and trembled with disgust and shame. He had pledged an oath, though, just like many of those same friends; he would be able to hide behind that oath for now, but he knew deep down that the words he would soon have to utter were poison to him.

He convened a crash meeting in the town hall. As soon as the escape ships had moored in the channel and the patrol boats had come ashore to pick up the troops and the general staff, Operation Sever was to be put into action immediately.

All of the island's children with local mothers and German fathers were to be collected and handed over to another high-ranking officer on the island straight away, with no questions asked. The parents were told that the children were needed for the war effort. But it was not specified to any of the parents that night which war they would be contributing to.

The parents reasoned and argued with each other. Tears fell, and angry words were thrown first this way, then the other, before the parents were finally given a good old Nazi ultimatum. They could either hand their children over to the secret Black Sun Division, receiving a first-class ticket on the next ship back to the Fatherland or a one-way ticket to South America in return, or they could refuse; if they chose the second option they would be left behind, and handed over to the islanders for retribution and punishment.

The choice was an easy one when it was put that way; after all, the children would be doing something valuable and meaningful, and they would all come home to be reunited with their families soon enough.

Of course they would. After all, they were just children; mixed-race children, admittedly, but still only children. They all believed the big lie. Or at least, they pretended to. The mothers knew, though. Mothers always know.

The Commandant promised them all, on his honour as an SS Officer and wearer of the Iron Cross with crossed swords and laurel leaves, that the children would be safe. They would become the future heroes of the Reich, bringing great pride and honour to their parents and families. But as he sailed away from the island later that night it wasn't the angry, choppy sea that was making him violently sick. He'd read those *bloody orders* in full, and he knew what was about to happen; he retched so hard that blood instead of vomit coated the deck beneath him.

It had been agreed by none other than the Fuhrer that the children were to be sacrificed for the greater good and the glory of the new German Empire. Their reward was great, but none of them would see another dawn or their parent's faces ever again.

The Commandant had sacrificed his honour that night – something he had never believed possible – and as he cried and rocked against the motion of the gunboat that was taking him away from the island for the last time, he saw the hopeful and reassured faces of the people he had betrayed everywhere he looked. They stared out at him from the puddles of water on the deck, and he saw the faces of the children in the spray of the ocean and the shape of the scudding clouds. They were everywhere, and they would not leave him even after he died.

Two months later the Commandant shot himself in the temple with his service pistol, saving the jury in Nuremberg the trouble of a trial, and the firing squad the regulation seven bullets.

After saying goodbye to their families that night, the children were driven away in soundproofed buses with blacked-out windows. The parents waved like inmates from an asylum, even though they could not see the faces of their offspring anymore. When the last bus had finally disappeared into the night, they collected their meagre possessions, boarded one of the fast patrol boats in the harbour, and were ferried from the shore to a waiting U-boat.

At exactly 01.00hrs the submarine submerged beneath the waves and disappeared.

At exactly 02.45hrs the children disappeared, too. Forever.

The children were taken for one last, moonlit walk along the coastal paths of their beautiful island home, around the high cliffs that lift Jersey from the waves like great dark, jagged shoulders, with views out to a sea that forgets quickly. When they reached the army's main observation turret – the largest on the island – they were given some refreshment before being told to change into their best Hitler Youth uniforms. Then, they all sang a song with made up words, before one of the men put on a cloak and wished them all good luck in a language that none of them had ever heard before. Then one by one, they were taken by the hand, and callously pitched over the cliff edge, into the dark night sky, and oblivion.

Hundreds of children disappeared that night; no bodies or remains were ever found on the beach, or returned to the land by the sea. The children had existed for only a short while. Some had only had six summers in which to run and play in the sun under the watchful eyes of their parents and guardians, making up stories and creating memories that they would never live to share.

The men of the Black Sun made sure of that. And after throwing the children to their death from the cliffs, they scurried away to the safety of their secret underground citadel, like the cowardly rats they were.

The tunnels that lead down to the dark city where the men of the Black Sun sleep are old. In Napoleon's time, the French and the English took it in turns to increase and enlarge the network , as they sought to build even stronger defensive positions to deter invaders, or to create places where they could hide the wealth or secrets of nations. These old rough, dark and dank passageways are still accessible today, and for the price of a week's half-board holiday in the Algarve you can walk them yourself, armed with a torch and listening through headphones to their history from a guide who has never seen them in real life.

The Germans needed to dig deeper than anyone else before them, because like all German plans, theirs were the biggest and the best. But the rock and stone down in the depths of the world is strong and dark, and to begin with it would not yield to the digging machines that the German engineers designed to eat it.

So, after a number of false starts, they decided to send the engineers away, and instead built their tunnel system with magic and with death. One day there were diesel engines belching out their poisonous breath deep underground, the next there were tunnels. Overnight they had appeared, miles of them, and in the morning the digging engines were tipped into the sea.

There are large open spaces down there that no sky has ever looked down upon. No rain falls on its streets, and no wind blows through the branches of a tree, because nothing can take root down there apart from sorrow, sadness, and despair. And there is a main square in this subterranean city, from which alleys, and buildings, and long, silent canals filled with dark, brackish seawater spread like arteries. This great parade ground is where all of the ghost children come to stand in neat lines, waiting for the future under great red, rotting flags that will never billow again.

Joachim emerged from the main tunnel into the watery light of the cave and looked around to make sure that no one was watching. They weren't, the coast was clear, so he set off. He hurried down the long, empty street to the bridge that spanned one of the outer canals. Once he'd crossed that, he took a short cut through Barracks Building Number 5, and emerged on the far side of the main square. He could see a few stragglers nearby drifting over to join the assembled ranks, so he fell in with them, casually taking his place at the front of his troop number.

Gunter, the flag bearer for the troop and his second in command, was standing in his usual position; he snapped to attention when he saw Joachim appear. Gunter had lived down the street from Joachim when they were alive. His father had been a member of the SS Intelligence corps, and Gunter had unfortunately taken after him. He was a nasty boy, really; a bully, and a bit of a bore. But he was a German soldier too. He gave the troop banner a quick mechanical shake, the small, rolled-up flag at the top unfurled, and the symbol of the ghost children's army appeared in all its faded glory. It was a silver lightning bolt on a red silk background, with a silver rod running through it.

All of the children were smartly dressed in their Number 1 Uniform. The silver on their buckles and belts looked white in the blue light. The leather of their belts and holsters shone and creaked as they shuffled into position. They looked incredible, but forlorn. On closer inspection you would say that even the sadness and despair in their eyes was uniform. Children fidget and gossip in whispers. Children play games and mock and tease and fart. But these children could not, and would not, because they were dead.

As Joachim stood rigidly to attention, listening to the rustle of banners and shrill piping of the bats overhead, he felt even more alone than ever before, so he practised remembering the faces of his parents and the names of streets and the things he'd seen when he lived up top. He imagined the wallpaper in his bedroom, the white dinner plates with the SS lightning bolts on the table, the rain dripping from his tent flap in the back garden. He pictured them all in his mind's eye and gave them all the detail he could imagine and remember, and after he had made them all, he clung to them like a lost soul on a life raft in the angriest of seas. It was at times like these, when he was with the other children, that he felt like he should just *give up*, as most of them had done already, and forget ever being alive. But there was something deep down inside him that whispered and cajoled and gnawed at him, and it would not let him rest.

The thing whispered to him, telling him that change was coming, that a rescue was being planned. And it told him that when it did, he would finally escape this dread underground city.

"Please let it be soon," he said under his breath.

"Sir?" said Gunter.

"Nothing, just clearing my throat. Eyes front, please."

Joachim looked up at the flags that hung from the roof of the cave. The once bright, blood redness of them had faded, and the sea salt had won its war against their fabric, turning them into weakened purple banners shot through with silver streaks.

Everything dies. The people fighting for a flag, the country that the flag flies over, and then the flag itself, he thought.

Directly in front of the assembled ranks was the main canal. It ran straight through the centre of the great hall like a solid black bar of night inlaid with black stars. When you looked down on it from the highest point in the hall, the canal looked like a long, thin trap door leading down to Hell itself.

The troops were lined up in perfect formation along the edge of the canal, and when Joachim looked down onto the surface of the water he got the impression that he was standing on a big black mirror. His upside-down self looked strange and alien, because there was hope in its eyes. While he was searching for life in the reflections of the other soldiers in his troop, the water began to heave and roll, splashing over the lip of the canal and running across the floor of the cave. No ghost child moved, or instinctively lifted a highly-polished leather boot; instead, they just watched as the water flowed right through their legs and feet, then drained away into the gutters.

Next, a periscope pierced the surface of the water, like a finger exploring a hole in a sheet. The single glass eye at the top swivelled and surveyed their ranks, then the flat stump of the conning tower emerged.

The ghost children snapped to attention as one. All those hours marching and drilling had turned them into a perfect military unit with all the discipline and rigour expected of the German child soldier. Their synchronised movements, culminating in a salute, were performed with such rhythm and precision that no visiting Field Marshall would find fault with their display today.

The submarine emerged from the depths and rocked back and forth for a second before settling. Its engines clanked and thudded. The noises it made sounded as if they had been wrapped in a thick sock.

Then it fell silent. The great round bubbles of white water that the ballast tanks pumped out settled, and turned grey on the surface of the water.

The forward hatch popped open and a column of light like a miniature anti-aircraft spotter lamp shot up into the darkness, giving the bats hanging there a heart attack. The flapping of their wings sounded like muted thunder, and rolled away just as quickly. A werewolf dressed in full Kriegsmarine uniform scrambled up a ladder from inside. It secured the hatch, then loped forward, cast out a bowline, and made the submarine fast to the quay.

Then Stranghold appeared. He was very smartly dressed, wearing a suit so perfect it would have made a Saville Row tailor weep with joy. Under his arm was a large, leather-bound rectangular object. The whiteness of his knuckles suggested that it was very valuable or very delicate. If the ghost children had known the importance of the object, and of what it would eventually cost them, they would have saluted again, then run away and hidden in the tunnels as fast as they could. As it was, the little man looked down on the children from the deck of the submarine and gave them a lazy salute in return. It was more of an arm flick, really, and he'd made it with his left arm, which as every good Nazi knows is the wrong side. He cleared his throat, and made a speech which must have taken all of five minutes to dash off; it was short, and dull, and would not have roused an elderly militia, let alone a youthful army.

"Soldiers of the Reich, we have returned! Here in my arms is the key that will unlock the miracle weapons! The weapons that we were promised for so long! Hoped for, yearned for! Now, they are truly within our reach.

"They lie sleeping deep down in the rock below us, but with this mighty tome we shall unlock their secrets, sending them out into the world and watching as they lay waste to our enemies. Soon you will be free; soon you will finally realise your potential, and understand why you are so important to the Black Sun and the future of our new empire.

"Our time has come, soldiers! This island, this place, this prison of yours for so long, will no longer hold you! Soon, my children, very soon, you will make your mark on this world."

Silence applied the full stop to his speech. Instead of wild, euphoric cheering, the only sound to be heard was the slap of water against the lichen-sided quay, and a ripple from one of the moth-eaten flags above. Joachim smiled and looked sideways at Gunter to gauge his reaction, but the face of the troop's flagbearer was set, and his eyes were locked on the swastika painted on the conning tower of the submarine.

The little man stood there, waiting for some sort of response. When none came, the expression on his face changed; it troubled Joachim. He didn't look angry; he just smiled the sort of smile you save for a horse with a broken leg, or the smile you spare a child that doesn't get picked for adoption. It was a sort of pity, but with something else nasty underpinning it. Joachim suddenly remembered where he'd seen such a smile before. It was a goodbye smile, and he'd seen it before on the faces of the men that had pushed him and the other children off the cliff long ago.

Stranghold surveyed the children once more, adjusted the package under his arm, and then climbed down the ladder on the outside of the submarine. When he reached the bottom rung, he stepped gingerly onto the quayside. The boat hissed and gurgled, as if to say goodbye; it could just have easily been good riddance – machines keep their own counsel, and rarely share it with the living.

He crossed the great hall quickly, walking with little pigeon steps, making for the huge, square opening that had been cut into the cold, dark stone of the cave wall. Above this doorway was the symbol of the Black Sun. It was big, bold, imposing and off-limits to the all but the men who practiced their dark magic down there in the lowest levels.

Joachim watched him saunter inside and become one with the blackness. He was about to dismiss his troop when two other men climbed up the ladder and stepped onto the gently rocking deck. They were not dressed like the other man at all.

Even from here he could see that these two were both strangers to any sort of sartorial style because they wore dark, ill-fitting suits with cream coloured shirts that in another life had once been white. Joachim didn't need to get any closer to know that the armpits of those shirts were yellow, and a line of brown grime would stretch across the inside of their collars. One of them was wearing a wide, red tie that swung rather than hung. Its point hung a good three inches from his belt, which was three inches too short for a tie according to any dress manual that he had ever read. The other man's tie, meanwhile, hung awkwardly, pointing almost diagonally across his chest.

Slovenly, thought Joachim. He could see their lapel pins shining in the gloom, and realised that they were of the Black Sun order, too. But they certainly weren't high ranking, that much was for sure. The faces of both men were instantly forgettable, because their features were blurred, and it had nothing to do with the light in the cave. It was almost as if you were looking at them through the bottom of a dirty glass; their eyes were smudges of darkness that shifted position on their faces and their mouths – or what Joachim thought were their mouths – drifted from side to side. Neither spoke, and it was obvious that they were under some sort of glamour, or spell, because they didn't even acknowledge the ranks of the ghost children arrayed in front of them; they simply climbed ashore and followed their master through the doorway.

Once they had gone, Joachim dismissed his troops. He watched them march across the parade ground and into the barracks, where they would drill, and sleep, and sit to attention, and wait.

From his position on the quayside, Joachim watched, as more and more werewolves ran up onto the deck; some would scratch and stretch, and occasionally one would look up, as if searching for the moon. They busied themselves unloading boxes, files, and strange-looking instruments. Then as quickly as they had appeared, they disappeared back inside. With two loud clangs the fore and aft hatches closed and locked, then they were gone.

All was quiet, then the Joachim heard a high-pitched whistle as the chief of the boat called the werewolves to their posts. Seconds later there was a whoosh, and the muffled sound of diesel engines springing to life. The boat was going to submerge. He was just about to go back to exploring the tunnels and listening to the sound of the wind and the reassuring hiss of the black pebbles, when another man suddenly appeared from behind the conning tower.

Joachim didn't know why he did what he did right there and then. Maybe it was the little whispering voice inside his head, or perhaps it was some sort of survival instinct, but he stepped quickly behind one of the huge columns that kept the roof of the cave from falling down on their heads, and watched and waited.

From where Joachim was hiding, he could see the man clearly. He was fairly tall, with black curly hair, and a round face that looked like it liked to smile a lot. He was dressed in a dark suit and, strangely, he carried a shoe in each hand.

The deck was cold and wet, so the man slipped his shoes on and gazed around the hall. It was obvious from the way he was dressed, and by the way he was acting, that he didn't want to be spotted. Was he a stow-away, or maybe even a spy?

Joachim should have sounded the alarm and called out the guard, but something told him not to, so he waited to see what the man would do next. After looking around the great hall and shaking his head incredulously a few times, the man climbed down the ladder and stepped on to the quayside. A bat came screaming out of the blackness, and the man ducked, instinctively. He shook his head again, then started to pace back and forth.

You're a long way from home, my friend, thought Joachim.

It was obvious that the man was not only lost, but also very confused. But then he saw the symbol of the Black Sun over the dark mouth of the tunnel, and he started to walk straight towards it.

Joachim had a choice to make, and not a lot of time to make it in; he crept across the hall using the columns as a screen, and followed. He got to the entrance a few seconds before the man and made up his mind. He knew what he was going to do, and damn the consequences.

"I wouldn't go in there if I were you," he said.

Ghosts don't do a lot of jumping, or widening of the eyes, or dropping of the bacon sandwich, because as a ghost you can see most things coming. But Williams nearly had a heart attack, or would have if he'd been alive. Because standing not more than five feet away from him was a young boy wearing a Hitler Youth uniform.

"I said, I wouldn't go down there if I were you. All of the ghosts that have done so have never returned."

Williams took a step back.

"Can you see me?"

Williams hadn't uttered a single word to anyone since he'd hitched a ride with Stranghold and his goons, and his voice sounded unnaturally loud in the darkness. He'd gone unnoticed and unseen by the whole crew of the submarine for the entirety of the short voyage; even the werewolves that crewed the boat had been unable to see him or smell him. So being addressed by one of the Hitler Youth in a cave underground was a jolt. A great big one.

Williams was urging his brain to reconnect with his mouth when the boy spoke again.

"Of course I can see you. And if you don't think fast, all of the other ghosts will be able to see you, too. I take it that you want to remain invisible and undetected by the Black Sun and the little man? If you do, then follow me, quickly!"

Joachim beckoned for the man to follow; he then ran across the slick, wet cobblestones without making a sound, and ducked into the nearest tunnel.

Sgt Williams of the Metropolitan Police Black Museum Occult Division, and DCI Judas Iscariot's right-hand ghost, had been through the life mangle over the past couple of weeks. He'd been in a WWII U-boat – one of Hitler's notorious Sea Wolves – and bunked down with a crew of men that were actually half man and half wolf. He'd seen giant archangels with flaming swords and a bad attitude fighting Jack the Ripper and John the Baptist on Clapham Common. He'd been murdered, then brought back to life – sort of – and now he was being asked to follow a member of the Hitler Youth down the rabbit hole. The part of his brain that normally filtered out the fantastic and the incredible had been retuned, so, he reacted the only way that he knew how, now, and went with the flow.

"Why not, what else could happen?" he said, and followed the boy inside the tunnel.

As the two ghosts disappeared the U-boat puffed out as much air as it needed to and started to sink. Within seconds it was gone, leaving only a collection of oily circles on the surface of the water.

40 minutes and several different tunnels later, Joachim drew back the heavy, rusted bolt of the blast door to gun emplacement SS10, and stepped inside with Williams. It was one of the last undiscovered gun mounts left on the island, the others having been commandeered by locals looking to make a fortune taking German and American tourists around them, showing them the old French artillery pieces that the Germans had liberated from them at the beginning of the war. Joachim had listened in to some of the commentary from these guides many years ago, and laughed at all the mistakes they had made. The men who served in these small, confined spaces weren't the crack troops everyone thought they'd been. For one thing, they stank like oxen in a sauna that was on fire most of the time. And as for the advanced and deadly sighting of the guns, half the time the gun crews would be on the field telephone, getting a dressing down from the Capitan of whichever German ship they'd accidentally fired upon!

SS10 was untouched. The bunks in the corner of the room were still there, as were the table and the chairs that the crews ate their dinner on. Some old black and white photographs had fallen to the floor, leaving a white square on the wall to prove they had once lived up there. The big gun was still present, of course, but it had been rolled as far back as possible, and a grey tarpaulin had been thrown over it; it looked like a small, black mountain that had grown inside a small, grey concrete box. The outpost was as far from the main hall as possible, and hopefully, Joachim thought, as far from the little man and the rest of his mind-reading brothers as possible, too. His guest sat down on the firing step of the cannon and loosened his tie, then looked down at his feet and started to chuckle. Joachim looked down, too, and saw why the man was laughing: his shoes were on the wrong feet. While he was correcting his mistake, Joachim had a chance to look at him more closely.

Joachim had remained standing, and seeing as he was the tenant and the man was a recently arrived guest, it seemed only right that he should be allowed to ask the questions first.

"So, who are you?"

The man tested the fit of each shoe and smiled. Joachim was right about his face; the man liked to smile.

"My name is Williams, and I am a policeman. I used to be a proper policeman, a real–life policeman, but as you can see, I'm not quite all there anymore. I'm following the dapper little German fellow who came here in the submarine. He has something that he stole from the organisation that I work for. It's a book I have to get hold of and keep safe until the cavalry arrives. That, in a nutshell, is who I am and why I'm here.

"Getting this book back isn't going to happen in the next five minutes, though, so before we go any further how about you help me out with something young fella? How is it that you can see me? Only a few living people can."

Now it was Joachim's turn to do something that he hadn't done for a long time. He smiled.

"That's easy. A ghost knows another ghost from afar," said Joachim.

"I think that we can help each other out, Herr Williams. At least, I know that I can help you get what you seek, but maybe you can help me with something in return? If I help you get what you want, will you try and help me get off this island?"

Williams looked up at the boy. Lots of strange things had happened to him recently and talking to another ghost shouldn't have fazed him, but this one was only a child, and that just couldn't ever feel right. He had nothing to lose, and everything to gain, and this strange little boy could have raised the alarm earlier but chose not to. He'd done him a massive favour by warning him about the tunnel with the Black Sun sign over it, too. But despite having had plenty of time to strategise during the last 24 hours, when he'd been hiding under an oily hammock in the torpedo room of a submarine listening to a man snoring and a werewolf farting, meeting a ghost child of the Hitler Youth was not something he'd planned for.

He had no idea of how to get hold of Judas, right

now, although he'd left him a note in the hope his boss had found it and was on his way. And he didn't know how to recover the book, either. He was going to need help. It didn't matter where that help came from right now, but first, he needed to establish some trust.

"What is your name, and why should I trust you? The little man is obviously some sort of German wizard, and here you are dressed up in the uniform of a Hitler Youth Sergeant, so I'm a bit suspicious, to say the least."

Williams watched the boy carefully.

The youth shuffled his feet, then adjusted the regimental scarf at his neck. Even though his eyes were pale and his body full of mist, there was something about him that shone in the darkness. He definitely looked like a true Aryan, but there was a sadness inside him that overpowered the arrogance Williams had expected to see.

"My name is Joachim Weiss, Herr Williams. And you can trust me because we both want to see the Black Sun destroyed. You want to stop them to make sure your friends have a future, and I want to stop them because they stole mine. Even the dead have dreams."

3 ICE IN THE EYE

Detective Chief Inspector Judas Iscariot of Scotland Yard's secret Occult Division, the Black Museum, looked around his office for what he hoped would not be the last time, and locked the door. He gave the handle an extra little pull and listened for the special click that the lock made when it was properly shut and not just pretending. It obliged, so he put the old, well-worn brass key back in his pocket. He had left everything in order, and more importantly, secure.

No one else was permitted or authorised to venture up onto the 7th floor of the Yard, and access to it was only possible from the stairway at the back of the building, through two sets of heavy double-doors secured with locks that could only be opened with a special pass key for each.

So far this year, only one ghost had been seen in the building. Lots had been heard, however.

PC Westinghouse was the officer who had bumped into one of the things that normally go bump in the night. He was the huge chap wearing the blue boiler suit and balaclava the viewers of London Tonight witnessed swinging the steel door lock smasher as the Special Crimes Unit made a surprise entrance to yet another drug dealer's abode at 01.00hrs one Saturday morning a couple of months ago. He was known to be a very brave man, so when he was found cowering in the stairwell at 04.00hrs that same day, gibbering about a floating person that wanted to sell him some lucky heather and a fresh child's head from the mass grave at Tower Hill, no one laughed. PC Westinghouse is handing out parking tickets in Brighton these days, and woe betide anyone who tries to sell him anything 'lucky' or mentions the words 'tower' and 'hill' in the same sentence. He was a loss to the unit, but it was a big improvement on the previous year when the Human Resources team had been bombarded with requests for transfers to other Nicks because of strange goings on at the Yard.

Thankfully, things on the 7th had been fairly quiet of late, but it wouldn't go down well with the Chief Super if one of the cleaners or a police officer fresh from the training academy were to take a wrong turn and ended up wandering around up here unescorted.

Judas looked through the thick, milky glass in the door, and gave the room a second once-over. All of the heavy, metal cabinets that he used to store his files were locked up. Inside these silent, metal sentinels were reports on London's witches, ghouls, angels, underground slave traders, assorted demons, magic portals and roads, and all the Fairy folk you could ever wish for. Judas never carried the keys to these cabinets with him. He always hid them deep inside the museum itself. The Black Museum housed a special 'Key Room'; in this room stood a table, and on that table lay artefacts and objects used by London's foulest and most famous criminals. Touching one of these objects could transport you back in time to the place where these criminals and monsters had created their legends. The characters themselves were safely contained in a time loop so that they could see their world but not interact with it ever again. It was the hardest prison you could imagine; a prison of temptation. The keys to the filing cabinets had been placed in the hands of a pickpocket called Amy Jones, who'd lived in London in 1576. She owed Judas a big favour and she could be trusted, unlike Jack the Ripper and some of his close friends.

There were secrets inside those files that would shock the heads of state of quite a few nations, and some that would have definitely brought down a government or three. Area 51 in the American desert was small fry compared to the secrets and stories contained within those cabinets. Judas knew where all of the bodies were buried, and where all of the most powerful and dangerous magical objects were stowed away, too. All this knowledge, and much more, was documented inside his files. If God ever let him retire he could make a fortune with one file and a quick call to the Daily Bastard on Fleet Street.

The oldest pages were covered in gold leaf, with phrases like 'Ye Olde' and 'Here Be Dragons' written on them, followed by page after page of street slang in Celt and Latin, then the original Cockney, and all the other languages used in London since its birth, until things got really basic, and less romantic, and incidents were written up in biro.

He had thought that the cabinets were bullet-proof, bomb-proof, spell-proof and everything else-proof, but one of them had recently been opened like a can of beans. He suspected that one of the inmates had supplied the knowledge required to bypass the intricate web of spells and state-of-the-art locks to the German Black Sun magician known as Stranghold. And the inmate in question was most likely Jack the Ripper.

That was something that he would rectify later when he got back; hopefully in one piece, this time.

Everything looked ship-shape and Brixton fashion inside his office, so Judas flicked the light-switch down. The office disappeared into the darkness and the glass pane in the door instantly became a black mirror. He stepped back and stared at his reflection, adjusting the dark blue wool tie that he wore over his white Kilgour shirt and smoothing his thick, dark, curly hair down. It had started getting unruly again and he needed it cut badly. The curls that flicked up over his ears had started to mutate into waves and it was only a matter of time before the deadly mullet would set in. He hadn't had a lot of time to himself recently, no space to take stock, or think about the future.

He had just fought a battle with the Black Sun magician Stranghold, his stooge John the Baptist and the ever-unreliable Jack the Ripper; it had taken a lot out of him, and it showed on his face. No amount of day cream would be able to smooth those worry lines away. If it hadn't been for God showing up in the olive grove all those centuries ago and making him immortal as punishment for sending Jesus to his death, he might have actually died at Jack's hand. But there was no time for reflection now.

The most important thing to do now was focus on the problem in hand. Herr Stranghold had stolen a very powerful book. It was at the heart of a mystery that began with severed angel wings and had ultimately taken Judas down into the depths of the city over the past few weeks, and face to face with some old enemies from his past. He'd just learned from the Angels of the North that this magical tome had been liberated from the great library in the City of the Heavens during the Second Fall.

It was reasonably common knowledge that Lucifer was responsible for the First Fall. The Morning Star, as Lucifer is sometimes called, had defied God, led a revolt, and earned himself a one-way ticket to anywhere awful as a result. The Second Fall was less well understood, however. The Angels of the North hadn't been very forthcoming about what caused it so far, but Judas was going to find out, somehow.

That was another thing on his to do list.

Judas had located the book with the help of one of his informants, an antique-collecting angel by the name of Ray, and hidden it inside the Black Museum. But Stranghold had outsmarted him; he'd broken into the Black Museum while Judas was battling the mysterious criminal gang known only as 'The 10' and their leader John the Baptist, at the battle of Clapham Common.

Stranghold was now heading off to Jersey with the book.

Apparently, one of the spells inside the book could unlock the fabled miracle weapons that Hitler had been obsessed with finding during the Second World War. Stranghold's mission was simple: find the weapons, conjure them out of whatever secret holding place they were located in, and turn them on London. He wanted to destroy the city, building a new 'Berlinopolis' in its place. Millions would die, of course. After London would come Paris, then Madrid, and so on, and so on, until the world was finally theirs.

"A magical Blitz! That's all I need," muttered Judas to the empty corridor. He took a deep breath, closed his blue-grey eyes and stood there for a moment to collect his thoughts.

He reached into his pocket and found the familiar silver coin, one of the original 30 he'd earned for his most famous act of treachery. He took it out and rubbed at the smooth surface, making circular motions with his thumb.

All the markings on both sides of the coin had disappeared, and it had got thinner and thinner over time. While some people clicked worry beads and others twirled a lock of hair, Judas just rubbed his coin. He slowed his breathing and pushed the air further and further down into the space at the bottom of his lungs, counting to ten with each rise and fall of his rib cage. The extra oxygen calmed and soothed him, and when he opened his eyes a few minutes later he felt more like himself.

Was he still that most famous and despised liar and

traitor any more, or was he actually turning into a good person after all these years?

God knows, he thought, and then smiled to himself.

At least, I hope he bloody well does.

At the end of the corridor was a door, and behind the door was a set of stairs that led up to the roof. Judas reached for the door handle, then stopped himself. He counted to ten, shot the cuff of his navy-blue jacket, and checked the time on his watch.

"Time flies, and it's about time that I did the same," he said out loud.

The angels that had flown him down from Newcastle after his meeting with the elders of the Angels of the North would be waiting for him on the roof of Scotland Yard, as ordered. Judas was supposed to be recovering the book from the safety of the Black Museum before being escorted back up north by the angels, to return the book whence it came. It would be safe up there in the stars, and Stranghold and his magical Nazi chums would never be able to find it again. They would be out of action forever.

That was the plan 24 hours ago, anyway.

The bad news was that the book was gone, of course, but there was at least some good news in that Judas knew where it was going; not only that, he had a man on the inside – or rather, a ghost on the inside – so all was not lost. His old partner Sgt Williams, a kind and caring family man who should really have been a supply-teacher for an inner-city school with discipline issues, had hidden himself inside the book. Apparently this was something that ghosts could do these days. He'd accompanied Herr Stranghold out of the museum and away from the Yard, without him knowing it, of course.

Williams had been killed at the battle of Clapham Common by John the Baptist, but had chosen to return as a ghost, to help Judas continue his fight against everything that goes bump, crash or bang in the night. Things had moved so swiftly over the past week that Judas had not had time to thank him properly, but he hoped he would get the chance to make amends very shortly. Williams was a good man, or *was* a good man, but now Judas was relying on him being an even better ghost.

He opened the door and took the back stairs up to the roof.

He reached the top, pushed the door gently, and stepped out.

The futuristic hinges that looked like space-aged bicycle pumps hissed softly as the door closed incredibly slowly behind him. The sun had dropped, and London's skyline was leaking upwards with the colour of the city. It wouldn't be long before the sky was full of blinking stars that moved gracefully across the night sky, attached to the wings of continental jumbo-jets as they took up their positions in an invisible line in the sky in order to land at Heathrow to the west. To the south, the red eye of the tower at Crystal Palace blinked from its side of the river, intermittently telling London that all was still well, like a silent town crier.

The gravel on the roof crunched underfoot as he walked across it. Then the sound of the pebbles rubbing against each other stopped abruptly, as he stepped onto the concrete lip that ran around the building's perimeter.

He stood on the edge and looked down; the hum of the city flew up the side of the building to say hello to his eardrums. Down below, on the road, the yellow and orange lights of the almost static vehicles created a series of links that bound all of the cars and buses and taxis together in a big chain. Traffic was heavy tonight, so the chain dragged itself down the road slowly. Judas watched the world go by for a while, and then he felt the angels' presence, long before he saw them. They must have been riding the thermals or whatever it was that winged things ride high on above him ever since he set foot on the roof, watching and waiting until the time was right to descend. He looked up and gave them a wave that HRH the Queen would have been proud of, and they dropped out of the sky like droplets of heavy silver.

The force of the downdraft caused by their muscular wings began to push him backward as they got closer, so he moved away from the edge of the building and took up position somewhere where he wouldn't run the risk of being blown off the roof and making a fool of himself. What Judas especially didn't want right now was his winged taxi service back to the north laughing and teasing him along the way.

All three angels landed softly on the gravel next to him.

Judas looked down at their feet. "How do you do that?"

"Do what?" the nearest angel replied.

"Not make any sound when you land," Judas

pointed at the gravel.

"Where is the book, Judas?"

The question came from Anzielle, the leader of this flight. He was one of the third order angels; not angel royalty like Michael or even Malzo, the former custodian of the Black Museum, but well-regarded amongst the fallen. Unlike a lot of his brethren, he had a sense of humour and a ready smile.

"Well, that's a bit of a long story, my flying friend, and it's one that can wait, to be honest. We'd better get going; circumstances have changed a bit, and the book has fallen into the wrong hands."

Judas delivered the bad news with a smile; it was one of his best smiles and he really meant it. Anzielle flexed his wings, reminding Judas of a sprinter stretching just before a race.

"Would it be possible for we three here to reclaim it? Do you know where it is?"

"The book is on its way to an island just off the south coast of England. I don't know how they are traveling, or what they are traveling in, so I can't help much there. We're definitely a match for them but as we don't know how to find them that's academic right now. Sorry chaps, I think we need to head back up north so I can speak to your master and to Michael, and make a plan."

The second angel, whose name was Andelas, produced the large leather sack that they had used to carry Judas down in from the north, while the third, Zaquiela reached into the small pouch that he wore on his belt and handed Judas a pair of unusually-shaped goggles. The lenses were dark green and shaped like inverted triangles, while the band that held them both in place was made of something that smelt like leather but shone like silver. Judas gave them a sniff and received a warning look from the angel with the sack.

"Sorry, old habit; wondered what the material was."

Anzielle looked up into the night sky and sniffed the air.

"The sky over London is clear now but it will fill up with rain and ice the further north we go. Put those on and your eyes will be spared."

"Fair enough, sounds painful" said Judas, and he put the goggles on. Or rather, he tried to put the goggles on. Angel's heads are bigger than those of a normal sized man, so they slipped down over his face and ended up hanging around his neck like a bulky leather scarf. He spent the next few valuable minutes trying to work out how to shorten the strap so that he could put them on properly. The angel with the sack quickly lost patience with him, and grabbed the goggles, set them to the correct size with nimble fingers and placed them back on his head. Seconds later they were in the air. Sure enough, within a few minutes of flying the temperature started to really drop, biting like a freezing dog; Judas hugged himself, and silently urged the angels to fly faster and faster.

They'd been flying for about 20 minutes when it happened.

Judas heard the sudden roar of the plane's engines, then felt a sickening thump. He must have lost consciousness for a few seconds, because when he came to and opened his eyes he knew straight away that he was falling.

The flight down from the north had been incredibly smooth, like flying in a Rolls Royce. The angels had the ability to read the air, avoiding the sudden pockets of dead pressure that make passenger planes buck and rattle like old rides at the local fairground. But that was when they could see properly. Tonight, the sky was full of ice and rain, and the wind was coming from all angles.

He knew he was going down fast. He was tumbling and spinning downwards. But he'd fallen from tall buildings before, and been thrown from the odd bridge or two; he always, always, crawled first, then walked away from it.

So he was ready for the ground, and not afraid to say hello to it.

The air whistled loudly all around him, and shards of ice floated in front of his eyes. Then came the silence that happens just before things are supposed to end. He sensed the earth long before he felt it, before he was launched into the familiar blackness that he had come to know as momentary death.

He had ended many, many times before. He couldn't be killed, of course; God wouldn't allow that. So stabbing, shooting, burning and the many other methods that would usually finish a human off just held him up for a bit. They were just irritations, really; his body absorbed the blade, or the fire, and then the spell or word that had been used on him by the main man upstairs just sent the pain and hurt away. The assassin's garrotte always snapped before it crushed his Adam's apple, and the poison from the murderer never did anything much. But it seemed falling from a great height was another story altogether.

There was a whisper, a creak of leather, and then absolute stillness. The blackness rolled over him like a really big duvet. Then he awoke and saw the flaming tree again.

In the moment between life and death everyone stands at the base of the tree.

It has a vast trunk and many branches that spread up and into the dark sky overhead. Its roots hold the tree to this moment in time. They go deep, and disappear into the blackness of the other world.

There are always people standing under the tree. Most know whether or not they will be climbing the tree to sit in the branches and wait for the sun, or if they will be going into the never-ending maze of the black roots.

Judas watched as one woman was sucked into the earth; he saw her life in an instant. Shelley had cheated on her husband with his brother. She'd started doing it on her wedding day and carried on, even though she knew that her husband knew about the affair. Brother had killed Brother, but just weeks later she had started using a dating site to find the next sap; something inside her was broken and she didn't care, so here she was.

A little boy that had been run over by a drunk driver floated up to the highest branch; he turned his face to the rising sun, and slept.

When Judas came to again, the tree was gone. He was somewhere else entirely. It was different, but it was all the same. Above him he saw some familiar stars. They did not blink, because they were frozen in time at a moment that he would ever forget.

He was back in the olive grove. It always looked the same.

The noose. His noose. He'd tied it, after all. It was hanging in the same dry, old tree, and the same leaves hung frozen in mid-air just above the hard earth. He could hear the storm revving up in the sky, and he could sense the anger that was making the storm come his way.

Judas gritted his teeth and closed his eyes as tightly as he could. He'd been here before, hoping each time that it would be his last visit. But this is what punishment is: the one thing you fear the most, over and over again, until whoever set the punishment decides you don't need it anymore. All things considered, Judas felt that he had done his time by now; but then again, who gets to kill the son of the Almighty and earn time off for good behaviour?

The storm arrived suddenly, and in half a heartbeat the air disappeared.

HE was here.

His shape appeared in the sky, and everything went crazy. Judas heard lots of sounds that crashed into each other, like duelling, kamikaze bagpipes. His ears bled and his tongue went numb. The pain went on forever, but only lasted a second or two, and then he was back.

"Not yet. There is more to do" said the great voice.

Judas heard the words wash over him and then he was in his own body again. He was whole; all the blood was on the inside, and he had the right number of limbs.

He looked up at the blue sky, took a breath, and

slipped away into the arms of a much needed friend – unconsciousness.

Anzielle had seen the passenger plane hit Andelas.

The smooth fuselage of the aircraft had struck the angel just between front facing deltoid and the nape of the neck, snapping it like a twig.

He could see from the way that Andelas fell after the initial impact, and from the spread of his wings, that he could not be saved. He'd watched him fall out of the sky, and knew that all of the life was gone from him already.

The low cloud and the sudden appearance of the passenger plane from the east had caught them unawares. Andelas, one of the strongest angels garrisoned with the Angels of the North, hadn't stood a chance. The goggles that the angels use for flying in conditions such as these were excellent, but Andelas hadn't been wearing his. He'd given his to Judas.

Andelas had died for being too good.

Each of the angels that were cast down in the Second Fall had a reason for challenging the status quo in the heavens. Some wanted closer ties with the humans. Some wanted to be more independent of the council, and the highchair and its master. Others had fallen in love with the wrong people.

Anzielle and Andelas had been lovers. Two of the mightiest angels, trained for combat, keepers of the peace respected for their discipline, had a secret that they had kept for a thousand years. But one night they had been discovered, either through fate, or by becoming too sure of themselves and letting their guard down. They had been making love when the angels of the watch had come upon them. Luckily their weapons and clothes were close at hand and in the confusion of their discovery they had been able to escape. They flew hard, knowing that their lives depended on it and eventually found a hiding place in one of the outer gardens of heaven. It wasn't long before the sky above the gardens grew dark with the beating wings of the host searching for them and they fled once again. There were no more hiding places for them though, not now. The Host had been turned out and the battle drums that rumbled like thunder beat on and on, never stopping. A purge had begun and battle was soon joined between those who believed without question, and those who believed that life was a gift to be lived and enjoyed. The fighting lasted for days and many brave angels were killed on both sides. Then, on the fifth day of fighting, a small number of angels escaped into the void and disappeared. They had been outnumbered from the beginning, but they had not been outfought. And now they were refugees on earth, but at least they could love who they wanted and be what they wanted to be.

Was Judas really worth all this? thought Anzielle, as he swooped down to collect the detective from the ground below.

Azruela, one of the highest of all the angels of the Second Fall, had already told them of Judas' strange gift of immortality. Before he had despatched them from the north, he had briefed them fully that Judas was to be treated with respect. But he'd added, in school ground parlance, that if it came to a fight he could handle himself.

Anzielle looked at Judas, lying on the ground. There was not a hair out of place or a single, solitary scratch on him.

The other angel grumbled and said something under his breath. Anzielle could feel the bitter resentment coming from him. There was nothing that either of them could do about the situation, though; they were on a mission that would give Azruela some much needed bargaining power against the power in the heavens if it was a success.

Anzielle saw the body of his lover lying in the grass nearby and his wings twitched and tensed. He felt the icy dagger of grief slowly piercing his heart and let out a small sob. Andelas was dead. The great love of his life was gone. He couldn't blame the plane and he couldn't blame Andelas for being his big, generous self. But he could blame Judas, and he would bring him to account. He let the grief become his shield, and closed his eyes and heart to the memory of Andelas.

"Only for the time being, though," he said to the wind.

He ordered the other angel to pick Judas' body up quickly, and to set off for the north. He watched him put the body of Judas back into the leather bag and take to the sky. When he'd disappeared into the underbelly of the low cloud he walked over to the body of his lover, kissed him once on the mouth, then picked him up. With one great thrust, he surged up into the sky.

4 IRON WINGS

Judas was unconscious, but he could sense someone, or something, talking. The words were just out of reach, and in between each sentence there was what felt like a great rush of air. He imagined a gigantic set of bellows being pushed together by two giants, each trying to push harder than the other. He opened his eyes and looked out on to a green world. His body ached, and his head felt like he was wearing a fully-grown sheep on each side of it. Slowly the sounds of the world caught up with him; he remembered where he was, and what he was doing. Try telling the guy next to you at the bar that you are flying north in a huge leather bag held by a flight of angels wearing a funky pair of green-lensed sunglasses. Well, that was where he was, and that was what he was doing.

Judas reached for the flap of the leather bag and opened it. The air rushed in, and so did the light of day. They had made good time. He could see the iron wings of the Angel of the North ahead. Newcastle formed a grey smudge behind it, and beyond the sprawl of the city was the belt of the forest where they were heading. Azruela would be waiting impatiently for the book. Judas looked left and right, and saw the wings of the angel that was carrying him beating up and down. They made a deep thrumming sound with each powerful beat.

Then he saw Anzielle and his heart stopped. Anzielle was carrying the third angel in his arms, and it was obvious that he was dead. Judas sat back inside the leather pouch and took off the goggles he was wearing. He'd learnt long ago that he was a grief magnet. It was drawn to him like moths to streetlights. If he hadn't allowed himself to be outwitted and played by Stranghold and Jack the Ripper, he wouldn't have had to make this flight, and the angel would still be alive. This was his case, and he was responsible for everyone and everything about it. Whether or not a death had come by accident or design it was still a death, and the numbers were racking up again. Stranghold was going to pay for Williams already; now he was going to have to pay for an angel, too.

Judas felt gravity at work, and minutes later the sound of the city disappeared to be replaced by the sighing of trees. The flap of the bag was lifted, and he stepped out.

Azruela was standing in a clearing, with the great wooden hall of the Angels of the North behind him. Grey sunlight shot through the branches of the trees like silver lances that buried themselves into the brown earth.

He stared at Judas for a few seconds and then spoke.

"So, *Judas*, your close friend and sometime companion travels with you again, it seems. You bring

Death with you everywhere you go. Unfortunately for members of my own flight, it is not your own."

Judas laid the goggles on the floor; he couldn't keep them, and he couldn't give them back either, so he put them down and hoped that they would be reclaimed later.

"I am truly sorry for the loss of one of your kind, Azruela. If I could swap places with him you know that I would. I can't. I've tried, but you-know-who won't have it.

"I wish we had time to mourn right now, but we don't. I don't want to sound hard or unfeeling, but we have a bigger problem on our hands."

Azruela looked down at Judas' hands, and his eyes widened. In an instant he knew that things were even worse than he thought.

"Where is the book?"

"I got back to London and things had taken a turn for the worse. John the Baptist and the rest of the Disciples had fooled me into thinking that they were the real enemy. It turns out that they were in fact being controlled by a very powerful Black Sun magician that wanted the book for other reasons. They broke into the Black Museum while I was on my way here, killed my Sergeant, and they've taken the book to an island off the south coast called Jersey."

"How do you know that this is where the book is headed?"

Azruela's voice had dropped to a whisper. Angels don't tend to show their emotions very often, but Judas could feel waves of anger coursing out from him as he spoke.

"We defeated John in the end, and managed to get everything out of him before Michael took him off to the North Sea for a nice cold burial.

"My old Sergeant Williams, now my *dead* Sergeant Williams, scribbled it all down and left his notes for me so we know where it's going and what it's going to be used for. I know this sounds a bit weird, but he wasn't killed completely. He decided to stick around as a ghost to help me out, and he's hidden himself inside the book.

"I was hoping that you might get Michael to come with me to get the book and return it here before things get any worse."

"Worse?" Azruela spat the word out with real energy.

"I have a dead angel to mourn and one of the most powerful objects on earth to recover; worse is not quite the word that I would use, Judas. And what makes you think that I have the power to summon an archangel? Come, we must go inside." Azruela turned and walked into the hall; as if on cue, the sunlight that had been cutting through the branches was turned off like a light switch, and the glade darkened.

Inside, the flames in the sconces flickered and sputtered, and shadows jumped and fidgeted on the walls. Azruela was already halfway down the hall; his grey and black wings were folded tightly against his back, and his head was bowed. He looked more like an angry vulture than the leader of the Angels of the North to Judas.

Azruela stopped at one of the long wooden tables at the far end of the hall. Ray was there already, leaning back in his chair with his feet up on the table. His eyes were closed, and his long blonde hair pointed down to the floor behind him. As Judas approached, he could just about hear the subdued bass sound that was coming from his oversized headphones. Azruela clicked his fingers, although the sound that came from his fingertips was anything but a click. Ray fell backwards, only managing to jump to his feet as a result of his wings flicking out reflexively. In one fluid movement he ripped the headphones from his head and dropped them onto the chair that he had just been sitting in.

"Great knowledge can be found on these shelves, Ray; enlightenment and spells that could change your life are only the turn of a page away. Yet you sleep your life away.

"And if I catch you with your feet up on these tables once more, you will be patrolling the moors in all weathers counting the sheep."

Ray smiled nervously, bobbed his head, and flicked at a spec of dirt on the surface of the table.

"Hello, Judas."

"Hello, Ray. How are you getting on?"

"Pretty good. Got the book?"

"I was just saying to Azruela here that things did not quite go to plan. We are up against it, again."

"Same old, same old, then?"

"It seems that way."

Azruela coughed politely and sat down.

"So, tell me what you plan to do then, Judas."

Judas sat down opposite the old angel and placed his palms down on the table. The wood was smooth and warm to the touch. Underneath the warmth was something else, a strange feeling; for a second Judas thought he detected a heartbeat, but the feeling softened before disappearing entirely.

Azruela saw the confusion on Judas' face and smiled.

"Everything in this place lives, Judas – in its own fashion, of course. Now, what is to be done?"

Judas sat upright and stretched his back, rolling his shoulders back and forth to loosen his weary muscles. He would have given anything for a tennis ball and a hard wall to rub up against at that moment. An old girlfriend had showed him how to remove knots and tension in his shoulders by placing the tennis ball between himself and the wall, leaning back onto it and shifting his weight up and down so that the ball targeted the precise area of the pain. But, alas, no tennis ball was at hand. His body was healing quickly, as usual, and he knew that he would be fighting fit again within a matter of minutes.

"I have to get to Jersey, find Williams, and then take the book off this little chap Stranghold. I'll need some help, obviously, and I was hoping that Michael would fly me down. He could pull Stranghold's limbs off one by one as part of the deal – he likes doing that. Once we've got the book, Michael can take it back up to where it belongs. I will deal with whatever else we find there myself."

Ray had remained standing. No one had offered him a chair, and after being caught with his feet up and sleeping on the job, he had decided that it was the best thing to do.

Ray was not particularly brave, but neither was he a coward. Judas had met him – and saved him – when he'd been getting a severe beating at the hands of one of the hate groups that had sprung up when the angels of the Second Fall had requested that London become their new home. Ray had been beaten up pretty badly by the time Judas had arrived on the scene that night, but he was not down, and he certainly wasn't going out without a fight.

The city was already seething with animosity towards migrants from Europe and Africa when the angels dropped out of the sky, and some people lost their marbles completely; certain members of the political ruling classes saw it as a Godsend, which is what it was from one angle at least.

Rival newspapers had already chosen their sides in this poisonous and nebulous argument, and were spewing their lies at each other with gusto, hoping that sales of their prospective rags, red tops and broadsheets were rising with each insult they traded. So the angels were invaders. The angels wanted to take over. The angels were going to be the end of the world. It didn't matter that in reality they were as far removed from this narrative as it was possible to imagine; the story stuck, hate groups proliferated, and angels like Ray, who liked the human race more than he liked his brother and sister angels, were first up against the wall.

The biggest of the hate groups was the called the Spears of Liberty. Better known as the 'Spears', they were being funded by some faceless bunch in the city with an axe to grind and enough poison to go around. Judas had been trying to get more information on the people behind the organisation, but they were well-informed and protected by some very highly-placed people in the present government.

When the pair met, Ray was bloody and bruised; some of his feathers had been torn out, and the Vivienne Westwood outfit he was half wearing was in tatters. For one of the smaller angels, he was giving as good as he got, but although Angels are deadly in the air, get them in a tight corner with enough numbers on your side, and things even out.

Ray was swinging right and left, but he was getting tired by the time that Judas waded in. After the first couple of punches the thugs got the message and decided to call it a day. That, and the fact that one of them had a foot and half of steel sticking out of his back from a blade that had been snapped in two.

The angel was wary at first. He'd heard about the immortal working at the Yard, and he wasn't sure what to make of Judas. Over time they had learned to trust each other, though, and on the odd occasion, Ray had been useful in locating the odd thing or two that helped Judas close a case or find a suspect. He wasn't a grass or an informer. He was just repaying a debt, because angels take debts very seriously indeed. Ray was eternally grateful to Judas for saving his life and when he said eternal, he meant it.

"I could come and help you," he said.

Judas and Azruela looked up at Ray at the same time, and Ray instinctively took a step back.

"I appreciate the offer, Ray, but it's likely to get a bit nasty. You sure you want to get involved?"

"I think it would be good for Ray to step into the fray, Judas. He offers nothing to us here, but he might be useful to you," said Azruela.

"I'd still like to ask Michael to come along as well, though; can you help me there?"

Azruela nodded and stood up. Judas got up, and together they walked down the aisle between the rows of wooden tables, towards the door at the back of the hall. Ray followed along behind, fumbling with his headphones as he went.

When they stepped out of the hall Judas saw that they had moved even farther into the forest. The air was still and heavy. Judas could sense that there were other angels here, just out of sight, watching and waiting.

Azruela waved a bony hand in the air; the branches of the trees creaked, and the leaves rustled and fell from the canopy above. Then they were all alone.

Azruela walked through the trees. Occasionally he would reach out and place a hand against the trunk of one, then he would listen and then shake his head. He was looking for something in particular. Judas thought he could hear him muttering, but decided not to interrupt.

After a short walk Azruela stopped. He had found the right tree.

"Please step back, and we shall see if anyone up there is listening to us."

Azruela's wings unfurled, then he stepped forward and plunged both of his hands into the trunk of the tree. They passed straight through the bark, and his forearms disappeared up to the elbows.

Judas had heard of this, but had never seen it done. He'd seen lots of spells and magic before, but this was a new one on him.

Azruela closed his eyes, and stopped breathing. Seconds later the tree began to glow and hum softly. The branches of the tree started to stretch and point up at the stars.

"He's making a call," said Ray.

"That's an angel's mobile phone then, is it?"

"Sort of."

"Not very portable, is it. I think you lot have got the wrong end of the stick when it comes to a mobile communication device."

Judas was about to make a joke about roaming charges when Azruela opened his eyes; he stepped back, and pulled his arms from inside the tree.

"He is far away, they say, on an errand for his master. He's not expected to return for many days. Michael will therefore not be able to join you I'm afraid, Judas. What will you do now?"

Judas looked at Ray and smiled.

"Well, I've got one angel by my side already, but I think I might need to get hold of a saint, too."

5 EVENOR

The journey back from the Angels of the North had been less eventful than the journey up. A different flight had been chosen to take him to London, and he could sense their angry indifference to him from the moment they leapt into the air until the moment they dumped him, unceremoniously, back on to the roof of Scotland Yard. He stepped out of the leather flying harness they had carried him in and was about to say thank you, but got a stone shower of gravel in the face from the down draft of their departing wings instead. Well, he'd been the most hated person in the world right up until the little Austrian chap with the stupid moustache had come along, and he knew what it was like to be shunned and reviled, so he'd better just get on with the job. There were bigger fish to fry.

Ray had told him that he wanted to go back to Islington, where he lived above the indoor market on

Upper Street, to get a few things that might come in handy. Judas wondered if there was such a thing as an angel bazooka or lightsabre made of feathers or something, as he made his way down the stairs and onto the seventh floor.

Everything seemed to be where he had left it.

He opened the door to his office, flicked the switch on the socket behind the kettle and smiled as it began to wheeze and splutter. He was just about to ask Williams if he wanted a brew, then remembered that he was no longer there. He missed his smiling face; the office was too quiet without him. Judas made himself a cup of tea and sat down. He blew the wisps of steam from the surface of the mug, placed it on the desk in front of him, and leaned back in his creaky leather chair. He was asleep before the kettle had cooled.

He dreamt of lightning. Not the black lightning he knew so well from the sky above the olive grove, but white lightning that searched the sky instead of diving down to earth. This lightning splintered and shattered the air, and in the middle of it all was a young boy who screamed white fire from his mouth.

The desk phone rang sharply, and Judas snapped up in his seat instantly. It was the main desk and a wrong number. He was awake now, and he looked up at the clock on the wall to discover that he'd slept for over ten hours. The world was turning, and time was flying. He went into the washroom, took a shower, and changed into fresh clothes. As he placed his old, dirty shirt in a plastic bag to be taken home later, he noticed that small shards of white ice were still embedded in the material, and the image of the dead angel's body flashed into his mind.

After making a fresh cup of tea and brushing his teeth, Judas called down to the main desk and asked for a car to be made ready, before heading downstairs to pick it up. The gates at the back of the Yard opened slowly, and the CCTV cameras that watch them slide away from each other turned around and looked down at the road from their perching points like robotic crows.

Normally Williams would do the driving, but today Judas was behind the wheel. He set off, pulling on to the bridge that marked the barrier between north and south London in good time. The traffic had been kind, for once.

Judas pulled into Iveley Road and parked. He got out and stretched. This part of London was always quiet. You could hear the traffic nearby, but the sound of it hummed rather than roared.

No wonder the house prices were out of reach to only the most senior and successful bankers, he thought to himself. He looked up and down the road, searching for one of the few short black parking meters that still existed. Judas found one at the end of the road and was happy to find that it still took coins – most would only save you from the legions of parking attendants if you called their big brothers online and spoke the secret code, these days. He rummaged in his pockets and took out a small handful of change. He was always extra careful when it came to spending gold and silver; there was one coin that he didn't want to lose. He picked it out from the pile and placed it inside the wallet pocket of his jacket. Then he fed the meter and listened as it swallowed all of his remaining cash.

St. Paul's church in the very heart of Clapham was more than just a place of worship. None of the locals knew of the secret tunnels underneath it that went very deep indeed, tunnels that were home to an ancient and very powerful army of highly trained warriors, the Saints of Clapham. The Saints had in lived in the area for a long time; they were its protectors, and they watched over it like muscular, magical hawks. It seemed like only yesterday that Judas had been here with Williams, looking for information about the sinister gang known as The 10.

They'd walked the invisible Church Roads from here to the Colliers Woods with the Saints, where they'd broken up a gang of slave traders that had held a slave market there. They'd fought the stunted, ugly little slavers in a pit under a building site, and saved a lot of young children who had been stolen to order. Buying them a pony or giving them a better life away from the poverty of the streets weren't part of the plans that the prospective new owners had for them, and Judas was happy when they'd smashed the ring and put the slavers out of business. After the fight they had interrogated them all in a particularly enhanced fashion, and after reducing a few to puddles of filth they had got the information they needed, uncovering who'd been behind the butchering of the angel they were investigating.

The leader of the Saints was a man called Thornton. He'd helped Judas to win the battle of Clapham Common against his old foe John the Baptist, and was in his debt. Now it seemed that Judas was going to have to ask for his help again.

Judas walked into the grounds of the church, spread his arms wide, and spoke to the gravestones.

"I am here to request an audience with Saints," he said.

A car alarm went off behind him, and a dog barked somewhere to someone that it didn't recognise. Then the wind blew, and the trees sighed. A leaf drifted down to the ground from a tree that hung one of its heavy branches over the iron railings that marked the boundaries of the church. It landed next to the highly polished toe of a very nice-looking men's leather boot.

"Hello again, Judas," said Thornton.

Thornton was a tall man. His hair was grey, and hung down to his collar. He had a scar down the right-hand side of his face that hadn't come from a shaving accident. He wore a sharp black suit and the whitest shirt Judas had ever seen. He'd have to ask him who washed his shirts or what powder he was using, if he had time.

"Thornton. I'm sorry to be back so soon, but things have taken a rather bad turn and I need your help. I've just come back from the Angels of the North and I have some news that might affect you and your family."

Thornton nodded, then pointed to a gravestone in the corner of the yard. It was covered in yellow lichen and green moss, and proudly told the world that Emily Robertson, proud and happy mother to Charles and Sarah and wife to George, was laid to rest in the place she knew as home. God rest her soul.

"Do you think she ever thought that you'd be using her place of rest as a front door, Thornton?"

"Your levity is a thin veil to your anguish and sadness, Judas" said Thornton.

"Oh well, it helps if you're me," replied Judas.

Thornton reached inside his jacket and took out a credit card shaped piece of thin metal. Then he scraped it against the gravestone. It made a ripping sound, but left no mark.

"Step forward then, Judas, and we can talk of things to come."

Moments later they were in a long corridor; the surface of the floor here was highly polished, the tiles were black and white, and they seemed to stretch on and on forever. Lining the walls on each side were wooden doors with shining brass handles. Thin bars of orange light leaked out from behind them, anchoring them to the floor.

As they walked down the corridor, Judas heard what sounded like gunfire from behind one door, and the low hum of rhythmic chanting from behind another. He tried to work out where he was in relation to the world above him, and came to the conclusion he was probably under the Picture House. Above him, people would be watching one of the foreign language films that the bohemian film-goers of the borough loved so much; either that, or a film where cars turned into warriors from a metal world lost in space, and blew cities to pieces.

Thornton stopped outside one particular door and gently pressed the handle downward. It gave a little squeak; one that wouldn't have bothered a mouse with a hearing aid. He held the door open and ushered Judas inside.

The room looked exactly the same as it had done when he'd last visited a few weeks ago. Judas sat down and stretched his legs, and waited for Thornton to take his seat. Thornton sat too, then motioned toward the small table at Judas' elbow. A cup and saucer, and a pot of tea had appeared; a little wisp of steam crept out of the spout and climbed an imaginary ladder up into the air, before disappearing.

"Thank you; much appreciated," said Judas, as he poured the hot dark brown liquid into his cup. He blew across the circular surface of the liquid and then set it down again; drinking tea was a ritual that had to be carried out precisely.

Thornton smiled as if he could read Judas' mind.

"So, Judas, what does the future hold for my kind?"

Judas sat forward, placed his forearms on his thighs, and let his hands dangle.

"When we fought The 10 on the Common, I thought we were just solving one case and discovering who it was that was killing the angels. But it seems that was all a bit of a smokescreen. The man behind it all, the man who had twisted John's mind into a string of sausages, actually wanted to turn my world upside down so he could get his hands on a special book that once belonged to the angels. While we were chasing The 10 all over town, he was whispering into Jack the Ripper's ear. Their plan was to break out all of the inmates inside the Black Museum, then while I was rounding them all up again he was going to use the book to locate some magical, miracle weapons that he would then be able to turn on London. World domination would follow, of course, and then we'd all die.

"Unfortunately, he has the book now, and he's on his way to Jersey. I had hoped that Michael would come with me, but he's off brandishing his fiery sword somewhere else right now. I'm here because I need your help. I'm here because I need some backup."

Thornton shifted in his chair and crossed one leg over the over. He closed his eyes, and Judas could see the tension in his forehead. He hadn't really noticed it before, but the saint was getting old. And not just getting on a bit, either; he was getting on a lot.

Thornton opened his eyes, and smiled.

"I cannot leave the city Judas, nor can most of my family, but there are a few of us that can travel further. I do have someone who needs to travel across the sea and into the east. She has a connection to the water that may come in handy; I think that she may be of some use to you. Would you like to meet her?"

Judas sat back, and sipped his tea.

"I'm up against some ruthless people, Thornton; there's a chance that I might not be coming back this time. Are you sure you can spare her?"

"Judas, you know of my people, and you know how long we have been here. You also know that this is not our real home. Most of us are settled here now and don't think of the past at all, but there are some who have questions that need answers, my friend.

"The one I speak of has many questions, and your mission, should you take her, would give her the opportunity to find some answers. She is more than capable, Judas; believe me when I say that if you are danger, she is a good person to have defending rather than attacking you."

Judas stood up, and offered his hand to Thornton.

The old man got up from his chair and grasped it. Thornton's grip didn't feel like it should belong to him; it was as if he had borrowed it from a circus strongman or swapped his own for that of a bear. It was solid, and dry, and dependable.

"If you think that she will come then I would be most grateful to you, thank you. I owe you more than I can repay you."

Thornton opened the door and they walked back down the corridor together. One second they had been underground, the next they were standing in the graveyard once again. Thornton reached inside his jacket pocket and produced one of his smart business cards. Judas took it, and turned it over so that he could read the inscription. In fine Copperplate type, on the whitest card he had ever seen, was the name 'Evenor', and a five digit number.

"Who prints these for you, then? Not that dusty parcel of scribes who live under the library?"

Thornton just smiled.

"Her name is Evenor, Judas. Call this number and she will come to you.

"Be well. If you are not successful, or if it looks like you will not be able to complete your mission, will we have any warning before the enemy descends upon us, or not?"

Judas opened the car door and got in. Once he had drawn the seat belt down over his torso and heard it make the reassuring click in the socket at his waist, he pressed the down button on the armrest, and the whirr of the small electrical motor inside the door panel pulled the glass window down ever so slowly.

"I will get word to you as soon as I can; if things get really bad, I will try and make contact with you through the Black Museum. One of the artefacts should be able to pass on a message to you via one of the guests in your graveyard. I will send you an angel called Ray in advance if I can, too. If he gives you this silver coin then you know that you are in mortal danger; make your own plans then, and save as many as you can. Thanks again, Thornton."

Judas put the car into first gear, checked the rear-view mirror, then let the handbrake off and started to pull away. When he checked his mirror again, Thornton had gone. The graveyard was still, as all graveyards are.

6 THE GRAVEYARD GRAPEVINE

Sgt Williams sat on the edge of the metal bunk and looked down onto the naked breasts of Greta from Frankfurt. The faded black and white poster was anchored to the floor of the gun embrasure by 80 years of dust, its subject still smiling after all these years. He wondered if she had made it through the war. He heard the boy cough politely, and he looked up at his new acquaintance. Joachim, troop leader of the ghost children army. The boy looked away from the poster quickly. He'd seen it a million times before, of course, but he still felt a little ashamed each time the young lady caught his eye. Joachim had never had a girlfriend. He often wished that he'd had the chance, but that was another thing that the Black Sun had stolen from him. He would never be able to fumble with a bra strap in the woods, let alone lose his virginity. In one way he was glad that they had thrown him to his death from the cliffs before he had had the chance to get involved with a girl, because if he had experienced something and liked it, then he would be even more tormented than he already was.

"We need – sorry, *I* need – to find out what the little man is up to, and what he plans to do next, Joachim," said Williams as he casually pushed the poster under the bunk with the side of his foot. "As far as I can tell, he can't see me or sense me, which is weird because he can see you and communicate with you. Maybe it's because you're both German, or something to do with one of his spells."

Joachim straightened his collar, and brushed an invisible piece of dust from his swastika as the breasts disappeared from sight. "The magicians work deep down in the lower tunnels. I can take you to the doorway, but I can go no further. As you said yourself, they can see me, and I'm not going down there unless ordered, or unless it means there's a chance to get off this rock."

Williams watched the boy carefully. He was still not sure whether or not to trust this Aryan youth, but as things stood, he was the only other ghost he knew.

"If I can find out what the master plan is, then I can try and send a message to my boss in London."

"How would you manage that?"

"Well, if I'm right, then there must be a very old graveyard on the island, or a place where criminals were tried, sentenced and punished. If there is, then I should be able to find an object there that I can talk through: a gibbet post or a hangman's noose, a murderer's knife or a poisoner's bottle, something like that. It will act like a kind of telephone, enabling me to speak to the ghost of the killer or the ghost of the victim. They in turn can then move through the time fields, from one century to another, as easy as pie, and get a message to the artefact room at the Black Museum. I did it loads of times when I was alive. You go in there on a random miserable Monday in 2017, then before you know it you're visiting 1550s London, then you wander over to York in the 1700s, then back to the present all in the same day. Easy. If I can use that technique here, then all we have to do is sit back and wait for the cavalry."

Joachim's eyes widened and his eyebrows shot up, as if somebody had turned the gravity off on his face. Then he tried ever so hard to pretend that he was not surprised at all. Williams had seen so many criminals and suspects do it in the interview rooms back at Scotland Yard that he nearly laughed out loud.

"Is there something or somewhere like that here, Joachim?"

Joachim turned towards the door, lifted the handle and pulled it open a fraction. He looked out and along the downward-slanting corridor. There was nothing save the hum of the wind moving about in those tunnels tonight. He looked around, and Williams saw that he had a strange little smile on his face. You wouldn't have called it a happy smile; it was more hopeful than anything else.

"Herr Williams, I will take you as far as you need to go and protect you as best I can if you will promise to set me free afterwards. Without me, you could wander around down here for years and not find your way to the Hall of the Lightning or to the Magical Weapons hangar, both of which feel like the sort of places you might need. I can get you in and out and show you the low tunnels that lead to the sea and the outside world. If you help me to escape, then I will help you to do the same."

William's first instinct was to say that no, he didn't want the boy coming to any harm as a result of his investigation. At least, that was what he would have said if he'd been able to turn the clock back a few weeks. He'd have still been alive then, protecting the public against the bad guys and standing between them and danger. But now he was a ghost, and so was this boy. It was a bit ridiculous to think of either of them being in harm's way now; it wasn't as if anyone could kill them, after all.

"Okay, Joachim, if you can show me where I can find the magic man and the book, I'll help you get away from here. I have a question for you, though: what do you want to do about the other kids, the other soldiers? Do they get a chance to escape, or do we leave them here?"

Joachim closed the door again, softly. Williams watched him closely as he paced the room. He could see that the boy was thinking about the others.

"I will speak to them and see what they want to do.

I have to know, though, are you certain they'll all be able to leave as well? I don't want to offer them false hope if there is none for them."

Williams stood up and tucked his shirt in.

"If they want out, then we take them all out."

Joachim smiled again. They shook hands, and Williams was about to throw up a right–armed salute as a bit of a wheeze, but thought better of it. This was no time for a Charlie Chaplin jig, or small Austrian moustache jokes. Joachim opened the door again and disappeared down the tunnel. Williams took a last look at Greta, then followed him.

They were going deeper and deeper down into the stone roots of the island. Each time they got to a junction, Joachim would always take the one that led downwards. As they walked on into the inky blackness, Joachim saw that Williams kept flinching, and ducking down at the sounds that came from the granite ceiling above them. When they reached the next junction, he whispered in his ear, and told him not to be unsettled by it; the eerie squeaking was just the noise of the bats flying overhead, criss-crossing in the air above them and making little whooshing sounds as they went home or chased insects. Williams nodded gratefully to the boy, reassured that there was not something untoward flying around them.

He followed Joachim closely, and as they walked he had the opportunity to think things through further. He was hoping that Judas was on his way, and that the scribbles he had left for him in his old Columbo-style coat were legible enough for him to work out what had happened in the Museum that day.

All the rest of the boys in the Flying Squad had laughed when he had been moved over to the Black Museum division. There were hilarious 'retirement cards' instead of 'leaving cards' stuffed into his pigeon–hole at the Yard on the day of his transfer, and oh how they'd all laughed at the japery and the tomfoolery. But even at the time Williams had thought, no, he'd *known* that he had moved up in the world. This new world was much more dangerous and exciting than the old one, in which he'd spent his days chasing old lags down the road with the contents of an East End jeweller's safe in a lovely recycled bag-for-life. And everything that he'd seen since was testament to that. When you cornered a common or garden criminal after a raid you could expect the chap to wave a reconditioned firearm with a 20 per cent chance of hitting its target at you; when you cornered an urban troll with a metal dustbin lid sharpened to within an inch of its life in its paw, there was an 80 per cent chance that you were going home with a leg, or arm, or both, wrapped up like an Egyptian Mummy's foot.

The last few years had certainly been colourful – at least five rainbows worth of colour if he had to quantify it – and now here he was, inside a great big grey rock surrounded by water following a ghost dressed in the uniform of the Hitler Youth. Happy days indeed! Williams followed the boy around what he sensed was a bend in the tunnel; as it straightened, he saw ahead the dim circle of fuzzy light that had to be the entrance to the lair of the little man, and the rest of his hooded chums.

7 SILVER SPEARS OF DEATH

Salt was attacking his person and he hated it. The foul stuff had crept into the weave and the weft of his beloved suits and shirts. The carnation in his lapel had withered and was about to disintegrate into a reddish dust. His razor-sharp creases were glinting with dirty silver smudges, and his cuffs were covered in flecks of grey. If he were magically transported to the middle of the Gobi Desert, he should be able to survive without water for a few days just by sucking the salt from his own waistcoat.

The small man was seated at one of the highly-polished tables in the high council chamber. The silence was heavy and ominous. Thousands of black and white photographs of the Reich were arranged in straight lines along the walls, alongside large oil paintings of ferocious wolves and dark, forbidding castles. One giant chandelier hung from the ceiling and sprinkled white shards of light onto the carpet and the curtains. It was huge, and it had travelled here across the channel in the hold of a Dutch fishing vessel. Like a lot of expensive furniture and fittings it came with its own history. A hundred years ago it had looked down on the finest collection of Black Magicians ever assembled in the main hall of one of Germany's oldest castles.

Where were they all now? Stranghold wondered.

The British and the Americans had kidnapped the most talented, or bribed them to betray their own people and their own kind with white beachfront properties that saw at least 363 days of sunshine each year in Miami. Some of them were already dead – they had to be.

"Good riddance, and curse them to the end of days!" he said to the empty room.

Stranghold was in a bad mood, and the salt wasn't helping. He had expected more of a welcome from the child ghosts, and the rest of the order of the Black Sun. Hadn't he recovered the book? Hadn't he masterminded the plan that pushed the Baptist and his Disciples against the Black Museum? The small matter of recruiting Jack the Ripper was worthy of high praise on its own! But no, the rest of the Brotherhood had just smiled politely and warmed their own palms with the slightest round of applause they could be bothered to make. No matter, he thought. And with that, he stood up and retired to his chambers.

His orderly was waiting for him in his room. He was

undoubtedly a spy. His name was Spitzler and he came from Dortmund. He had been 'given' to Stranghold by one of the inner circle many years before and they had never spoken. Stranghold despised him, because he was dirty and stupid. He was also clumsy and forgetful. In fact, he didn't have a great deal going for him. It was a good thing that a hot bath had been run already or he would have punished Spitzler. It was fortunate for the manservant that the scent of starch hung in the air and a selection of crisp white shirts has been laid out on the bed, waiting with their arms open and collars unbuttoned. He gave a little shudder of delight. He was in love with his own appearance, of course; he was a narcissist of the highest order and he knew it. He dismissed Spitzler almost immediately, and twisted the brass head of the key in the lock until it made a comforting click. He pressed his ear to the door, and swiftly identified the soft swoosh that Spitzler's lank hair made against the other side of the wood. One of these days Stranghold might just use a spell to fire a sewing needle through the keyhole and blind Spitzler. He heard him shuffle off down the corridor, his over-sized feet making hushing noises as he dragged them across the lush red carpet.

Stranghold placed a secrecy spell on the room and sat down to look at his prize. He stroked the cover with his fingertips and then stopped immediately as he saw the greasy smears on the leather caused by his dirty hands. He sat back suddenly: if a deadly, venomous snake had just slithered out of his shirtsleeve and hissed at him he would have moved more slowly. Dirt was his true enemy. Seconds later he was in the bath and scrubbing like Lady Macbeth on acid with the ghost of Duncan banging on the door.

After he had bathed and dressed, he sat at his writing desk. It was a huge walnut affair with scrollwork that ran down into the carpet like wooden ripples carved from dark chocolate. He reached for the leather–bound book and slid it gently toward him. It made a sound when touched, a sound that you felt rather than heard, almost like an echo underwater.

He took a deep breath and tried to open the book, but of course it was locked with some form of high angel magic. Judas would know how to unlock it, as would the scrawny angel creature he had tried to buy it from in the flea market in London. But both were far away, and would not give up the secrets of the book easily if interrogated.

Rest, first, though. The leagues underwater were as strenuous as those on the road, he thought, as he drifted away into the cold embrace of sleep.

If the time he slept for was hours, they were dwarf-hours, because it felt as though as soon as his head hit the pillow there was a loud, rhythmic banging on the door.

Spitzler's fingers appeared first. They slithered around the edge of the door and hesitated before making physical contact with it. His head followed. The lights in the room were off, and the heavy velvet curtains stopped any light from trespassing from under their skirts. The loathing between the pair was mutual; Spitzler hated the little man and was of course reporting back to the high council every move he made and every letter he wrote. He could see a lump in the bed; a very small one, as if a child were asleep. If the council had ordered him to kill the sleeping magician this would have been the perfect moment. He stepped into the room and closed the door gently behind him. In his imagination, he slipped his shoes off, drew the long-bladed knife from his boot, and crept across the room, listening intently to the rise and the fall of the man's breathing. If it remained steady, he lifted his foot and stepped closer; if there were a grunt or a ruffle of sheets, he would have turned to stone. His imagination could play as long as it wanted to, but Spitzler had orders for his master, so he coughed quietly into the hollow of his hand.

"I heard you coming down the hall," said the little man. "If you're going to wake me in the morning by huffing at the door and infesting my boudoir with your cheap pomade and bad breath, at least have the good grace to come armed with a big pot of strong black coffee."

Spitzler felt a small surge of pride – he would save the large wave for when he saw Herr Stranghold in a puddle of his own vomit and bleeding from his eyes – because he had anticipated this and prepared a pot of the finest coffee, alongside a bone china tea cup on a bone china saucer, replete with the shiniest teaspoon that ever was. He wheeled the trolley inside the bedroom and parked it just where the little man liked it best, then waited for another insult. It didn't come. The little man had taken himself off to the bathroom, so Spitzler left to celebrate his moral victory with his own kind.

Stranghold scrubbed at his pale flanks until they turned an ugly pink. Then he soaped himself with a bar of soap that was made from seaweed and cost more than a nurse can expect to earn in a week. After drying and applying a combination of creams and ointments, and spending at least 30 minutes in front of his wardrobe deciding on which combination of shirt, tie and cufflinks was in order, he left the room with what he hoped to be the last piece of the puzzle under his arm.

Orderlies and fellow practitioners passed him as he walked down the dimly lit corridor; he saw all of them but didn't really register their existence, because the book was vibrating against his ribs and he imagined it was trying to talk to him. It was unnerving at first, but he relaxed as it seemed first to quieten and then to throb ever so gently, until it fell into step with the beating of his heart. He reached the great stone arch that led down to the lower rooms and passed through it. The sounds of the underground city were switched off immediately. Even the shrill piping of the bats could not pierce the enchantment that prevented the living from entering the lower halls. Flames flickered from torches in sconces that never went out, casting erratic shadows across the floor. Hooded figures appeared out of the gloom and then disappeared twice as quickly, opening invisible doors in the dark that seemed to be known only to them.

The little man continued walking, his in-built navigation system leading him through the dark without fail. He turned this way and that, over stone bridges that traversed deep chasms in the rock that smelt of dead water, through great black hallways with ceilings that couldn't be seen and cried small, evil tears down on whoever passed below them until, abruptly, he reached the great hall of the inner circle of the Black Magicians Guild, and stood before the door.

Something made a sound in the tunnel behind him and he turned quickly, expecting to see an enemy bearing down on him. But there was nothing there. He stared down the tunnel for a short while, slowing his breathing until the loud beating of his own heart reduced and he could listen to the darkness, probing it for noises that had no right to be there. If anything had been there before, it was not there now. The dripping continued, and he sensed a shift in the flow of the air around him, but he could not detect anything untoward in the cave. He turned around, straightened his bowtie and readied himself.

Stranghold muttered a spell under his breath and a wooden door opened before him, throwing a shaft of greyish light back into the hall. He walked in and prepared to present the book: his trophy, his seat at the high table, the key to unlocking the magical, master weapons and defeat the forces that had once dared to stand against the Reich.

The door closed behind him. The great long table that once belonged to the Bismarck family stretched all the way across the hall. A large, four-sided lamp hung by a thick steel chain from the ceiling. Inside it, a blue light fought to escape, but could find no path to freedom. Around the walls were great shields that belonged to the warriors of Siegfried's time. They were all dented and cleaved; dull insignia were painted across them, and the leather harnesses that men used to carry them hung down like withered intestines behind them. The chairs that lined the table were antiques, too. Withered armrests poked out from skeletal wooden frames like the immobile arms of static zombies. The little man reached down toward the shiny wooden surface of the table and knocked once with the metal of his ring. In the darkness all around him, a chiming sound reverberated off the walls. It was a soft sound, a gentle sound, quite out of place down here in the bowels of the earth; but it had the desired effect, and within seconds, grey shapes started to form around him.

The Black Magicians did not wear great robes in the chamber, each of them either dressed in their military finery or they wore clothes as befitting their station; all in all, there were some very fine suits on show. These men took up position behind their seats, and waited. There was a rustle, then the servants appeared. The ghost children of the Reich, replete in their Hitler Youth uniforms, glided out of the darkness and pulled the chairs out for their masters.

First, the Master of the Order took his seat at the head of the table, then the rest of the men took theirs. The ghost children floated among them, bringing refreshments and lighting candles. One of them was halfway across the hall when the tray he was carrying fell from his grip, and the contents of the tray smashed onto the floor. The nearest magician seemed perplexed, and beckoned the ghost child over. He took the child's ghostly arm in his hand, and peered at it. Then, he shook his head, calmly placing a thumb on to the child's forehead and whispering something that only the boy could hear. The boy screamed out in pain, and began to fold in on himself. It was like watching a piece of paper being folded over again and again, until it had reached the size of a stamp. Then, when it was physically impossible to fold any further, it burst into flames, until whatever was left of the boy turned to dust, and drifted away into the dark of nothingness above the table like a puff of smoke from a cigarette. The man who had killed the boy looked down at his hands and smiled. He looked pleased with himself.

Stranghold took his seat at the table and placed the book down in front of him. All heads turned in his direction, and he felt an impossible surge of pride and triumph rise up inside. The man who sat at the head of the table started to clap, and one by one all of the others joined him. Stranghold stood up and bowed to each of them in turn. Silence descended

The ghost children were given their orders and

dismissed; they saluted, then disappeared through the walls.

"I have tried a basic spell of opening and as expected, my fellow practitioners, it did not work. Understandably, the magic that keeps the book locked to us is very strong. If, as we surmise, this book was created by some other powerful force, then a spell will not be enough.

"To resolve this minor irritation, I have obtained a key of sorts."

Stranghold reached inside his suit jacket and drew out a beautiful white feather. Some of the magicians hissed at the sight of it, and recoiled, but Stranghold just placed it on the table next to the leather-bound book.

"This feather was obtained by one of our operatives earlier this year, John the Baptist. The Baptist is no longer with us I'm afraid – he fell in battle with the first deceiver, Judas Iscariot, who as we all know is an agent for the Black Museum. Before he was laid to rest, the Baptist passed this feather to me. It looks just like an ordinary feather – albeit a rather large one. I believe that it can be used as a primitive sort of conduit, and that if we focus our collective power on it we will trick the book into opening for us. We shall have to summon all our strength to do this, and some of us may not survive the opening; we have all had to make sacrifices over the years, but this could be the most heroic yet. Gentlemen, shall we begin?"

All of the magicians rose as one and congregated

around Stranghold. Then, without speaking, they all raised their right arms and made a Nazi salute. They held the position for a few seconds and then, slowly, lowered their hands until all of them were pointing at the book on the table. Stranghold placed the large white feather on top of it and started an incantation in German, interspersed with clicking sounds and whispered phrases. Time passed, and as the candles on the table burnt down they were replaced by blonde ghosts wearing Nazi armbands. Stranghold continued chanting; beads of sweat formed on his brow, but his resolve never faltered. Meanwhile two of the black magicians perished, falling down dead where they stood with one of them smashing his head on the edge of the table, leaving a puddle of blood on the floor. Stranghold reached down, took the feather in both hands, then kissed and blew on it gently.

The feather started to glow and swell, then to wilt and melt as the dark spell coursed through it. It had shrunk to half its original size, and turned a nasty urine shade of yellow; its purity had been sucked from it entirely, and it began to fizzle and steam. Another one of the Guild fell to his knees and toppled to one side, with flames shooting from his eye sockets. The mood of the collective was very nearly failing, but suddenly there was a sound like the crashing of waves, and the rumble of thunder in a desert. It travelled swiftly, starting softly in the distance before racing up to them with unparalleled fury. There was a huge boom and what sounded like the wrenching of shoulder joints, then all of the magicians fell to the ground; all were utterly spent, and some were unconscious.

Stranghold was the first to return to his feet. He looked down on the book and let out a faint sob. The feather was just a blackened stump now, but he picked it up gingerly and replaced it inside his jacket pocket; it may come in useful again at some point, he thought to himself. Then, he reached out to the book. His whole life had been spent searching for the power to crush the enemies of his beloved Master Race, and now it was here in front of him.

Or was it?

He hoped with all his being that the spell had worked. Failure now would mean the end for him personally, and all the planning and sacrifice would count for nothing. His fingers were trembling as he stroked the leather-bound book, then he curled his fingertips under the lip of the front cover and gently lifted his hand. The gasps he heard all around him told him that he had been successful. He felt their joy, and he swelled with pride.

The pages of the book were unusually crisp, and the writing was as black as night. Stranghold touched the bottom right-hand corner of the first page and spoke a word not heard in many thousands of years. The pages vibrated, then flickered up and over, turning rapidly until they suddenly stopped, and the information for which the small man had searched the world for the best part of his adult life appeared. He would have called the moment orgasmic, but that was an alien concept to him, so he preferred to describe it as a fulfilling moment of great clarity, instead. He looked down at the page and read the words on it voraciously, from the first letter to the last full-stop, then sat down in his chair and closed his eyes. In his mind, flags were waving, and giant tanks rolled past with legion upon legion of super-soldiers marching behind them in well-ordered squares. Overhead, aircraft that flew without wings roared past, and turned the clouds around them to wisps of white straw in the air. Next he saw the great cities of the modern world on fire, and above them floated a fleet of great Zeppelins, with hundreds of razor-sharp stakes protruding from their metallic bodies. A ghost child was impaled on each stake, and from their mouths lightning rained down on the earth below, burning anything that it touched.

Finally, he understood why the children had been sacrificed all of those years ago. They were the conduits from which the dark magic written in the book would flow. The author of the book described the great floating forms adorned with sacrifices of an unholy nature, firing upon targets hidden in the earth, guided by some sort of homing beacon.

So, that was what the rods were for.

The little man felt all of the missing pieces he had locked away in his sub-conscious start to fall into place. The day was coming, soon; there could be no doubt about that now. All he had to do, along with the rest of the order, was pour the dark spells in the book down the throats of the children. The Zeppelins, he knew, were tethered in giant stone hangers, hidden from sight in the cliff faces all around the island.

His attention was drawn back into the room as he heard the scrape of the great empty chair at the head of the table being pulled out and away from it. He opened his eyes, and saw the remaining members of the Black Magicians Guild lined up on the far side of the room; each one lifted their arm in a Nazi salute, then one-by-one they pointed at the empty chair. Stranghold stood and walked up to it. The old Master of the Order lay on the floor next to it, dead. Nine knives had been plunged into his back. Stranghold smiled, and took his new seat.

"Fellow magicians, we have a lot of work to do…"

8 DESTINY CALLS FROM THE DARK

Williams had left Joachim behind at the bend in the tunnel when the little man had stopped in front of the wooden door on the far side of the cave. The boy was being helpful, and any suspicion that he was leading Williams into a trap had disappeared when he'd quickly stopped and pointed to the badge in his lapel. It had started to glow red. The boy had whispered urgently that it was a summons from the enemy and he could not turn it off, stepping back into the dark with both hands pressed tightly over his breast; the badge and the light had faded away with him. Only when Joachim was completely hidden did Williams move.

He walked forward, making sure to avoid the puddles and the gaping holes in the cave floor, and had nearly crossed to the other side of the cave when the little man had whipped around and stared straight at him. Despite being a ghost and thus physically incapable of such things, he thought he could hear his heart beating ten to the dozen, and the blood rushing around in his ears. One thing he could definitely still feel, and feel very keenly, was fear. It turned out to be the best thing that could have happened, because it rooted him to the spot like a harpoon gun through the toes.

After what felt like a long, long time, Stranghold had turned away and opened the door, and Williams had followed him through into the room beyond. He had passed so close to him, in fact, that he could smell the pomade that the little man was using on his Errol Flynn moustache.

What he saw and heard inside had chilled him to the bone.

He'd watched as some of the men in black robes had fallen to the floor, completely empty of life and spent of all their magic. And when the book had finally opened and the pages had started to flicker backwards and forwards, he knew that what was in essence a book rescue mission had just turned into a full-on search, rescue and then destroy mission. After witnessing the little man taking his seat at the head of the order, and the Caeser-esque death of the previous occupant at the hands of the little zealots who surrounded him, Williams knew that he had to take a breath, wait until the coast was clear and then get out of there as fast as was ghostly possible. He needed to warn Joachim what was in store for him and his Hitler Youth friends. He wasn't sure that anyone would thank him for saving some junior wannabe Nazi troop, but they were children after all, even if they were ghosts.

Williams waited for the black robes to file out, and for the bodies to be dragged from the room, before he moved a muscle. He still found it strange that he could move about without anyone seeing him. The magicians of the Black Sun could see the ghost children, but they hadn't observed him. He'd try to work that out later.

He found Joachim hiding at the back of the tunnel, looking down at a bat with a broken wing. It gave off little whistles of despair, and tried to flap the immobile wing to fly off, but after a few seconds it died, and Joachim turned away. Williams thought he heard the boy whisper a few short words, perhaps it was even a silent prayer. After a few seconds, Joachim looked up at him.

"I saw the little man and the rest of the black robes pass down the tunnel to the library not more than 20 minutes ago, Herr Williams." The boy was not afraid, and he was clearly already keen to get moving, but Williams reached out and motioned for him to stop for a second. The boy was quick on the uptake, and stood still.

"What did you see, Herr Williams?"

"Joachim, do you know anything about some great silver airships?"

"Of course, we all do; they are in the great hangers in the cliff. A long time ago, we were told that we would be taking a trip in them across the seas to the

South Pole to meet up once again with our parents at one of the secret hidden ice bases; but of course it was another lie spun by the magicians and the Lightning Troops of the SS."

When Williams heard the words 'Troops' and 'Lightning' in the same sentence he got excited, but at the same time he felt an ominous feeling of dread, because he knew where the rest of the conversation must take him.

"Joachim, do you know why you were brought here? To the island?"

"We weren't all brought here, Herr Williams. I, and many others, were born here. My Mother fell in love with a German officer, as did many of the other women of the island."

The boy looked around at the tunnel, just like any other boy thousands of miles away might look at his street or a house, and anchor himself to the place of his birth. He belonged on the surface under the sky, not under these endless stone clouds, thought Williams. He felt for the boy at that moment. Here he was, in full 'I love Hitler' fancy dress, a prime example of the master race: tall, blond, muscular, and with shoulders wide enough to make a school sports teacher dream of rugby cups and football trophies. But he was a ghost. A pale, mirror of a soul, held in the balance of time on some evil hook. Williams knew then that he would help the boy do whatever it took to escape this place and, if at all possible, to get away from the Black Sun.

"Joachim, I heard a few things in there that I'm not sure you want to hear."

The boy straightened up to his full height. He wasn't that much shorter than Williams, and his police brain-radar started to ping. This was the moment when bad news either set a light to the blue touch-paper of anger, or placed a huge reassuring hand on the shoulder of whoever you were talking to.

"Listen, Joachim, I appreciate that I wouldn't have got this far without you. I'd still be wandering around the streets of the necropolis up there, wishing that I had a German phrase book on me to read the signs if you hadn't volunteered to help. You've been really helpful, and what I'm about to say will hurt. Those idiots in the big black dresses have something planned for you, and it doesn't involve flying you South for a family reunion, I'm afraid."

The boy's discipline faltered for a second; he shifted from side to side in the tunnel, and after a second or two his hand reached up to the pin on his lapel. Williams watched in silence as the boy scratched at it like some sort of immortal scab that fell away and then grew back again and again. He picked at the meaning of it and its symbolism, but he couldn't remove it; it had become an evil albatross to him. In that moment, Williams saw a lost, murdered, little boy wearing a flag that was too heavy to bear. The boy was at war with himself; his head turned this way and that, and Williams mistook the indecision for doubt.

"I know that the future of the ghost children of

Jersey is not going to turn out well, Herr Williams. We all knew that our time down here under this grey, rocky sky that never moves, was not a prelude to something wonderful. When you have been ghosts as long as we have, you learn to accept your fate, and hope that you get an opportunity to change it. I would rather do something that defines me, Herr Williams, than fade away into the gloom like so many of the others. I will never see my family again – they are surely dead by now – but I do not want to end my time in this form without doing something that I can be proud of.

"Death does not come on speedy wings down here; it seeps towards you like the damp on the walls of the caves that surround us. I fear it, Herr Williams. I would prefer to hear what you have heard, and then make my own decision, please.

"So, tell me what you have heard. If it is something that can change the flow of this twilight existence then I will act. What the others choose to do is their own concern. I will take your words to them and give them the opportunity to choose their own fate."

Williams admired the boy for his calm, measured words and stoic attitude. He hadn't been a ghost for long – a mere heartbeat in the life of a ghost in fact – but in that moment, he realised that any sort of life or existence without hope is to be dead when alive. Being a ghost had its advantages. Not many, but there were a few, and now he must make the most of them. He hoped Judas and the cavalry were en route, because he was about to throw a verbal truth grenade into the massed ranks of the Hitler Youth ghost division.

If they were lucky, then the blast would take out most of the enemy, and he'd be back at the Yard and the Black Museum, giving Jack the Ripper a hard time over a mug of NATO standard tea and a macaroon.

Williams crouched down and motioned for the boy to drop down beside him; when they were both comfortable, he started to tell him everything that he had heard.

9 BLACK FIRE IN THE SKY

"Joachim, what Stranghold read from the 'Book' described a master weapon; a devastating, evil weapon that worked like some sort of super lightning conductor. At first, I thought he was talking about some sort of missile, or a ray beam. Then, as he explained the way it worked and the devastation it would wreak, I started to get a better idea about what he meant when he talked about the fuel cells that would power the weapon. It's you and the rest of the ghost children. You've been stacked up down here like some sort of paranormal arsenal. The airships that are hidden in the cliffs have been modernised; right now, they're sitting there, each equipped with 111 metal spikes sticking out from around their circumference. Like giant, silver, stretched hedgehogs of doom, if you like.

"Then – and this is the bit that made me shiver – then comes the bit where you and the rest of the troops feature. The Black Sun had you all sacrificed for a reason, Joachim. They knew that the war was lost, but they persuaded Herr Hitler to approve their plan and have you all killed. Written in the 'Book' is a spell that requires the ghosts of pure children to make it work. It requires true believers, and rabid, flag followers. You have to believe that you are the avenging angels of the Reich. You have to feel it and want to be there, otherwise the spell won't work. The Black Sun are relying on the fact that the Hitler Youth will see it through.

"Stranghold read that you'll all be taken to the hangars where the airships are hidden, where there'll be lots of flag waving and trumpet fanfares. There'll be flowers thrown in the air like a military parade, a rousing speech, and then, just as you think you'll be walking up the gangplank and setting off for battle, you'll all be taken to one side and impaled on the spikes. Every single one of you, from the oldest to the youngest. Apparently, the spears have been magically charged with Black Sun energy or whatever nonsense they like to call it, which means that when the airships are over London, the little man can use you as a sort of super-conductor to focus something he calls the black lightning. The spell will connect the lightning to beacons hidden inside some of the bigger and more prominent buildings of the city. These beacons have all been hidden already, apparently. When the airships appear and Stranghold speaks the words, cold fire will rain down on the capital and its people.

"Because the airships are magically protected, no radar will detect them, and it'll be pointless scrambling the squadrons of the Brylcream boys of the RAF once the firestorm begins, because there'll be nothing left to protect apart from grey smoke and the smell of burning. The little man said that you had all been stored down here like grains of magical powder to fuel the lightning strikes that would ultimately wipe out the children of Albion.

"Nothing of you will be left, Joachim. Nothing at all I'm afraid. I think he used the word 'melting' at one point. It sounds incredible, but it also feels *true* if you can understand me. I'm not sure why I'm telling you all this, actually. No, that's a lie. I do know. I want to help you. I don't know how you and the rest of the youth are going to react to this news. Maybe you'll all turn on the Black Sun, maybe you'll fight on with them, I don't know. I hope that you'll all find another way to escape, though part of me thinks that if the Hitler Youth are still crazy about the Reich and want to kick-start the 3000-year version they might want to volunteer and help. I don't know. What do you think?"

Joachim had been quiet all the time that Williams had been speaking. He'd even kept quiet when the big British policeman had been searching for words that he felt would not offend the boy in front of him. He was dying to jump in and shake this man, to tell him that he, Joachim, was no *proper* German; he was a half-breed, he had been born on a little island that had had some military and tactical significance a long time ago to a Jersey woman and a German soldier. His parents would never have even bumped into each other or fallen in love unless the world had been at war. When people said he was a war baby, he thought that they meant that he was born during the war; it was only after his death at the cliffs and his new life had begun under them that he realised that what they actually meant was that he was a baby that had been born because of the conflict of nations. He had no real reason to be alive.

Joachim no longer felt any pride in the unholy future project that he and his friends had been told about again and again by the dashing German officers in their striking uniforms. They wore black leather harnesses that shone like dark, liquid gold and their black uniforms cut them out of the backgrounds of the streets they walked along. They were handsome and terrifying at the same time, just as their Austrian seamstress had intended. He had heard their orders and their dogma barked out, again and again and again.

He remembered looking out of the corner of his eye at the children either side of him at the drill classes they had all volunteered for. The wind was causing the green grass to create waves of silver that coursed over the ground and disappeared over the cliffs. Seagulls flew overhead, racing away from a storm or a bird of prey. The clouds overhead ran past like sprinters, all energy and punch; here one minute, the next over France to the south east. And here they all were, standing to attention, and looking to the future via a holocaust and a scorched Earth. In each face he saw, whether it was to his left or his right, there was only the same wild, manic, look in their eyes. Come on! Last one dead gets no glory! They should have all been playing football or trying to kiss girls, but instead they were part of some rabid dog, panting and scratching at the earth to fight and bring death to anyone that was not carrying a red flag with a white circle at its heart and an ancient Indian symbol that had been subverted for evil ends.

If only the purists in the party and the 'youth' had known where their beloved symbol had come from. If only the people of Germany had seen their children being hurled to their death from a cliff on an island that had no relevance to Germany, to become the ammunition required to kill the world long after the Third Reich had faded from history.

Joachim wanted to purge himself of what he knew and felt about the people he had blindly followed, the people that had shone in his youth, like great suns that floated through his formative years, moulding and sculpting him with their tunnel vision of racial purity and Teutonic arrogance. He wanted to cleanse himself of their poisoned views and their black dreams of a singular, straight-lined society, and either die properly or bring down his murderers and see them punished. He wasn't really all that bothered about how it happened, only that it did, and that they suffered.

The tunnel was dark. Williams' words came straight and true, and they bounced off the walls to land firmly in his mind. There was no light down here, but he could see the plan clearly in his mind's eye and he liked it.

Hopefully the others would approve, too. If they didn't, he could see a fair few of them turning nasty. Could a ghost kill another ghost, he wondered? He was about to find out.

10 THE TURNING

Joachim listened to Williams as he explained the last part of his plan. He couldn't explain why he liked the words he was hearing, or why the big, open face of the man who had only just arrived on the island without any shoes only hours before made him feel balanced and centred. Was it just that he was having a conversation that didn't revolve around drills and flag waving? Or was it that the conversation was about movement and actions? He'd been down here for so long with only his hope for company. Had the tiny spark inside started to glow, and grow?

Joachim made some notes in his pad, and his hand trembled as he wrote. The thoughts flowed down through his arm and covered the pages. As the words filled the spaces between the light blue horizontal lines, a memory that had been buried deep down in the dust of his mind came bursting through his consciousness like a phosphorous shell exploding right in front of his eyes.

The day was bright and clear, the green grass of their lawn had just been watered by the gardener, big fat droplets of water bent the backs of the stems of the rose bushes, and the clouds hung in the air as if pinned to the blue sky. His mother approached, smiling. She had both arms locked behind her back. Joachim knew that she was hiding a gift there. Her eyes were bright, and her beautiful face was radiant. He felt the surge of excitement that only mystery brings. When she presented the gift to him, he was elated.

As a member of the Hitler Youth, a senior and decorated member at that, one must always have a notepad for dispatches and orders. So his mother had purchased a beautiful leather-bound case for him. She'd wanted the finest leather on the island, and no expense had been spared; it had the best binding, lots of pockets for maps and orders, and most importantly – a monograph. He had never had cause to use it, though. He was dead before he had a chance to scribble anything inside it.

When Joachim looked down at that first page, it was virginal and pure. No smudges or graphite gashes had marked the surface. 'Nothing to report,' said those slivers of white cartridge paper, 'No news here.' The next holocaust was on hold and the war was over, lost; no plans to be taken note of right now. For that, he was more than grateful.

Williams finished talking and sat back against the

wall of the tunnel. Joachim stood up and made himself presentable, and placed his notepad back in the pocket of his field-shorts.

"I will take you back to the gun room. You'll be safe there, the black robes never go up to it. I'll go back down to the main square afterwards and on to the barracks, where I'll speak to the other commanders and their troops. If all goes well and they agree to join us I'll come to get you. Then we can find a way to destroy the Black Sun."

Williams closed the large iron door after Joachim had departed. The boy looked energised; it was almost as if he had become more solid. When Williams had first seen him he was almost transparent, his clothes were washed out, and all the colour in them had gone. Now, he was fuller and easier to see, even in the gloom of the tunnels. He sat back on the metal bench and thought of Judas and Michael, wishing they were here right now. Of course, that was the next step; he needed to get in touch with Judas, to get word to him about the Zeppelins and the lightning strike, but hadn't a clue about how to do it. He picked up the dusty porn poster from the floor of the gun room and started to construct a paper plane. Or perhaps that should be a paper Juncker, he thought to himself, as the grey light that seeped through the hole in the stone wall of the cliff turned to black.

Joachim had walked down through the tunnels with a spring in his step. Rather than take the direct route as he normally did, he laid a false trail. He was the only one who ever explored up here, but he didn't want to take any chances. He was nervous but excited at the same time and yet he felt uncomfortable too. His whole life, or at least, the brief period of time for which he'd been allowed to live, had been spent in support of the Nazi faith. He had wanted to be a soldier; a builder of the new society of the Reich. He hadn't asked to be killed, or turned into a magical weapon; a ghostly magazine, attached to a lance on an airship that would wipe out people who had no connection with a war that had ended long ago. As for the Black Sun, he had eavesdropped on them many times and the stories that they had brought back into the deep of the citadel from the modern, outside world, did not sound like the actions of a people or race intent on making the world a better place. Far from it. Some of their stories had left him cold.

He stepped out of the main tunnel and stood on the pathway that would eventually lead him down to the main square and the silent canals. He looked down on the rooftops of the barracks and saw the troops marching up and down, waving their flags and sounding the occasional bugle. If they all came, then collectively they would have a chance; if they turned on him and handed him over to the Black Robes, he would be incinerated – turned to dust in a heartbeat.

Joachim set off down the pathway, crossed over the main canal, and turned right into the main square. One of the sentries snapped to attention and saluted smartly. Joachim returned the salute and carried on. He reached the main barracks; a large, square, four-storey building. The windows were huge, and the glass in them had turned a shade of deathly ebony. The design was half Bauhaus, half Bavarian Wolf's Lair. The builders had decided it was safer to nod to the past and wink at the future at the same time when it was constructed. Over the main door hung the flag of Joachim's troop, a bar of iron had been sewn into the fold at the bottom so that it hung straight and true. On either side of the door stood two more guards, holding rifles at the high port that looked like they had been surrendered to them by two friendly giants. The stocks reached down by the knees, and the bayonet clasp hovered just above their heads; grown-up rifles for grown-dead children. Neither moved or registered his presence, as he passed through the door and stepped into the main hall. The rest of the brigade were all here. Bunks of beds, 20-feet high, reached up towards the rafters and the ceiling. The bedding on them was perfectly folded into rectangular parcels, with swan white pillows resting on top of each like a crown. There were a series of long tables that stretched the length of the hall, each seating 100 soldiers on each side. The boys that sat at them now did not eat, joke or talk with each other. Their hands rested palms down on the surface of the table, the space between them filled not with a metal plate and a field can of beer or water, but with dust and memories. Joachim walked up to the company bugler. He had forgotten his name a long time ago, but didn't even bother to read his shoulder flash to find out what it was.

"Bugler, call the brigade to order. I want to make an announcement."

The bugler gazed into the middle distance, raised his musical weapon up and stared down its barrel. Then he took a small breath, or pretended to, and blew into it. The note filled the hall, and every one of the child soldiers scrambled off their benches and bunks, forming into ranks in the centre of the hall within seconds. Joachim walked out in front of the massed ranks, threw out a vigorous salute to the Swastika flag on the wall, then turned and addressed them all.

"Soldiers! How many of you know what is hidden in the stone hangars on the far side of the citadel? For those that know I beg your indulgence, but for those who do not, hear this.

"Hidden in the great hangars are airships. Giant, silver airships! They will soon be readied for flight, and the doors in the cliffs will be opened for the first time since we have all been stationed here. The first time since we lost the war, since we were defeated!"

There was a faint rumble of dissent from the ranks; a few voices could be heard muttering angrily.

"They will be fuelled with power cells from the Black Sun, and they will be targeted at the beating heart of our great enemy, the city of London!"

The atmosphere in the hall was strange; it felt unbalanced and threatening. There was some cheering, of course, because some of the soldiers did not know if they should or should not. Joachim felt the hostility in the air but pressed on regardless, he knew it was a forlorn hope but if he was going to get out, then each and every one of those in front of him deserved the same choice.

'Victory! Victory!' the shouts started at the back and grew louder as they got closer.

"Quiet! Pay attention! Those airships will be carrying secret, magical weapons that will flatten London like a rat's head under a shovel. But before you cheer yourselves into a frenzy, let me tell you something.

"The fuel that will power those weapons will come from whatever soul you still have left! It will be ripped from you by the Black Robes. First, you will be impaled on a silver stake on one of the airships. Then, when the airships are in place over London, the energy of your souls will be dragged out of you; you will be burnt in the heart of a lightning bolt, and smashed into the earth!

"Our deaths have given the Black Sun the power they need to win their battle. But is their battle the battle that we all volunteered to fight? Where are our parents? Where are our flights to the South and to a new world? Lies! All lies!

"The Black Robes have used us for decades, but now we have a choice: if we turn against them and bring them down, we can all board those airships and be free of this island tomb forever!"

Joachim finished his speech and scanned the faces of the front rank. He was looking for any sign that they were with him, or that he should make for the nearest door quickly. The echoes of his words were still retreating away through the halls, getting smaller and smaller, until only the drips of the stalactites were talking.

The ghost children stood perfectly still; in better times he would have been proud of how disciplined they were, and of how well turned out they looked. Joachim wanted to tell them all about Williams, and how he'd listened in to the conversations of the Black Council, but if he were to reveal the other ghost's existence and presence in the meeting the rest of the troops would smell betrayal first, and the truth a poor second, and put an end to both of them. Or worse still, they'd hand them over to the little man and his zealots.

Perhaps it was the thought of Stranghold that had summoned the little man, or maybe there was some sort of spell that alerted him, because the next thing Joachim heard was the soft, perfectly-regimented sound of hands clapping, then there he was, in the flesh, the new leader of the Black Sun. He was the same size as many of the children, so he was able to get pretty close to where Joachim was standing before being spotted. He stopped clapping suddenly. It was strange, because he stood there with his hands in mid-clap position, as if he was carrying a small invisible box that was so precious he mustn't make another movement lest it break. Joachim locked eyes with him. What he saw answered his question unequivocally. He turned, and ran as fast as he could.

In the blink of an eye all hell broke loose, and wave after wave of the ghost children surged forward. They moved at a terrific speed, but because there were so many of them and they were all squeezed into a fairly small space, it was inevitable that one or more of those at the front would stumble, or trip the boy or girl next to him or her, and a few went down. Some of those behind were quick enough to halt or jump to one side, while some simply ran over the person in front. It slowed them down a little, but it didn't stop them, and soon they were all taking turns to let each other out of the main doors to continue the pursuit.

Joachim sprinted across the main square, making for the small bridge over the Uber Rhine. This was the smallest of the canals; some of the boys had tried to jump across it as a dare once, but no more than a few had managed to make it across. Joachim reckoned the bridge would act like a funnel, thinning the numbers in pursuit still further. He had to make it to the tow path that ran alongside the furthest submarine dock with a gap of at least 20 seconds or he would be caught, and some of the boys were faster than he was so he needed every advantage he could think of.

Once he'd traversed the first bridge he ran into the main magazine building, which lay ahead. He briefly tried to slam the great iron doors behind him, but swiftly realised he would waste too much time trying to get the two huge doors closed and the holding bar dropped to lock them together, so he just carried on through, hoping that his pursuers would think he was hiding somewhere between the tall shelves that sagged under the weight of weapons that had been cleaned, but never fired. It might fool a few, but not all of them, so he leapt over the counter where the quartermaster normally stood and ducked inside his office, wedging a chair up against the door handle and climbing out of the rear window to get to the next bridge. He didn't cross this one, even though he could hear the shouting and the pounding of boots on the wooden floor of the building he had just escaped from. Instead, he ripped off his swastika armband, placed it neatly on the first step of the bridge, and stepped to one side, dropping himself over the edge and into the canal, under the arch of the stonework. The water flowed right through him. It was a strange sensation, to see the water without feeling it. The dark of the underside of the bridge hid him from sight, and he smiled as he heard the thunder of who knew how many leather soles pass over him.

Joachim slowly dropped fully into the water, and drifted away from the bridge. If he was correct and his plan was good, then they would double back just as he was passing them in the other direction. Hopefully, they would be looking past and over him and wouldn't see him bobbing along beneath them.

It wasn't long before this hope was put to the test. The shouting, which had become more distant when he was hanging from the bridge, was getting louder once again, and he tried as hard as he could to become invisible. He almost burst out laughing as the thought formed in his head. How can a ghost wish to be more invisible? he thought, as the reflections of the torches the other ghost children carried gnawed at the surface of the water.

His plan worked. The troops were all so fired up with catching the traitor that they passed him by. Moments later, he was climbing up the ladder he had seen Williams clinging on to earlier. Had he somehow known then that that was the moment he'd been waiting for? Was it just curiosity, or was its curiosity's wilder brother, recklessness, that had convinced him to follow the man? That was a question for another time. He had to get into the torpedo tunnel on the far side of the submarine pen as quickly as possible. It was tight, and rose steeply, but Joachim knew that if he could get up it as far as the first loading bay then he would be able to block the shaft and make his escape. It was a big if, but it was the only if he had.

He was just about to enter the mouth of the tunnel and disappear when he heard someone call to him from out of the mist. The voice was weak and thin, and it crept rather than carried. Joachim knew instantly whose it was. The tunnel's entrance was mere feet away, but he would have to reveal his hiding place for a second before he could get to it. So, he waited. The voice slithered out of the darkness once again, but this time it was nearer.

"I don't know your name, little soldier, but if I were you, I would stand very still. You're already dead, in a manner of speaking, so threats may not work on you. But believe me, if you don't surrender to me right now, and tell me what you know and who you heard it from, then dying will turn out to have been the most pleasurable thing you've ever experienced."

The mist dissolved. Or rather, the mist sank swiftly towards the ground then disappeared into the earth. One second you couldn't see a hand in front of your face, the next, you could see everything. It was so clear that Joachim could see the symbol of the Black Sun that was carved into the wall on the opposite side of the main square.

The little man stood in the doorway of the nearest barracks; he looked wispy, and weak, like a little boy wearing his father's best clothes. His size didn't matter a jot though because his words were heavyweights in the evil intent division, and they crossed the space that lay between the two of them like a thunderclap. His frame might be slight, but his words hung heavy in the air.

"Where is that Jewish deceiver, the one they call Judas? Where is the good Lord's bloodhound? The secret protector of England and his Black Museum?"

Joachim took a deep breath and revealed himself. It was no use hiding anymore; he had been run to ground, and it wouldn't be long before the others arrived en masse to subdue him and hand him over to the Black Robes.

The little man smiled, and started to walk towards him. Joachim began to panic, but a voice at the back of his head urged him to be calm. He had a chance; it was only a slim one, and its success would depend on whether the little man had read the Hitler Youth escape and evasion manual, as Joachim had done on so many occasions.

He started to run towards the little man, and pretended to stumble. He hoped this little ruse-de-guerre would buy him at least half a heartbeat. Even a quarter beat would do, because the next few seconds were crucial; everything depended on this moment. He had to make the small magician think that he needed to get past him to make his escape.

The newly anointed leader of the Black Robes had positioned himself in the middle of the only passageway that lead away from the submarine dock, away from the black water and the stone wall, and up into the main square. It appeared to be the only escape route available, but while he knew the layout of the citadel, he evidently didn't know the layout of the tunnels that ran likes roads into it. He was guarding the wrong exit.

Joachim dropped to his knees; it brought him to within lunging distance of the tunnel. He had to concentrate on Stranghold and not to let his eyes betray him, so he started to talk, in the hope that his ramblings would distract the little man.

"Were you there when I was thrown off the cliffs that night? Were you one of the smiling, friendly men in robes of midnight black? The ones who wanted to show us the stars and the heavens, and reveal our final destination – the point on the horizon where the pole star nicked the boundary of the sea and air?

"Away to the south it was, a place so far south, you said, that we would be free to build another world. It was going to be a land of ice and mountains and deep underground places where we would join our parents, away from the allies and the impure. I'll bet that you were, you look like the sort that only fights children!"

Joachim was hoping that a low blow to the man's honour, so low in fact that it scraped along the floor like the heels of a dragged cadaver, would do the trick. He wanted to get him either to relax, to get angry, or to stir some other distracting emotion, then he might have a chance to throw himself into the tunnel and climb for all he was worth.

"Boy, little boy, scared little boy…"

Stranghold's voice curled across the floor like a snake with a mouth full of honey.

"Of course I was there, boy. It was my plan, after all; I alone constructed it. A plan that would not come into effect straight away, sadly, but a plan that would need a power source never before seen.

"You are of one of the Jersey Children, are you not? You are one of the lightning children? I looked into your eyes when you flew into the dark from the cliff edge. How much noise you all made when you suddenly realised that you weren't leaving the island after all.

"I am the last thing you saw after your mother's shiny, tear spattered face. Remember how she hugged you and said goodbye? Remember her soft, light smelling perfume? She cried just like all the rest. Her beautiful but flawed half-Aryan child. Her baby: blue-eyed and strong-limbed; bright and caring; the right sort of boy born into the wrong time.

"Then remember, little bird of Jersey, how we made you fly; over the cliffs, and into the white thunder of the crushing water that smashes into and over the sharp black rocks.

"You were dead the moment you were born. Your German father, and all the German fathers of all the children born to the inhabitants of this, tiny, ugly, cold and wet island were always going to die, too. It was written in a book that grew heavy under the dust of centuries long before this war started.

"Your father, and lots like him, were told to take lovers here; none of them wanted to of course, it was abhorrent to them to mix their good blood with English and French mongrels. But they did it for their love of the master race, and for the creation of the Second Reich. They did it for the rebirth of the Black Sun as the only power worthy to rule the world!"

Joachim had had quite enough of the man's ramblings and looked him in the eye, hopefully for the last time. He could have responded, or pretended to get angry, but he had already guessed what Stranghold was planning, and it didn't include reinstating him to the command team of the ghosts of the Hitler Youth. The little man raised his left arm so that it was pointing just a little higher than Joachim's head; he was about to raise his own salute in return, but realised at the last moment that it wasn't a salute at all. Stranghold was mumbling something, and instead of holding his palm flat to the ground he was bending and interlocking his fingers while the air was blurring all around him. Joachim dived to his right and rolled into the mouth of the tunnel. Rather than trying to stand and run up the shaft he pulled himself along the ground, and at the very last moment he jumped like a frog into the darkness of the tunnel.

The world suddenly turned upside-down. There was a noise like air escaping from a thousand burst tires, quickly followed by what he could only describe as the sound of a giant rubbing two huge rocks together. And that was before the blast, and the explosion. Joachim was only a metre up the tunnel when it hit. The ground shook, and the dust rolled over him like a dirty blanket that shed shards of rock as it passed. The light disappeared immediately, and Joachim almost smiled because his plan had worked; the little man had closed off the only means of pursuit, and all because his pride had required that he show a boy how powerful he really was.

The tunnel below was blocked, so no one was coming up that way for now. The other ghost children would get through eventually, of course, they would drift through the rock in a few minutes if they could be persuaded. It didn't matter yet, though; he was on his feet before the dust had settled and was already running down the second tunnel, completing the first part of his decoy run. He was going as fast as he could, and had a head-start; the others were far behind and he knew the tunnels better than anyone else. But something felt wrong, so he stopped and cleared his head.

Was he leading them to Williams? He had only been thinking about one thing, and that was getting away from the Black Robes and out of this dank prison. He had to be smarter; Williams said he could get him out, but what good was that if they were both burning forever in one of the Black Sun magician's spells?

He set off again, leaving more false trails now. He was almost at the last tunnel junction when he heard the sounds of pursuit far away. He could hear the stupid, piercing whistles of the sections calling out to each other in the darkness. This was going to help him out, this was going to be his shield; the more they peeped and let out their shrill whistles the better – he could pin-point their movements and lead them away from Williams.

It wasn't long before he was walking back up the tunnel to the gun room. He slipped inside and found Williams looking at the breasts of a pin-up model wearing a Valkyr outfit on a poster that had been stuffed into the mouth of one of the spent shell casings. He looked embarrassed and quickly dropped her, but instead of falling away from Joachim she landed at his feet. Joachim picked her up, and placed her back inside the shell where she belonged.

"Herr Williams, we must get away from here. The Black Sun now knows that I have discovered their plans and they are after us. They should be over on the other side of the island by now so we have a little time, but not much."

Williams crossed the room in a flash, which was fast for him; he opened the door an inch, and peered down the tunnel.

"Nothing coming. Quick, tell me what the others said – are they with us?"

"I'm afraid not, Williams. I barely escaped the little man, and the others are lost, I think; they won't accept that the Black Sun are going to use them and then discard them. We are on our own."

Williams paced backwards and forwards; he was trying to think, but he kept getting side-tracked by the breasts he had just seen.

"We're not alone Joachim, we just need to be sure that word gets to Judas. If we can do that, we'll have some muscle and power on our side, too.

"I tried to fill him in on where I was headed and what was going on before I left, but perhaps we should try to send a reminder. What I really need is another ghost. Preferably one that's committed a nasty crime and has done some time in gaol."

Joachim was confused.

"Why do we need another ghost?"

"If I can find another ghost – the ghost of a murderer, for example – I can pass the word to Judas across what we call the Time Fields. In a room called The Black Museum back at Scotland Yard, we have a big table with lots of odd–looking objects on it, and by touching one related to that murderer, we can travel to the time and the place where they lived."

The boy looked confused, so Williams tried to elaborate.

"If we have a magical serial killer case that is proving difficult to solve, we speak to a famous serial killer like Jack the Ripper so we can understand what makes people like them tick. Jack is a full-on narcissist and hates the idea that anyone will take his crown, so often he betrays them, telling us who they are or where they're planning to kill next.

"There are thousands of killers, occultists and weirdos spread all over the Time Fields. They talk to each other, and conspire with each other to cause us harm or muddy the waters if they can. They can't escape, and they have to relive their lives over and over again but without the chance to kill, so they go crazy.

"If we can find an equivalent room to the Black Museum here on the island, or an object infused with the remnants of its murderous owner, then we may be able to warn Judas and get him to bring the cavalry to rescue us. If we can use whatever we find to get the jungle drums sounding in the Time Fields we may get someone or something to alert Judas.

"The Castle of Mont Orgueil!" shouted Joachim.

"It's a tourist attraction now, but it's 800 years old. It overlooks the harbour, and has models of French soldiers guarding the ramparts – fat lot of use they were. There's some ancient occult stuff buried deep down in the earth beneath it – the Black Robes did some digging there once, but gave up on it. I spent some time wandering around the tunnels after they left, and then went back again in the 60s.

There are rooms where the guides never go, and with good reason. In the old days, they hung witches from the battlements then set them alight. They'd take their ashes and whatever was left over, pack it into strongboxes, and move them to the cellars. The locals wouldn't allow the remains to be buried near the town, and the fishermen said no thanks to their ashes being sprinkled over the water because it would curse the fishing grounds. So they ended up being stacked up against one of the walls in the cellars, where they also chained up the odd murderer, or packed a thief or two inside a small metal cage and promptly forgot about them.

"You can feel the bad energy down there, Herr Williams. It's not as potent as the atmosphere the Black Robes live in, but you can feel it, even through the walls of the tunnels nearby. If you wanted to find something or someone that lived and died badly, that's where you'll find them. We can get to it in an hour if we go quickly."

Williams thought that it was the best option, and said so. Joachim checked to see if the coast was clear, while Williams had one last look at some faded German breasts. If his wife knew what he was doing, he'd be a dead man.

11 THE WAVE KILLER

Williams and Joachim ran as fast as they could through the tunnels that led up to the surface. Williams tucked in behind the boy and stayed out of his way – the last thing they needed was to trip each other up and lose time, or alert their pursuers. Although the tunnels were quiet, neither could shake off the feeling that something was coming after them, fast. The boy seemed to know every inch of the tunnels; how long he'd spent searching them all was anybody's guess. This knowledge was what was going to save them, thought Williams, or at least give them a fighting chance.

Ghosts don't get out of puff, which both surprised and motivated Williams. He'd always found a way to get out of the Met's annual fitness test, because he knew that he was too many sausage rolls down the wrong track to run a mile in under seven minutes.

They had been running for about 40 minutes straight when they encountered their first patrol. Joachim held his hand up and closed his fist. Williams had watched enough war films to know that this meant stop and hold your breath, so he did just that. Joachim had flattened himself against the wall of the tunnels, and inched forward until he could see around the corner. He could just about make out the forms of some of his comrades about 20 feet away. Thankfully, they were looking the wrong way; they must have thought their quarry had gone to ground and stayed there. Furthermore, although the tunnels were well-maintained up here near the surface, the ghost section that had been assigned to the position hadn't turned on the lights, which worked both for and against them. The little man would have something unpleasant to say about that, thought Joachim.

The light switch was on the opposite side of the tunnel, only a few feet away so well within reach. Joachim calmly stepped towards it and flicked it. The sudden burst of light set the tiger amongst the pigeons, and Two Section of the Jersey Hitler Youth brigade fell over each other to ready themselves. The section leader, a boy Joachim recognised as Heinrich, whose father was also an SS Officer, shouted at his soldiers and pushed them into position. Joachim motioned for Williams to cross the tunnel, and pointed to the turning on the left a few feet away. Once Williams had disappeared around the corner and was safe, he flicked the light switch down again; the tunnel plunged into darkness, and all he heard as he ran to catch up with Williams was the sound of confusion behind him.

They found a ladder that led up to the old castle moments later, and climbed it as quickly as possible. They opened the hatch that led to the castle's cellars, swiftly entered, then did the decent thing and hauled the ladder up after them. Without its rungs marking the opening, no one would know this was where they were hiding. In front of them were some steps leading to the cellars; Williams followed Joachim up them into a large, dark room that smelt of mould and something that he couldn't quite identify.

Joachim wandered around the room. Occasionally he would stop and stare at a fixed point on the wall for a few seconds and then move on to another. Williams sat down with his back against the wall and tried to put his predicament into some sort of perspective.

It had been a long few weeks, and lots had happened. The U-boat had been cramped, smelly, and full of werewolves, while the island's tunnels had been dark, dusty and full of the smartly-dressed ghosts of the Hitler Youth. He had stowed away and put himself in harm's way far too easily. He'd jumped out of the frying pan and into the fire, then leapt out of that and into the forge for good measure.

On the positive side he and Joachim had learned all about the Nazi warlock's grand plan, and were doing their best to thwart it. But there was something niggling at him, and whatever it was, it was making it hard for him to concentrate, so Williams stood up and began to pace the room as well.

The battle of Clapham Common and the final destruction of John the Baptist seemed very distant; his world had been upside down even before he was killed and became a ghost. Working for Judas and being a part of the Black Museum brought its own fair share of danger and oddness, but now it felt like he had been express-lifted up to a whole new level of weird. As he walked and thought, his hand – guided by the patron saint of doing everything by the book – went in search of his trusty, reliable and standard issue Met notebook.

It wasn't there, of course, so he started to mumble to himself instead and pretended that he was reading from his notes.

They were safe for the time being.

He stopped mid-pace and almost burst out laughing at the sheer stupidity of what he was saying and thinking. They were in the cellar of a very old castle where the cursed and charred remains of medieval witches, killed without a fair trial of course, had been bricked up for all eternity in lead-lined boxes with only each other for company. They were surrounded by the angry and yet disciplined ghosts of the Hitler Youth and Hitler's WWII magicians, who wanted nothing more than to burn alive anyone who opposed them.

If that sounded like a mountain to climb, Williams had already embarked on the K2 version of events.

Williams and Joachim were hoping to speak to the spirit of a 400-year-old murderer, if they could find one. In New York, Johannesburg or the Favelas of Rio, you'd have a pretty good chance, but they were in Jersey: nice, quiet, and not a murder capital of anywhere, Jersey. The chances of finding anyone with a connection to the 'Object Room' here were so slim they were almost transparent.

What Williams and Joachim needed was the opportunity to communicate with another one of history's bad-but-slightly-good guys. Someone like Dick Turpin, for example. He was a nasty piece of work when he needed to be, but it was said that he lived to a code of sorts; he wasn't exactly Robin Hood, but he wasn't Reggie Kray either. This was the type of spirit or ghost that Williams and Joachim really needed to locate. Williams flipped a page in his imaginary notebook and paced on.

Now at least they knew why the 'Book' was so important. It was worth killing for because it could kill a whole nation in one fairly nasty lightning attack.

At the beginning of the investigation the good guys were looking for a serial killer or killers that liked chopping the wings from angels, wrapping them in polythene, and dropping them off at the nearest witches' coven or on the steps of Scotland Yard. Then, the good guys discovered that a secret Nazi organisation was responsible for the whole thing, not some lone wolf or some odd anti-heaven group that had a penchant for blood. John the Baptist had spilled the beans about it all, just before he'd taken a swim to the bottom of the ocean and made his bed there for all time. He and the Disciples had been used as a smokescreen to facilitate the location and the retrieval of the 'Book'.

The Black Sun, as those investigating the case now knew the real perpetrators to be, got very close to acquiring the 'Book' when, by either good or bad luck, it found its way to Judas and the Black Museum. But now they had it.

Now the supernatural forces of law and order knew who they were up against and just how powerful they were. All in all, this had to be a bonus point for the team in blue, at least. He was just about to turn around and do another lap of the cellar when he noticed the boy and stopped dead in his tracks.

Joachim was on the far side of the room, facing the wall, a light grey smudge in the dark. Williams had only known the boy a short while, but he had stopped moving, and because of that he could tell that something was wrong. Very wrong.

The boy was always active, searching for something

or looking for a way out, or a way away, from the island. This was the first time since Williams had set eyes on him that he was stationary. The hairs on the back of the hairs on his neck stood to an impressive Horse Guards Parade level of attention, and he thought at first that the boy was listening to someone or something through the wall. His head was slightly cocked to the right, and he kept nodding as if in acknowledgement.

Williams couldn't hear anything in the cellar; to him it was as quiet as the grave. He walked over to investigate, and was about to tap the boy on the shoulder to ask him if he was all right, when he began to hear the low murmur of a conversation. Joachim clearly heard it, too, and was transfixed. He bobbed his head up and down mechanically, and his fingers twitched uncontrollably. Williams edged closer and he began to catch the odd word or two. He could hear mostly female voices; they whispered and giggled and cajoled, and he began to nod in agreement, even though he had no idea what he was agreeing to. He saw the boy's head start to loll backwards and forwards, as though the energy supply to his ghostly form had gone on strike. A movement in the shadows behind him caught his eye, vanishing as quickly as it had appeared. He turned back to the boy, saw him drop to his knees, twitch his head slightly, before his forehead came to rest on the wall with a slight thump.

Joachim didn't respond. He didn't look to be in pain or distress, just fast asleep. At least, Williams hoped that it was sleep, and not something more sinister.

Without his spectral wingman at his side, Williams was starting to get scared. The voices he'd heard were overlaid on top of other voices emanating from everywhere now; it sounded to his untrained ear as if odd dialects and ancient accents were vying for supremacy in the air all around him. It might just have been his imagination, but it seemed as though the shadows were fighting with each other in one corner, and having sex with each other in another.

The murmuring got louder; it felt as if the cellar were alive with it. Williams spun around, half-expecting to see hundreds of people and dark forms that used to be people trying to squeeze into the space between him and the surrounding walls.

He started to feel a bit light-headed himself; a voice nearby told him that he was sleepy, and could do with a rest. He was just about to nod in agreement when he realised what was happening, and who the voices belonged to.

The iron boxes that held the spirits of the witches had been buried down here, and it was their voices he was hearing. Judas had told him many times – or rather warned him – about listening too hard or being conned into listening to the voices in the Black Museum back at the Yard. He'd been caught out once before by Jack the Ripper and would've paid the price had it not been for his boss. Having been down this dark alleyway before, he had a word with himself in no uncertain terms, and focused.

He reached out, grabbed Joachim's collar, and dragged him away from the wall into the centre of the room. The boy was as limp as a window-cleaner's chamois, but his eyes were wide open. He looked particularly odd, and Williams was about to ask him why he was so heavy, him being a ghost and all, when his own strength evaporated, and he dropped to the floor like a stone, with the mother of all headaches and his ears ringing.

Joachim woke, feeling strange, and found Williams laying on the cellar floor next to him. He looked down at his arms and examined his hands; even in this poor light he knew that they had grown more transparent, and less dense. He was beginning to fade away; something had sucked away some of the life he still had left in him.

He gave Williams a nudge; Williams snuffled, and opened one of his eyes.

"Why are we on the floor?" said the boy.

"You were attracted to something over there by the wall and had fallen asleep or unconscious, I couldn't tell which; I just grabbed you, and this is where we ended up. I think, for once, we fell out of danger instead of into it."

The boy stood up and straightened his uniform.

"I heard voices, Williams. Women's voices, whispering and telling me things, and then I woke up here with you."

"At a guess I'd say they were the lost spirits of the witches, Joachim. They must have fused with the very fabric of the castle after all these years, a bit like the Sirens that attempted to lure Odysseus to his doom or something like that. Let's get out of here in case we start hearing them again."

Joachim helped Williams to his feet, and together they climbed the stone stairs up, and out of the cellars.

The Castle of Mont Orgueil was something akin to Alcatraz or Colditz to the locals who lived here hundreds of years ago. Then it was a cutting-edge, high-tech holding pen that men and women feared. Now it was a tourist attraction of course, and Joachim and Williams had entered an exhibit room within it.

What remained of the weapons of mass bodily destruction were on display; all of them had been cleaned until they looked sore, then laid to rest on purple velvet cushions. Yellowing bits of card that described which orifice a device was normally aimed at during an interrogation had been tied on to the exhibits with brown twine.

The walls displayed faded pictures that had all seen too much daylight. Posters that were reproductions of reproductions shouted at them in French and English to fight the good fight against a number of conflicting enemies. The German posters –much better designed than the others of course – informed citizens that resistance was futile, told them to wear their rifle butt bruises with honour and pride, and warned them not to forget that it's Hitler's birthday next Friday so take a bath and comb your hair. Jersey had seen its fair share of guests, tenants, invaders and gits over the years, and someone had taken great pains to show all of them in their worst light here. Apart from the English, of course, who were forever riding to the rescue.

"Where do we find this cage, then?"

The enclosure they were looking for had to be big enough to hold a man, or men, and there certainly wasn't room for something of that size inside this room as far as he could see. Joachim pointed at the large faded tapestry that covered the entire wall behind them. Jersey was pictured there in all its glory. Everything from the odd riptide on the bay, to the lost church on the cliff edge that wasn't really lost at all.

"Look behind it, Herr Williams."

Williams moved one of the cases of pokers and pincers to one side, and pulled the cord that moved the tapestry back and forth along a brass pole that had been screwed to the ceiling. A hundred years' worth of dust and mites filled the air; if Williams had been alive it would probably have killed him. Once the tapestry had been pulled aside, Williams could see a small wooden door that had been concealed behind it. There was no key in the lock, so he turned the metal hoop handle; the door gave a little embarrassed squeak, then opened. They both stepped through the doorway; once inside, they made sure to pull the tapestry back to its original position and close the door.

You would have been hard pressed to squeeze an adult-sized table tennis table into the room. It was so small that Williams could reach each wall with outstretched arms just by standing in its centre. Mind you, it would have cost a fortune back in London.

Against one wall was a cage. Iron, definitely. Too small for any normal-sized man of course, and because of its small size, and its lack of headroom and legroom, it would have been very painful to spend any time inside. So this was the cage where all the really bad people did their hard time, thought Williams.

Joachim moved back to the door, and put his ear up against it. After a few seconds he gave Williams a nod, and made the thumbs-up sign.

"Here is the cage I spoke of, Herr Williams. On the wall are the names of the men who died inside it."

Williams saw the faded old list on the wall, and bent forward to read it. None of the names stood out, he'd never come across any of the them in the Black Museum's archives. He wasn't surprised, though. Interpol hadn't been invented back then, so why on earth would he recognise any of them?

"Pot-luck it is then, Joachim!"

"What is pot-luck, Herr Williams?"

"We'll have to guess, and hope that one of the characters on this list was mad and bad enough to leave part of his essence or soul behind.

"It's the way it works back at the Black Museum; evil attaches itself to people, and sometimes it's so strong that it continues to live on after their physical form has died in the clothes they wore, or the instruments they used. We can speak to Jack the Ripper, Spring Heeled Jack and any other well-known nasty piece of work from any period of time just by holding an object that they used, or that we've been able to imprison them inside.

"Do me a favour. Pick a number from one to 11 for me."

Joachim waggled his head from side-to-side and raised his eyes to the heavens in that way that little boys do when they pretend to think hard about something. Williams watched him as he struggled to choose a number, and it struck him just how young the boy really was. He had lived –if you could call it living in the tunnels and the dark spaces of the shadows and the Black Sun citadel – surrounded by mad little Nazi wizards that wanted to impale him and the rest of the see-through Hitler Youth on an invisible airship, then send millions of volts of lightning through them all. He had become friends with the boy, and hoped he would be able to get his message through to Judas in time to save him, as well as London. Williams' own wife and child were still living in the capital, and he had a duty to serve and protect the public, whether he himself were dead or alive.

"Try number seven."

"Seven it is, Joachim. Looks like he's a lovely sounding chap – Wilfred Benoit, also known as the

'Wave Killer'. He's thought to be the island's first serial killer, and an altogether disgusting and criminally insane individual. He was a highwayman by trade and was very successful, it seems, avoiding capture for many years. He developed an appetite for drowning the people he had waylaid on the roads; murdering them, then stripping their dead bodies, placing them on the beach and drawing what local law enforcement at the time thought were magical symbols around them. For magic, read black magic, and then Satan.

"Apparently there was an island-wide search, and Benoit was captured in the dead of night under a full moon in August; he had a stick in his hand, and was trying to finish his last pattern in the sand around a local woman's freshly drowned body. He was then forcefully invited to stay in the cage, naked of course, and made to rest without a pillow until all the locals had taken it in turn to spit and urinate over him. Once the Islanders had all used up their week's supply of bodily fluids, Benoit was taken from the cage to the Mont Orgueil and tortured to death. And just in case he hadn't seen the errors of his ways, his dead body was placed back in the cage, and hung from the battlements until October. There was very little of the carcass remaining afterwards, but the men tasked with taking the cage down said that as they dragged it down the stone steps of the castle they heard what sounded like someone laughing hysterically as they carried it away. He sounds just like our man."

The cage was cold to the touch. This was odd, because the room was well heated by a pair of giant wrought iron radiators and the windows were all double or triple glazed, so it should have been at room temperature at the very least. Williams hoped that there was something left of Benoit living deep down inside the steel, and both men could start to feel as much as they dragged the cage into the centre of the small room. Underneath the lattice of iron bars they could also sense something else. It was like swimming in the sea and feeling two currents at work beneath you; all you had to do was put one foot a little further down towards the sea bed, and half your leg would go numb.

Joachim heard something that frightened him, and it wasn't coming from the cage. He dashed to the door, opened it, and pushed the tapestry aside and disappeared out into the exhibit room; the small door closed with a soft bump and he was on his own.

Williams had a good idea about what had caused Joachim to react in this way, and started to talk to the cage. He'd seen Judas do it many times. But that was back at the Black Museum. This wasn't the museum, and the cage might not be personal enough to Benoit; it wasn't an old keepsake, a mask or a favourite pistol, but it was their only chance to get a message out to Judas.

"Benoit? William Benoit? My name is Sgt Williams…Is any part of you still here inside the cage?"

Nothing happened, so he tried again.

"Benoit, can you hear me? We need your help, and if you do as we ask, we may be able to do something for you. Speak to me, and we might be able to get you…"

Suddenly, the sound of the sea rushed into the room. A few seconds passed, then it came again; this time there was also the sound of the surf being stroked, and wet sand being scratched.

Williams was about to start talking again when he remembered how Judas used to work on the evil spirits, making them feel as if they were getting something in return for the information that he wanted. The scratching sound stopped, and the temperature in the room dropped so that Williams could see his breath waft across the room. Then a voice from far away began to talk.

"What do you want of me?"

The accent and the pitch of the voice itself reminded Williams of sword swinging heroes from the Saturday Morning Picture Show at his local cinema when he was a boy. He saw powdered wigs, and bright red coats with heavy leather holsters full of pistols and swords, with huge hand protectors that curved over their handles.

"Benoit, you were once a highwayman on this island. Did you ever travel abroad, to England, perhaps?"

He heard the sound of something smashing in the room outside and knew that time was not on his side – again.

"I have travelled far and wide in my time. I've lifted purses on all of England's highways, whether it was my patch or not! What's it to you?"

"How would you like to be freed from this cage, to go back to those roads and to ride them forever?"

"Too many maidens have I put to sleep under the waves, stranger; this is my resting place now, and none can free me from it."

"What if I could do it? I only need you pass a message to someone for me in return."

"There are no others here with me, only the shimmering walls and the echoes of the dead. I cannot pass your message to anyone."

Williams could detect sadness in Benoit's voice, but

also hope, and his heart lifted.

"The shimmering walls you can see are just the borders of your small world, Benoit. They can be pushed back. All it would take is for me to borrow a small token from you; if there was something here in this room that was important to you, I could take it away with me, and place it at the heart of a place called the Black Museum. There is great power there, and it is connected to the City of the Heavens. If I place your token on a great table there, we have the power to make the space you live in much bigger. There will be ghosts of your past there, although you will not be able to harm them. All I need is for you to pass a message on to someone I know, or to persuade someone else to pass it on to them."

The sound of the waves increased; when they landed on the beach, the boom they made sounded like vast drums being beaten from a long, long way away. Benoit's voice became a whisper, and Williams had to strain hard to catch his words.

"How do I know that you will keep your word? You could walk away from here and leave me to my torment in this empty place. I can hear voices and I think I see people in the mist that rolls off the sea, but hundreds of years of solitude have made me mad. How do I know that this voice, your voice, is real?"

Williams heard another thud followed by a crash from the room outside, and rushed over to the door. He opened it, and lifted the corner of the tapestry carefully. There was no sign of Joachim in the outer room, but the cellar door was open and from it there came the sounds of battle from the tunnels below. Bright flashes of light illuminated the stone walls of the cellar, and smoke crept up and out of the darkness like long thin fingers searching for handholds on the walls.

Williams was torn between leaving Benoit and his cage, and charging down the steps and into the fray. If the boy was captured and the Black Sun burned what was left of his soul, he would regret it; the boy was brave and true, and without him Williams would not have got far. He knew all this, but he also knew that if he didn't get the message out to Judas then a lot of boys of Joachim's age would be joining him in the spirit world prematurely.

He turned away from the din of battle, and stepped back into the room with Benoit the Wave Killer.

"Will you pass the message on, Benoit?"

Williams shouted his request into the air above the cage. If Benoit had gone again, then Williams could have lost his chance to save London and lost Joachim as well. In the silence that followed, he feared the worst. But just has he was about to turn the cage over and throw it against the wall, he heard Benoit's voice.

"Take the leather garrotte with the small polished stone attached to it; that weapon of mine is as much a part of me as my own blood. If you are true in what you say, then that will summon me to this place of power, the one that you call the Black Museum. I will pass your message on at the shimmering walls, to the shapes that live beyond them. Then I shall await your summons."

"Thank you, Benoit."

Williams quickly passed his message on in full to the spirit, then pocketed the leather garrotte and rushed away to rescue Joachim.

12 STANDING AND DELIVERING

A crow landed on the rotten wooden rail right in front of where Dick Turpin, England's most famous highwayman, was swinging by his neck and dreaming of riding his horse, the legendary Black Bess, again. Dick was part of the time fields. Like a number of gentlemen thieves and likable rogues of his time, Dick was an honest criminal; he never harmed anyone if he didn't have to and he was never a greedy man. Some of his victims drank to his good fortune even after he had robbed them, because he always left them with something to get home with; their purses would definitely be lighter, but never ever totally empty. Dick was one of the good bad guys, and he was the intended recipient of Williams' message. Turpin could climb down from the noose whenever he wanted to, but like all the inmates of the time fields and the Black Museum, he had to be punished from time to time. He could be riding Bess hell for leather one minute and then he'd be swinging from the gibbet and experiencing the pain of strangulation the next. That was just the way it was.

The crow had a bird's nervous tick, and its head and neck would have qualified for the St Vitus' Dance world championships such was the speed and energy of its movement. In this part of the time fields, birds flew and horses whinnied just as you'd expect in the real world, but the differences were apparent for all to see: the colours of life had been rubbed away, and a cold, wet mist hung to the earth like upside-down clouds.

The crow hopped from its perch and landed on Dick's shoulder. A maggot was trying to hide itself underneath his neckerchief, but the bird had seen it already, casually nipping its rear end and snatching it away. Lifting his head, the crow made one throaty screech and swallowed the maggot whole.

"Watch that bloody neckerchief you little thief! That was a present from the Queen of the Gypsies down Hampstead way!"

The crow wasn't expecting to hear anything from the withered old carcass that was swinging in the breeze, and nearly coughed up the maggot in surprise.

"Go on now bird, away you go. It's time for Dick to stretch his legs."

The crow was just a black dot in the silver sky when Dick slipped his neck out from the noose, landing with a muffled thud on the wooden planks that made up the platform of the gallows. He cricked his neck and turned left, then right, to restore his vision. He lifted a bony hand to his neck, and examined the neckerchief.

"A little tear, no more. It still looks as beautiful as they day I won it at the Devil's Punchbowl point-to-point horse race."

Dick placed two fingers into his mouth, and whistled long and hard. Then he sat down on the bottom step and waited for Bess. She wasn't long in coming, and within the hour they were racing down the road towards London.

They had been riding for almost a day when Dick heard it the first time. There was something just on the edge of his hearing, like voices arriving from far away. He reined Bess in and they left the road, trotting towards the silver wall that marked the edge of Dick's world. The wall ran down through a stream and up the other side of the bank, then passed straight through the centre of a giant oak tree before disappearing, along with the rest of Dick's world. If he were to try and ride into that darkness, he would just find himself back at the gallows.

The tree was making the noise that he could hear. Bess sniffed at an acorn that she found at the base of the trunk and nibbled at it. Dick dismounted, and put his ear to the wood. The voice he heard was familiar to him, but he couldn't place it straight away. It was only after a few seconds had passed that he recognised who it belonged to.

"Well, well, well; if it isn't Jack with the spring in his

heels! Jack! We haven't spoken in quite some time, have we? You still running around town with those springs in your shoes, ripping bodices and tearing dresses and shifts?

"Spring Heeled Jack, indeed! What's all this noise about then?"

Black Bess lifted her head and went off in search of some decent grass; she didn't like being this close to the border between such different times in history. On this side of the wall she could enjoy the countryside and open roads, on the other it could be anything at all – grimy Glaswegian streets, perhaps, or the dangerous docks of Liverpool. She saw a nice patch of fresh grey grass and gave the situation no more thought.

Meanwhile, Dick kept his ear to the tree, nodding occasionally in agreement with something that Spring Heeled Jack was telling him from a few hundred years into the future. Bess was enjoying the grass when her master suddenly called for her. She knew from the pitch of the whistle that it was urgent, so she stopped nibbling at the turf and galloped over to him; sure enough, there he was, pacing up and down and slapping his black tricorn hat against his skinny little legs.

"Back to the gallows, my Black Bess; fast as ever you can run my lady! We need to get a message to the Inspector, and we got no time to lose!"

Bess was off and running. She churned up the mud of the road with her powerful hooves, sending clods flying into the air behind her. She ate up the miles greedily, Dick easing her back every now and again by squeezing his knees together; they knew each other so well that a little nudge was all it took, and that worked both ways. They reached the top of Gallows Basin Hill, and there in the hollow were the gallows. Bess had once made history by racing from London to York faster than any other horse had ever done, and looking back at the hill, the road that led over it, and all the way to the shimmering wall by the giant oak tree, Dick thought to himself that she'd have set another record if she had been timed for this ride. Dick removed his saddle from Bess' back; there was a fine sheen of sweat there, but she just trotted away to have a rest, as if she had just run to the stables and back.

Dick climbed the steps of the gallows, reached up, and grasped the rope that had once robbed him of his breath. He closed his eyes and concentrated. This wasn't something he'd had to do for a long time, and he hoped that he was doing it correctly. He could feel the strands of the rope in the palm of his hand – they reminded him of Black Bess' mane – then an unusual but vaguely familiar sensation began to whisper to him from somewhere in his past. Both his eyes were closed, but he could sense that the sky above the gallows had darkened drastically; the blackness behind his eyelids seemed to get deeper, and if he were a fanciful man he might have supposed that if he were to let go of the noose he would drop into the void and disappear forever.

He held the noose even more tightly and thought

about the mask that he had surrendered to the Black Museum all those centuries ago. The custodians of the Museum had said that when he stood on the gallows and held it with both hands, it would be just like one of those magic mirrors you'd find at one of the county fayres. They would be able to see him, and he would be able to see them, and if he helped them then they would set him free. They'd brought Bess back as a show of good faith and freed him from the bite of the noose, and because of that he was now forever in their debt. Hanging from a noose on a rickety old set of gallows for the rest of your days was punishment enough, and there was no arguing with the fact that he deserved to be punished, but earning your freedom back and then, just maybe, eternal rest for him and Bess? Well, that was something he would risk all for.

The first time he had been summoned to the gallows and seen the giant angel and the immortal man, he had been petrified. This time, he was still frightened, but there was something else hovering nearby in his consciousness that made the experience not nearly as terrifying.

In the old days, when he had been alive and whole, he would have called it 'hope' and after all this time swinging in the breeze playing host to maggots and crows that used his shoulder as a WC, he was going to do everything he could to realise that 'hope', by doing the right thing. He'd robbed from thousands who'd probably never done a bad thing in their lives, taken hard-earned money, and swiped the family jewels. And now he had a chance to give it all back – metaphorically speaking, of course.

I'd bet a sovereign that I'm the first highwayman that is just about to stand and deliver to someone else though, he thought.

He tried to relax. The gallows creaked underneath him, and the crows croaked and cackled with each other from the branches of the trees across the meadow, but nothing was happening, and the noose would not talk to him. The immortal man had said that it might take some time to connect with the Black Museum, but time was not on his side right now. He wanted to get the message that Spring Heeled Jack had passed on to him, to Judas, as soon as was non-humanly possible. He was just about to give up when his arm went numb, and his eyes started to burn with the brightest light he had ever seen. From far away he heard voices, lots of them, cursing and shouting at each other.

13 YOUR MONEY OR YOUR LIFE

Detective Inspector Judas Iscariot was sitting at one of the plastic tables in the Yard's canteen, minding his own business. He was counting the coffee circles that had been burned into the table's surface over and over again. The clock on the wall above his head goaded him with every tick and every tock. He was sitting as far away as possible from the 'Instant Response Team' that had taken up residence at the tables nearest the doors. He loathed their over exaggerated muscles, on-trend tattoos and wooden heads. It wasn't just that they were noisy, arrogant and liked to wear their veins on the outside, looking like surface-level skin spaghetti stuck on with cellophane; it was their utter belief in the power of their weapons that got on his nerves. Guns and steel were formidable weapons, but there were far more dangerous things out there than a bullet.

The female PCs on the team had even bigger testicles than the guard dogs, and the conversation that flowed across the room from their tables would have earned groans and raising of multiple eyebrows from a secondary school debating society.

The coffee in the plastic cup in front of him had turned to brown milk a long time ago; he wished he were somewhere else, but he couldn't leave the station. There had been no word from Williams, Ray or even Michael. Whenever the big winged bruiser showed up it usually meant bad news, but it was funny how Judas was actually coming to rely on him now. Having Michael around freed some space for him to think, and to plan ahead instead of constantly reacting to situations; his presence gave Judas time to exist.

He was thinking about Williams and John the Baptist. Two people: one from the past, and one from the now. He'd been responsible for the destruction of both. One of them had lost his life, while the other had been turned mad by an evil little bastard that wanted to set fire to the world.

He'd spoken to Williams' widow and seen the look in her eyes when he'd told her of her husband's death. When he'd been resurrected by God, one of the many weapons he'd been given by the almighty was an ability to read the thoughts of others. He didn't use it often, but there were times when a little peek into someone or something's thoughts could save the day, and give him the upper hand in dangerous situations. He couldn't hear everything, but what he did pick up gave him a little snapshot of their feelings, hopes and desires. More often than not it also revealed a lot of hate and fear.

This thought-reading ability *was* a gift, but also a curse. He'd known people in every decade and century that he had lived through, that had prayed, murdered and risked all for the gift of eternal life or the gift of the second sight who would agree; when it had been gifted to them, they had only realised at the end what sort of a *gift* it really was.

When Judas had gone to see Williams' widow he'd left feeling much sadder than he'd been when he'd arrived. He'd expected a grieving widow, with little black mascara rivers coursing down her face and scrunched up tissues thrust up both cuffs. Instead, all he'd found was anger and hatred.

It had never occurred to Judas that Williams' wife had been anything other than a staunch, caring and strong wife. But he discovered at that meeting, in their home, that she'd hated Williams all her married life. She told Judas over and over again about how Williams had been the ticket out of Wales that she'd craved; he'd given her one willingly, and as it turned out, stupidly. She said, in between angry sobs and shouting at the child, that he'd never loved him at all. As he sat there in their two-up, two-down house, styled in the latest Scandinavian flat-pack, the waves of negative energy smashed into him like an angry tide. He could see the fear growing and growing inside her, like a balloon filling with helium. She had been having nightmares about losing the house every night since Williams had died. And here she was, alone in London: a young widow with limited opportunities and lots of stretchmarks.

In her mind, all this was true, all Judas saw was a lonely, frightened young woman looking for a new tunnel with some light at the end of it. Regardless of how she felt about Williams, he would make sure the Met looked after her. There were different rules for the Black Museum, and he hadn't asked for anything in well over two hundred years. Also, the current Superintendent was a good man, he knew what sort of things went on inside the Museum and what sort of crimes Judas and his team investigated. He liked to know that the crimes were being solved, but he didn't like to know about who was committing them, which was fair enough. He would make sure that she kept the house, and he'd divert a few quid into her bank account from one of his reserves. It would be enough for her to live well and put an end to her dark thoughts.

Judas suddenly became aware that the noise in the canteen had dropped to a manageable hum. The 'Instant Response' team had obviously responded in an instant to something that required a show of *farce*, and the canteen was blissfully calm. He was about to get another coffee when his scar started to itch. That meant danger. He fed the recycling bin another empty coffee cup on his way out.

At the end of the corridor he saw that the lift doors were closing really slowly, like two oil tankers on a collision course, and he was able to get in before anyone started pressing the inverted triangles button as fast as they could. Once inside he reached over and pressed the black button that was sandwiched in between those marked six and eight. As expected, the occupants of the lift all shuffled backwards a step or two. Only the Black Museum team got off on the black button floor. Thankfully, the uncomfortable silence that followed didn't have to last too long, because the lift itself moved a lot faster than its doors. As soon as it had shuddered to a halt and he'd been released by the sound of the exit ping, he ran down the corridor to the Key Room as fast as he could. The itching of his scar had become an uncomfortable throb now, and the intensity of the feeling itself was starting to really worry him.

He stopped outside the door to the Key Room, pulled the black credit card-sized key from his pocket, and swiped it through the metal lips of the lock. The door opened with a soft hiss and he stepped inside, straight into a wall of noise.

The Black Museum was London's most secret prison. Only a few people knew of its existence. Even the Prime Minister and the Secretary of State were kept in the dark about it, lest one of them babble about it when they were in their cups at their private Mayfair club.

The inmates of the museum were all dead. Each one of them had committed such revolting crimes when they were alive that after they had been hanged, drawn and quartered or stoned to death, their spirit was sentenced to an afterlife of torment. And once you were locked up inside, you were there forever.

They lived inside the museum in row upon row of glass cases and filing cabinets. Looking down on them from the walls were photographs of London's worst criminals and the scenes of their most heinous crimes. The museum had a full set of Jack the Ripper's knives, lead pipes wrapped in blood-stained bandages that had once belonged to a minor member of the Royal Family, and cut-throat razors that had cut a lot of throats in the East End.

The weapons were infused with the spirits of those that had wielded them; they could speak to each other, and they did so in the embodiment of their crimes. So blackmail letters tried to turn anyone that would listen to them mad, and jars of poisons whispered about nagging wives and regicide. Meanwhile, rubber tubes and nooses spoke in gasps and choking noises, while leather gloves grunted and struggled to get the strangled words out.

The problem was that they all liked to talk all at the same time, and when they'd been left alone for too long they all went a little crazier than what counted for normal in this place.

Judas slammed the door behind him; it gave a reassuring mechanical click as the lock activated.

"All right now, settle down, settle down!" said Judas.

The voices stopped their bickering and the room

instantly fell silent. Aside from the odd mumble and the creak of a cabinet, all was still and quiet.

His scar was going crazy now, so he started to walk around the room and up and down the rows of glass cabinets, stopping now and then to place a palm onto the cold surfaces, searching for a clue to the source of the disturbance. Then from somewhere close by he heard the flash and smash of a flintlock, the creak of well-worn leather, and the sound of horses snorting and stamping. The sounds came from the Key Room, and Judas knew exactly who was responsible for making them.

He passed through the outer room of the museum, and went straight to the Key Room, and looked for the black leather mask that a certain Mr Richard Turpin wore to work. There were lots of keys arranged on the huge table inside. They weren't keys in the normal sense of the word, but items that provided access to prison cells in the Time Fields; they were housed here for safe keeping.

Dick Turpin's key was the mask he wore as a highwayman. It was a crude covering, made of a single piece of leather with two misshapen eyeholes cut out.

Judas scanned the surface of the table, wishing that he'd paid more attention to the angel called Malzo who had, until very recently, been the former Warden of the Black Museum. The evil that was locked up inside the Museum was potent and powerful, and it needed a strong pair of wings to keep it all under control. Malzo had been an important angel once, respected and revered, but he'd nailed his colours to the wrong mast in the one and only celestial leadership contest in the City of the Heavens. He should have known better, but the candidate that secured his vote – Lucifer the Morning Star – was very persuasive; you only had to ask Adam and Eve.

After the battle that had ensued between Lucifer and his supporters and the Archangels, led by Michael of the flaming sword and really bad anger management issues fame, Malzo was not just on the losing side, he was cast out of the City of the Heavens in disgrace. The other angels had shown him a modicum of mercy and had only clipped his wings for him. This was not the same has shearing them off completely, which would have meant they'd never grow back. No, they'd let Malzo keep his, because at one time he had been a loyal and good soldier of the Host. His real punishment hurt much more than the temporary loss of his wings, though; he was banished to Earth where he was to take-up the position of a turnkey and warder at the prison known as the Black Museum.

Malzo served his time at the museum stoically. He patrolled the time fields diligently in the beginning; and once his wings had regrown he flew across them again and again, keeping watch over the killers and the rapists of old London Town. He kept two-eyes on the worst, and occasionally turned a blind one to some of the others. He did his time alongside the inmates, knowing that there was no early release for them but dreaming endlessly that there might be one for him.

Angels live a long, long time – much longer than a mortal can imagine or understand – and Judas eventually came to understand the true magnitude of Malzo's punishment. When he had first entered the museum, the angel was distant and angry. It would not speak to Judas or anybody else unless it absolutely had to do so, communicating instead in rumbles and distant thunder. It would slam doors and lock them, and even make the museum disappear for weeks on end. But over time, Malzo had revealed himself to Judas, and had even saved his life by stopping one of the museum's most evil of inmates from escaping.

Jack the Ripper was that inmate. He'd found a means to unleash centuries of evil on present day London, and he would have succeeded had it not been for Judas and Malzo. The angel had been grievously wounded by Jack, but he had redeemed himself through his actions and had been allowed to return the City of the Heavens.

Judas wished he was here right now, because his eyes were starting to get tired. He'd never really realised how big this table really was before. It stretched on and on. It looked like it was a square table from one angle, but as you walked along one of its sides, it began to stretch, becoming more like a long thin rectangle. He'd originally thought that perhaps a few hundred keys lay on it, but now he could see that there were thousands. He could be here all day, and if the throbbing of his scar was anything to go by, he didn't have half as long as that. He stopped looking at the table and closed his eyes for a second.

There had to be a way to get the right key to identify itself.

Then, a thought came to him. He'd met a few highwaymen in his time and each of them claimed to have a 'special way' of doing their business. They didn't want to be caught or identified, of course, but if an act of derring-do was to be performed then the public should know who was responsible.

Judas span round, and with his best highwayman voice shouted:

"Stand and deliver!"

He felt like a complete idiot, but it was worth a try.

Nothing happened in the room for a few seconds, then from the far end of the table, he heard the voice of Dick Turpin reply:

"Your money or your life!"

Judas traced the sound of the voice, and there in the corner of the table, just next to a vicious looking claw-hammer, was a leather mask. He reached over, picked it up, and closed his eyes; when he opened them again, he was standing on a set of rotten wooden gallows, looking straight into the one good remaining eye of one of history's most famous highwaymen.

14 SILVER SWORDS IN THE SKY

"Got a message from Spring-Heeled Jack, Judas. Not heard from him for a long time.

"Anyways, he calls to me through the boundary of his world into mine, and says he has a message for me. Strange type he was, his voice started high up in the trees, then the next you know he's down at eye level. Up and down he went, and it was hard to hear sometimes but the gist of it is this:

"Williams is in Jersey and needs your help desperately. There's a tunnel city underground, and he's under attack there from a small magical man. The book is unlocked, and London will be destroyed by silver swords from the sky. Oh, and bring the angels.

"That's all, I think. Yes, that was all he said."

"You're sure, Dick?"

"Absolutely, sir. I may be half-eaten by worms and

crows, but my noggin is still sharp."

"Good man, Dick, I'll make sure you're rewarded for this."

"Whatever you think is right, sir, although my old body as it was would be something…"

"I'll see what I can do, Dick."

Judas closed his eyes once again, and when he opened them he was back in the Key Room. He placed Dick's mask back on the table where he had found it, and ran back to his office. Once there, he rummaged through the pockets of his jacket. The first thing he found was his silver coin. He placed it on the table in front of him. It might be more of a silver disc than currency now, but it still had the power to remind him of his painful past in an instant.

But now was not the time to dwell on that.

He found what he was looking for in the right-hand pocket of his suit jacket.

It was a plain business card with a London mobile number on it and one word written in a forgettable sans-serif typeface – Evenor.

He dialled the number, and after three short beeps he heard her voice.

"Yes?"

"I have need of your services, Evenor."

"I will be ready."

The line went dead. Judas returned the card to his pocket, picked up his silver coin again, and rubbed it. His mind was racing: the scar had calmed down a bit, and he knew that Williams was alive, albeit in grave danger. He also knew that the little man had opened the book, whatever that meant. And what were these silver swords that Dick was talking about? Judas got up, took his long dark blue coat from the peg on the wall, and put it on. He went through the same departure routine as always, locking the door to his office, and making sure that the fire exit that led onto the seventh floor could only be activated and opened by someone who was museum-briefed and museum-friendly. Health and Safety would have had a field day with him, but people would have been safer with the fire than with what lived behind some of these doors. He waved to the Duty Sergeant as he walked through the foyer, and stepped out into what Londoners amusingly referred to as sunshine. He had an idea about how he and Evenor could get to Jersey as quickly as possible, and it didn't involve travelling in anything with four wheels or a combustion engine, so he took the Northern Line to Clapham Common.

The church was quiet; thankfully today the conveyor belt of weddings and funerals hadn't been turned on. As he approached it from the Common side, he could see a woman in a sharp black suit and matching sunglasses standing beside a gravestone. She was neither fidgeting nor moving around, just waiting. It had to be Evenor. Judas opened the gate and walked up to her.

"Evenor?"

She nodded.

"Are you ready to go?"

"Of course. Where are we going?"

"Jersey. I'll need to speak to Thornton quickly about taking the Church Roads south to the coast, first. If we travel by them, we can get there in half the time. We have to get to Jersey as soon as possible; my partner Williams is in danger, and so is London itself."

Judas realised that he was talking quickly, maybe too quickly, but Evenor seemed to have processed everything already.

"There is a place not far from Whale Island in Portsmouth where we could find a boat that travels along currents not known to even the wisest fisherman; it runs all the way to Jersey.

"We will have to navigate the ghost ship market, though. It has always been a neutral venue and a good place to uncover information that is hard to come by."

Judas listened intently. He'd been thinking of asking Michael to fly them over to the island, but Evenor obviously knew the secret ways of the sea, and this way seemed quickest, particularly seeing as Michael was away somewhere and uncontactable.

He was about to take his coin out and scrape it along the edge of one of the gravestones to announce himself to the Saints of Clapham and begin his parley with Thornton, but the man himself had already appeared. Word obviously didn't travel far in these parts without its greatest defender hearing of it.

"Judas. How do you fare?" Thornton talked as though he were two hundred years old.

"Much better for hearing that Williams is alive and

where our enemy can be found, Thornton. I need to get there, save him, and stop whatever it is that Herr Stranghold of the Black Sun is cooking up for us."

Thornton looked at Evenor. At least, that's what Judas thought he was doing – both of them were wearing sunglasses, so they could be looking over each other's shoulders for all he knew. Something clearly passed between them, though, and quickly, because Thornton swiftly turned around and made his way across the graveyard to a small headstone in the corner. The stone itself was covered in lichen and the name of the current tenant was undecipherable. A kind and caring soul had placed some fresh flowers in a beautiful little vase, though. Thornton reached down and brushed some dust away from the face of the stone, revealing a representation of a small 'Folds Anchor', carved there long ago. A Latin inscription ran underneath it; unlike the other words chiselled into the stone, it was clear and pristine.

It read 'Per Mare. Per Terre.'

"It means 'By Sea. By Land,' Judas. The man who lays here was once a soldier. None of his friends knew what or who he really was. He came to these shores thousands of years ago, when London was just a collection of mud huts and trading markets. He was a soldier from a place that is no longer on any map we use today. There are many like him in this graveyard.

"He was perhaps a little like you, Judas. But no matter. The fact that he lies here proves that forgiveness can be earned. As his first love was the sea, perhaps we can gain access to the Church Road that leads south from here to the coast using his last resting place as your departure point."

Thornton reached down and placed his index finger into the vase of fresh flowers and dipped it into the water. After he had removed his digit, he drew what looked like a circle on the stone surface of the headstone.

A few minutes passed, and Judas was starting to think that maybe the road would not open to him again; he'd travelled down one of them recently in order to rescue some stolen children from a slave market in Colliers Wood, and maybe there was a toll that needed to be paid, or some sort of restriction in place. But then there was a sound like wood being dragged across pebbles, and the hiss of surf rolling over seaweed. Thornton had been able to fashion an opening for them. He casually placed a hand on Judas' shoulder, and pointed to a hazy patch of blue just by the metal railings that marked the Church's perimeter; it hung in the air like a balloon seen through an empty glass bottle,.

"Safe journey to you both. Evenor will do her best to guide you, and will counsel you should you need her help. Farewell."

Thornton stepped to one side, and Judas was about to walk past him when the leaves on the ground were whipped up and into the air by the downdraft from a pair of powerful angel's wings.

Thornton and Evenor reacted first, and leapt to one

side. Judas turned quickly, and saw the shape of the angel backlit by the sun. On any other day he would have attacked first and said sorry later, but the angel that was descending on them was slight, and carried no weapons. It landed, and the brown leaves that were filling the air like brown static settled on the ground.

Ray folded his wings back. He was bare-chested as usual, showing off his well-toned physique to all and sundry, and wearing an enormous pair of wireless headphones. He was listening to something with the volume setting on loud because Judas, Thornton, Evenor and anyone else in this particular postcode could hear the bass.

"Judas! Caught you! I've been flying back and forth from here to our friends in the north. The place up there is in a mess; angels are being sent to every corner of the country searching for the Black Sun and the book, the library has been packed up and moved somewhere secret, and they're all on full alert. Those boys and girls mean business Judas; they're armed to the teeth, and I wouldn't want to be on the wrong side of them – unless I was Michael, of course – then it would be even. Where is the big fella, anyway?

"I was told to keep an eye on you, not that you need it of course, but I'd like to do my bit to help. I saw you jump on the tube in town and guessed that this might be where you were heading, so I waited up there and dropped down when the Saint of Clapham town did his opening trick with the gravestone. Where are we heading?" Ray was a funny, excitable angel, a little on the small side, and a big hit with human women. He was particularly excited now, though. Judas could tell. He'd also just set eyes on Evenor and had flexed his wings out like a peacock.

"Ray, meet Evenor, Evenor meet Ray. You can get to know each other on the way down," said Judas, trying not to notice Ray's obvious and frankly embarrassing courtship signals.

Judas thanked Thornton for his help, then he, Evenor and Ray stepped through an invisible door behind a gravestone and out onto one of the invisible Church Roads that criss-cross the country. This one would take them south to Portsmouth, England's historic naval port, then on to Whale Island, a small island with no whales.

15 THE GHOST FLEET

As they walked, the shadows of cars passed by on either side, and occasionally a commuter train would rush past making no sound at all. The Church Roads were as straight as a Llama could spit. Judas and Evenor had travelled along them many times, but this was a totally new experience for Ray, who liked the open sky and at least one good escape route. It was a little bit like walking through a thick, grey glass tube; the light from the world outside seeped through, but no noise was allowed to trespass here. For the first hour they walked in silence; Judas was lost in his own thoughts, trying to imagine what Williams was doing and what Stranghold had in store for them all. Evenor said very little at the best of times, while the only thing that Ray was thinking about was Evenor. Soon, the sharp edges of the towns they passed through drifted away, and were replaced with the long, dark smudges of hedges and fields. Portsmouth was an hour and a half from London by car, or 45 minutes if you drove like Williams, and it would have taken much longer to walk it in the real world. But the Church Roads, created by the ancient druids so that they could walk across Albion fair without getting butchered along the way by warring tribes, had a funny way of shortening journey times. Judas had once walked to Wales in 30 minutes. When he'd told Williams this, his loyal Sergeant and a true son of the valleys had spat his tea over two desks in disbelief, which was nearly a record at Scotland Yard.

Judas checked his watch and was about to announce that they were nearly at the exit, when he noticed Evenor staring at the scar that ran around his neck. It had happened before. The scar from the rope that he had used to hang himself with in the olive garden at Gethsemane would never fade; it was another one of his gifts from God. In the past people had just stared and then averted their eyes, hoping that they hadn't been caught looking, although on one occasion a well-meaning member of the public had approached him and pressed a Samaritans card into his hand, telling him that help was never far away. Judas had taken the card and given the well-wisher a pat on the shoulder along with one of his best smiles. He'd deposited the card in the business card jar of the East End pub he'd been drinking in later on that day.

Evenor didn't try to avert her eyes, and continued to stare.

"He can end your life in a lot of ways, Evenor. Sometimes he lets you kill yourself then brings you back to do his dirty work for him, and sometimes he strikes you down with lightning or a savage quip. You can never tell which one it's going to be. I'm used to the scar; but you should see the one on my chest – that's really something. Exactly how he scooped up my entrails and shoved them back inside my rib cage still confuses me, though."

Evenor said nothing and walked on. Her expression didn't change; it was as if someone had just told her about a new restaurant up the road.

"The scar story normally gets them interested doesn't it, Judas?"

Ray had ambled up beside him; he was light on his feet, even for an angel.

Judas just smiled. Ray was obviously very interested in Evenor, but she wasn't remotely bothered about him, which had put the handsome angel's nose out of joint. At the same time it had cheered Judas up no end. He even managed a raise of a solo eyebrow.

Evenor had stopped walking about 20 feet ahead, and was staring down at the ground when Judas and Ray caught up with her. They could see why. The road stretched on ahead, straight and true, and they could have walked on and on forever, but she'd spotted an opening on the right–hand side of the glass-like tunnel.

On the ground just in front of the opening was a symbol. It was an anchor that looked very much like the one Thornton had pointed out on the gravestone back at the Church on the Common.

"Here, I think" suggested Evenor.

Judas nodded in acknowledgement, and stepped

through it.

The British Empire owed everything to its sailors and ships, and regardless of where they were born, Portsmouth was their spiritual home. Everywhere you looked in the city there was an homage to the vessels and the men that had roamed the seas, bashing the French and the Spanish whenever the mood took them and carving off great chunks of land that didn't belong to them.

Whale Island sits snugly inside Portsmouth Harbour, with its big brother Portsea Island only a stone's throw away on the starboard bow. The name sounds romantic, conjuring up visions of Nantucket and the great whaling ports of New England, but the reality is somewhat different. Linked to a naval base, row upon row of single-storeyed buildings with metal corrugated roofs and brown creosoted walls spread out in long lines like spider's web ladders from the main gate. Cleaners in tiny road sweepers patrol the island in packs, feasting on the red leaves that drop from the trees, and naval instructors amble around in navy trousers and jumpers and white rimmed peaked caps with small highly polished brass cap badges on them.

Most of the huts are lecture theatres now, inside which the theory of naval warfare and the reading of brightly coloured flags is taught to freshly scrubbed naval recruits. Judas, Evenor and Ray walked past the buildings, following their noses to the gently lapping sea; they had to be somewhere before the tide turned.

The Gay Hornet was a pleasure boat. It had two masts and a lovely dark blue hull, with a new cordage that glowed white against the light grey of the dock. The sails were down, of course, and tied up neatly in tight bunts that to the trained eye would have told you a lot about the skipper. The boat rose and fell gently, giving a little kick every now and again as the forces of the tides tried to confuse it. Judas didn't have to ask if this was the one they were looking for; none of the other small vessels in the harbour came anywhere near it, its owners choosing to tie-up further down the dock. These other craft were working vessels – dirty and scuffed up, with lobster pots swinging from yellowed ropes and cabins covered in tarpaulins. Names like 'Betty-Sue' and 'Wave Rider' were painted on their sterns, with no discernible care being taken on the artwork.

Judas stopped in front of the Gay Hornet and waited. He knew the sea well, and he knew her customs. Ray flicked his wings and ruffled them into shape. Evenor, on the other hand, had suddenly become more animated. She seemed to have come to life: there was colour in her cheeks, and she had removed her sunglasses. Judas could not help staring at her eyes, which were a golden-brown colour and almost feline in shape; the gold was very golden, and the brown was very light, and they seemed to catch the light and then refused to release it. She saw them both looking, and quickly put her sunglasses back on. Judas realised that it was the sea that had brought about the change in her, and like a very heavy penny falling through zero gravity he knew where she was from. She had mentioned that her homeland was far away across the sea. He'd thought she was from Australia, but now he knew without a shadow of a doubt that she was much older than she looked, and a lot more dangerous than he had anticipated. Thornton had said that she had business in the west, and that she had particular skills that might be useful on their journey. Given what he'd figured out, he almost had an urge to push her into the water to see if what he had heard was true, but before he could ask her the million dollar question, the cabin doors aboard the Gay Hornet opened, and a young man with the world's best kept beard stepped out of the gloom and onto the pristine deck.

The Captain of the Gay Hornet gave old sea dogs a bad name. He was dressed to the nines, and didn't have a stitch out of place. He eyed Judas, Evenor and Ray warily, staring hard at each one in turn, then smiled, and his teeth put the rigging to shame.

"Well hello, there. I take it you won't be needing the booze cruise or the coastal cliffs quickie? You look like you might be heading into deeper waters."

"We need to charter your vessel, Captain and we hope to sail with the tide for the island of Jersey, if you can accommodate us."

"Captain Conny at your service; please come aboard. The gentleman with the wings can bunk up front if he likes – we can move the storage bulkhead forward and open the roof of the cabin so that he can stretch out. As the lady is of the sea, she may choose where she likes to bunk. And you, sir, well you may bunk where you like, too. If you want to catch the tide we had best make haste, she's a bit of a tart in these waters. We'll talk payment on the way to wherever it is you want to get to."

Judas clambered aboard, while Ray unfurled his wings, flew over the main jib in one leap, performed a little bank, and glided to the front of the Gay Hornet, disappearing with alarming speed and accuracy down into the hold through an open hatch. Evenor had already stepped neatly across the small gap between the dock and the deck and was sitting with her back against the main mast. Between her and Captain Conny, it was hard to tell who looked most at home on the deck of the Gay Hornet at that moment.

The Captain moved quickly about the ship, seeming to be everywhere at once, lifting a hatch here and pulling on a rope there. Judas couldn't see any other crew members, and realised soon after the boat disengaged itself from the dock and drifted precisely where it needed to go that the vessel was not your average craft. Evenor didn't move from the mast, not even when the Harbour Master's launch, crewed by two surly looking chaps and a young man that looked barely able to lift a razor let alone shave with it, hailed them from the deck of his own little floating kingdom, demanding to know where they were headed.

She just kept looking at the sea and smiling.

Once they had cleared the harbour walls, the breakwater started to act up a bit. The Gay Hornet gave her odd little kick on the downward roll to starboard again, and Captain Conny decided to let her have her head.

He sauntered past Evenor, who was as still as the

mast she sat against, and made his way to the wheel at the stern. He carefully scanned the grey, white-flecked waves in every direction before he made any adjustment to the Gay Hornet's course. He had an easy manner, and he shifted his weight from foot to foot in perfect time with the rise and fall of the deck. Judas watched him carefully; wherever he went on his beloved craft, he seemed to merge with the timbers of the vessel the moment he stood still, becoming a part of it.

In a gesture born out of habit, Captain Conny touched two wrinkled fingers to the white band of his cap to Judas, who had taken up residence on the rather luxurious padded seats that hugged the fine curves of the Hornet's aft a few feet behind the wheel. Judas returned the compliment with a nod of the head. The Captain smiled with a mouth full of the whitest teeth Judas had ever seen. If ever they were cast adrift and needed to signal for help in the dead of night in the cold embrace of a raging sea, all they'd need do would be to get Conny to open his mouth and smile in the direction of their rescuers; they wouldn't be able to miss the sheer brilliance of those pearly whites.

Once he was happy with the trim of the Hornet, Conny took hold of the wheel and started to hum to himself. At first Judas thought that the humming was just a tuneless distraction, but as the waves grew choppier as they headed out of the channel and into the sea, he realised the skipper was singing, softly at first, then louder. He noticed that as the waves advanced on the hull of the Gay Hornet, the singer's voice grew louder, just for a beat, and whichever wave was nearest would drop under the hull and roll off into the distance. He did this a few times, then suddenly the sea all around started to behave strangely. Captain Conny stopped singing and smiled; even though the waves were choppy for as far as the eye could see, the water that ran along the sides of the Gay Hornet was so flat and calm they could have been on a boating lake.

Conny turned around to Judas once the Hornet had left the land behind.

"So where are we headed, what's our course, and who, if I might enquire, are you?"

Judas ambled over to the Captain. He still hadn't made his mind up about what sort of person the man was, but with Evenor and Ray close at hand he thought he was on safe ground, even if it did keep shifting underfoot.

"My name is Detective Chief Inspector Judas Iscariot of Scotland Yard. My two companions are not on the 'force', but they are helping me with my enquiries. We're heading to the island of Jersey; we have to get there as quickly as possible, please. The angel could fly there in a fraction of the time, of course, but the lady and I are flightless, as you can see."

The Captain nearly blinded Judas with his smile, and gave a little sideways nod of the head to show he understood that this charter would not be like most of his normal voyages.

"What do you think of the Hornet, DCI Judas Iscariot? Is she not a wonderful vessel?"

The Captain was in love with his ship, of course; sea

captains often did develop unusual feelings for their boats. But Judas could see that there was something else at play here, and it made his scar prickle. And whereas an angry pulling sensation meant danger, a prickle often signalled magic or something otherwise hard to explain. His first thought was that Captain Conny was joined with the ship in more ways than one. He just got that feeling that should he take a knife and slash at one of the sails or smash one of the decking planks to pieces, Conny himself might start to bleed.

"She is a very fine craft, Captain. Lovely lines, sails true and fast, and she has spirit. She gives a little kick every now and then, doesn't she? I say that as though I know the sea, but to be honest with you, most of my experience has been in small fishing boats in mostly fine weather. You, on the other hand, seem able to talk to the weather."

Now it was the Captain's turn to return the compliment; he did so with a little wave of the hand. The Hornet leapt forward with joy as he did it. Judas could see that Conny was no stranger to passengers like him. It would have been strange if he wasn't.

"To Jersey it is, then, and you want to get their fast. I can crack on a bit, if she lets me, and we could make landfall early tomorrow. How does that sound, Inspector?"

"It sounds good. I was going to ask you if we could be of service, but I don't think you need it, or that she would allow it."

"You're right there, Inspector. The Gay Hornet and I have an understanding, and it would take you years to get to know her little ways. I will go about preparing her for the trip. If I should be hard to find onboard, or out of earshot, please do not be alarmed – no harm will come to us, the sea will treat us fair, and the Hornet will let me know if the sea starts playing up. Is that okay?"

"It's your ship, Captain. We'll stay out of your way."

For the next few hours, the Hornet picked up speed again and again, until they were clipping along at something close to powerboat speed. The ride was still as comfortable as before, maybe even more so; the deck kept its slight roll and kick, and Evenor stayed motionless beneath the main sail, always looking towards the horizon for a continent that had disappeared long ago.

Judas spent most of his time thinking about Stranghold and the book. The little man had caused Judas and those around him a lot of pain. He'd also used some sort of magic spell to poison the mind of John the Baptist.

John and the rest of the Disciples had followed Judas out of the desert after the great betrayal. God had other plans for them as well, but the Disciples chose another path and became The 10, a notorious, shadowy crime syndicate that won their spurs fighting for whoever could afford them. The Borgias were afraid of The 10, the Genovese family trod carefully around them, and the Krays trembled when they heard that The 10 were coming for them. They'd been committing crimes for an age, poisoning their own minds as the number of misdeeds grew; John had already started to go mad long before Stranghold got his hooks into his old grey matter.

The Black Sun had ordered Stranghold to find the 'Book', and Stranghold had searched the world for it. He should never have found it, because it was safe in the great library in the City of the Heavens, far out of the reach of humankind and its trigger-happy attitude to destruction and war. But the book was stolen during the Second Fall of the Angels, and it passed from wing to hand, then from hand to hand, until Ray came across it in an old antiques market in Islington. He knew as soon as he saw it that it was something special. At first, he thought only about the financial reward, but then he became aware that he was being followed, which was when Judas had entered the fray. He'd come to Ray's rescue then and now here he was, sitting at the back of a living ship, with a sharp-suited assassin wearing Tom Ford sunglasses and Ray himself, cruising at speed towards the island of Jersey and certain danger.

Judas pulled his coat more tightly around him to keep out the curious breeze, and watched a seagull preparing to land on the deck of the Hornet. Just as it was about to stretch out its little skinny drumstick legs and place a webbed foot on one of the highly polished wooden gratings that ran the whole length of the craft, a coil of rope on the deck unravelled like a snake and whipped the seagull's wing; the bird disappeared into the grey sky like a white rocket. Judas smiled briefly, then his mind pulled him back into the darkness of the present day.

Stranghold wanted the book badly, he would never

become the leader of the Black Sun without it. But he'd proved himself shrewd, and careful, and he had what all great tacticians have in abundance – *patience*.

Was this just a ruse to get him to the island? And what would he face when he got there? Hopelessly outnumbered? Of course. Backs against the wall? Most definitely. But why? If they went in to tackle the Black Sun and their evil magic, he should plan for that and load the dice in his favour for a change, being proactive and not reactive. He had Ray and Evenor, of course, while Williams was already there with a new sidekick, which made five. But five was not nearly enough. Judas took out his silver coin, making the familiar circular motion across its surface with his thumb; he started to plan ahead.

The waves passed by and the wind made the rigging sing, while the hum of the sails was like the Hornet's baritone section, joining in to provide the soundtrack of their journey. The hours passed by with the seagulls, and Judas would have rubbed the coin flat if it hadn't been for Ray's interruption.

He was wearing a very figure-hugging t-shirt with the name of the ship on the front. The letters were depicted with twists of rope and sailor's knots, while an embroidered image of a golden hornet buzzed away on one of the shoulder sleeves.

"I've been thinking," said Ray.

"Of running away to sea?' said Judas.

"Nice. No. We are headed right into the tiger's den."

"It's the lion's den, Ray."

"You know what I mean. But we need some heavy weapons, some major firepower, Judas. This is going to get really messy, and I think Evenor might need some back-up."

If anyone needs some back-up, Ray, it's you. Evenor can take care of herself, don't worry about her. What's on your mind?"

Ray unfurled his wings for a second, and at that same moment wished he hadn't, because a sudden gust of wind blew in from the starboard side of the vessel, picking him up off the deck; it was in the process of blowing him overboard and into the drink when the Hornet's boom arm swung across incredibly quickly and Ray, instead of going for a swim, landed comfortably in the furls of the billowing main sail. The sound he made as he hit the canvass reminded Judas of a cricket game he had attended at Lord's, when the wicketkeeper had caught one of the fast bowler's quickest efforts of the day. It was a soft, hard thump, if there could be such a thing.

"Keep your wings tucked in when you are on-deck, angel! If it hadn't been for the Hornet's quick thinking, you'd be taking a long cold bath right now!" bellowed the Captain from somewhere else on the ship.

Ray tumbled to the deck and quickly gathered in his wings. He made a show of flexing them and checking them, but Judas could tell that he was embarrassed; angels don't like looking foolish, and they take great pride in being able to read the wind. Unfortunately for Ray, Evenor had been looking on. She smiled at Judas, then at Ray, then sat back down again to watch the sea rise and fall.

The light was beginning to fade and soon there would be no difference between the colour of the night sky and the water all around them. The ship must have been keeping an eye on the sky, too, because one-by-one the lanterns started to glow, and at the very top of the mast a green light started to blink like a giant invisible cyclops. Captain Conny reappeared. He had changed his clothes and now wore a heavy camel-haired overcoat and a cosy-looking woollen hat pulled down over his ears. He took the wheel, and gave the Hornet the once-over; everything was in its rightful place, and the ship was cutting through the water like a dolphin on steroids.

"May I have a word, Detective Chief Inspector?"

"Of course, Captain." said Judas.

"You will have noticed by now that the Gay Hornet is not your run-of-the-mill sort of ship; she has something about her that makes her special. When I take normal folk out for a sail, she behaves and keeps quiet, but when there are *special* passengers onboard, she knows, and she has a tendency to show off a bit. What makes her truly special, however, is that she sort of feels what the passengers are feeling. She can read their thoughts, if you like, and because I'm her Captain and we know each other so well, she passes some of their thoughts on to me. So, I suppose what I'm saying in a roundabout sort of way, is that I know that you need some physical help, a bit of muscle. Is that about right?"

Judas sat up, then stood up. He buttoned his coat,

and rolled his shoulders back and forth to release some of the tension that had stowed away on board with him.

"You're right, captain. We're heading into the unknown, but whatever we find when we get there is likely to be of a life-threatening nature. I won't deny it, because if what you say is true then you already know what I've been thinking about, or at least the Gay Hornet does."

The ship banked slightly, then righted herself so that she was on an even keel again. Captain Conny laughed, and took a folded map from one of the huge pockets in his coat.

"That's her apologising for reading your thoughts without asking, Inspector.

"If you come inside the cabin, I can show you a spot where there will be a gathering of seafaring folk sometime tomorrow morning. We call it the Ghost Fleet, and I think you might be able to find yourself an army there, or at least a ship and crew capable of bloodying a few noses. If you want me to change our course, it will take us out of the way a bit, but I think the Hornet will step up and get you to the Island in much the same sort of time, should you choose to go."

"I think we should chance it, Judas."

Evenor had appeared at Judas' shoulder without making a sound.

"I have heard of this fleet; sunken galleons and Norse longboats, submarines and destroyers, Gin Palaces, yachts and fishing boats, crewed by spirits and wraiths, werewolves and ghouls. Some of them might come in handy, don't you think?"

The Captain nodded and smiled at Evenor, and for the first time since Judas had met her she smiled, a rare show of emotion, directed straight at the Captain.

Ray was going to be heartbroken.

The Gay Hornet had her head now, the change in course had moved the stars around in the sky making Orion and his belt shift over to starboard, and her wake was long and white. The Captain had taken the wheel as soon as Judas had decided to make for the Ghost Fleet's meeting place, and he was making his beloved ship work really hard. On any other vessel, the crew would be roaring around all over the deck, taking in one sail and releasing another to steal as much of the wind as possible, but the Hornet did it all by herself. Each time the wind changed or dropped, she would sheer away and find it again, so that by 22.00hrs they were approaching the necessary coordinates on the map.

Judas watched the sea rolling past. Ray was in a mood because he'd seen Evenor and the Captain talking to each other, and had retired to his cabin to preen a bit and sulk a lot. After they'd all left the cabin Evenor had taken up a new position on the deck; she'd vacated the space directly in front of the mast, deciding that standing next to the Captain was much better. Judas thought that the Hornet might get jealous and start slowing down, but she tore on into the black on black of the sea and the night.

"There we are!" shouted the Captain. Judas was by his side in an instant, staring at a small patch of green light in the darkness ahead. This remained a dot for the next 30 minutes, and Judas got the impression that although the wind was blowing hard the ship had stopped; then, with the equivalent of a parachute ground-rush, the dot suddenly ballooned into a glow the size of a football, then before they knew it they found themselves gliding slowly alongside a WWII German U-boat that itself was at a standstill next to a large white, single funnelled yacht playing host to what appeared to be a party in full swing. The sound of music and laughter and the clinking of glasses swam across the water between them; as they coasted along, a couple of boat lengths from the two craft, they could see the partygoers onboard turn to stare at them for a few seconds, before becoming disinterested and turning back to their conversations and canapes. Next, Judas spotted a number of other vessels that had been hidden from view behind the two boats appear out of the darkness. There was a really sleek clipper, two or maybe three fishing boats, a number of small yachts, a steep-sided British Navy frigate that looked so old Nelson could have learned the ropes in her, and lots of different types of merchant vessels. Their decks swarmed with dots of white and brown and yellow, that became the faces of their crews as the Hornet drifted nearer. Judas could make out the blue frock coats of the Navy Captains, the Malay head-hunters, the Chinese coolies and sailors from each and every sea-faring nation.

Each of the craft had lashed itself fast on to its nearest neighbour, and the individual ships now formed one great floating hulk. Trading was going on between the ships, and occasionally there would be the flash and sparks of a repair taking place.

They came to a halt, and drew up against the U-boat's long hull. A figure stepped out of the darkness behind the conning tower and loped along the sub's deck towards them. Judas and Evenor tensed, ready to repel boarders if required, but the Captain placed a reassuring hand on Judas' shoulder and gave a small, almost imperceptible shake of the head. The figure reached the end of the U-boat, and in the red light of the Port-side lantern they realised it was a werewolf, in full German Navy uniform, tailored specially to the creature's hunched body and long arms and legs.

The beast reached down to the deck, picked up a large boathook, and used it to deftly fend off the Hornet before bringing her to within a few feet of the submarine. When he had made her fast against the U-boat, he motioned for them to hop across with one very dangerous looking claw. Captain Conny went first, Evenor followed him, then Judas stepped across the small black void between the two crafts. The iron plated submarine beneath his feet felt very different to the highly polished, wooden deck of the Hornet. The U-boat seemed heavy and solid underfoot, which of course it was, whereas the Gay Hornet felt like it was part of the sea itself, not just a craft riding on top of it.

"Obergefrieter Lindelhoff at your service, Kapitan," said the werewolf.

"Please pass along the deck, and you will be able to walk across to the Flying Ruby and join the party. My

Kapitan will be there. You will know him when you see him, of course."

Captain Conny saluted the werewolf Lindelhoff, and walked past him towards the prow of the vessel. A very sturdy-looking bridge made from two wooden ladders had been slung between the two ships, and tied off with Germanic precision. Judas followed Evenor, who was only one step behind Captain Conny. They traversed the space between the two, floating worlds of the Gin Palace and the U-boat easily, and joined one of the strangest parties that Judas had ever been to.

The last time Judas had been surprised was when he'd stumbled upon a partner-sharing club taking place in a giant culvert under Mayfair. He'd been investigating some gypsy smugglers at the time; they'd been bringing drugs into the capital via some of the old WWI evacuation waterways that the Government of the time had built in secret, just in case they lost the war and needed to get the city's inhabitants to safety. Judas had turned a corner, and had nearly been decapitated with a sword by a very effeminate looking gentleman wearing the uniform of one of Napoleon's Hussars. The swinger of the sword could have been deadly, if he hadn't already been deadly drunk. Luckily the blade only sliced off a corner of the collar of the Kilgour overcoat he had been wearing.

Judas was angry about the wounding of his coat at the time, and had knocked the old soldier out cold because he knew how much the tailor would charge to make it good again.

The smugglers had been bringing some nasty blends

of tobacco leaf in from the West Country; it was so strong that even the magical population exercised caution when it was being shared around. Unfortunately, the 'Taint of Tavistock', as the leaf was called, had found its way into the hands of some party-goers in Hounslow. Later, these same party-goers tried just a little bit, to be sure it was okay, and found out to their eternal regret, that although it was indeed okay, it was only okay for a unicorn or a wyvern or even a spectre or a ghoul; it certainly was not fit for human consumption. The ones that had survived the tasting were still counting and recounting the one-inch tiles on the walls of London's most secret sanitoriums.

The tricky little gypsy responsible had given him the slip that night, and Judas had stumbled instead into a gathering for a very select group of individuals. There were at least 200 different breeds of magical creatures already there, and they were partying hard; members of each race lined up to get off with each other, and some of the pairings that had already been made caused Judas to shake his head in confusion. How they were going to do what he presumed they would be doing took some thinking about, and he wasn't sure at the time that he wanted to go there.

The Lord Mayor's band were in residence, playing K-Pop tunes with their brass instruments for entertainment. Some of the humans in attendance, meanwhile, should really have known better, and there was much hiding of faces behind masks that they hoped would help them to blend in, as Judas searched the crowds for the gypsy creature. He had long gone, but Judas decided to stick around anyway and make everyone feel uncomfortable.

That had been quite a night but what he saw right then on the ghost gin palace made his brain hurt. There were at least two hundred sailors from all over the world and from all over time, drinking champagne from crystal flutes and wooden tankards bound together with steel hoops, while delicate cups made of brightly painted porcelain were being lifted to the lips of oriental princesses by stern looking Conquistadores. Everybody was devouring delicate looking little canapes and pastries, held aloft by monkeys wearing 'I Love Gibraltar' t-shirts. Ghosts passed through the crowds, beasts of all types ran up and down the deck, and the uniforms of every single navy ever formed rubbed shoulders with pirates and merchant navy crew from every country under the sun. Polar bears stood upright and chatted to Inuit tribal elders, half of Ye Olde England's naval heroes kept their sabres in their scabbards and slapped their French counterparts on the back, sharing amusing stories. Everyone and everything here was enjoying the party, no old wounds were being opened, and it looked to Judas like a lot of whiskey, gin, potions and shots were being imbibed, along with enough grog to choke a donkey.

Captain Conny took Judas' arm, and steered him and Evenor toward a gap in the throng near a ship's funnel that had been polished so hard it looked like a black mirror. He appropriated three glasses of champagne from the nearest Gibraltarian ape

"I've been here many times in the past, so perhaps

it would be best if you allowed me to suggest a course of action, Detective Chief Inspector?"

Judas drained his champagne, and was about to set the empty glass down on the nearest hatch when a little ape shot across the deck, snatching it up and placing it on a silver tray before running up the nearest bit of rigging and into the darkness aloft, where it disappeared without dropping a glass or spilling a drop.

"I think that approaching the island as quietly and covertly as possible will give you some advantage, which we'll need of course. We'll also need some fighters that can work as well by night as they can by day, so I'm going to try and enlist the help of the U-boat and its ferocious crew of werewolves. What do you think, Detective Chief Inspector?"

Judas thought about what the Captain was suggesting. It made a lot of sense, but there was one thing that Conny had not thought through: would the German Navy fight the Black Sun – Hitler's notorious occult division?

"I don't think the Black Sun is going to start trembling if I approach on the Hornet flanked by three British frigates crewed by men in white wigs and hats that look like they are on the wrong way around. I know they'd be game, but cannons and shot are no match for that lot. See what you can do, Captain. Evenor, will you go with the Captain and advise where you think necessary?"

Judas had only suggested this because it would drive Ray mad. And where was the angel, anyway? He'd said he had come to help, but all he'd done so far was give

Evenor the puppy eyes and then sulk like a child when he'd been rejected.

Conny smiled, and was about to go off in search of help, but stopped and turned back to face Judas.

"We haven't talked about my fee for this enterprise, have we? I will go and find the U-boat's Kapitan, and attempt to persuade him to help you if I can. I will also take you the rest of the way to Jersey and then return you to Whale Island afterwards. As for payment, I'll consider it settled if Evenor agrees to sail with me for one cycle of the moon, after you have completed your mission."

"Evenor does not work for me, nor does she obey my command. She volunteered to help me, but she decides where she goes and who with, so I cannot make that a condition of our agreement because it is not within my power. Ask me anything else, and I will see what I can do."

Evenor removed her sunglasses, folded the arms back, and then placed them inside her jacket pocket. Her irises had lost their flickering golden flame now, and they danced with a cold fire. She looked incredible, and at the same time quite intimidating. A couple of Arabian Corsairs had been meaning to come over and try to engage her in conversation but as soon as the sunglasses had come off, they decided to try their luck elsewhere. The look on her face told them that they had made the right decision.

"I will come with you afterwards, Captain Conny, once the book is reclaimed and the Black Sun are destroyed. We will sail together for more than one turn of the moon if you wish it, because I hope to see a place that disappeared some time ago – a place that was old when the Druids and the Celts were young. If you help me search for it, I will come with you for as long as you want me to."

The Captain, smiled broadly, then turned on his heel and waded into the melee, looking for a German U-boat Kapitan with a crew of flesh-eating werewolves that enjoyed a bit of rough-and-tumble and liked howling at the moon.

16 THE BADGE OF BETRAYAL

Williams landed with all the grace of a tranquilised bull elephant at the foot of the stone stairs. He wasn't sure whether the projectile had been a spell or a grenade, but whatever it was, it had missed him by a country mile. The blast, however, caught him side-on, and bounced him against the wall of the cellar with such force that he was now laying on the floor with a savage ringing in the ears. The dust from the blast had come to his rescue, at least, and as it was settling, the boy he'd come to save had saved him instead. The dust enveloped everything, from wall-to-wall and floor-to-ceiling, so there was zero visibility in the cellar, but Joachim had seized the initiative and grabbed him by the shoulder, heaving him behind the stack of boxes he'd erected as a barricade before the attack from the tunnels below started again. He managed to get Williams to his foot now, and they started to climb the stone steps once again. They'd nearly made it to the top when the badge in Joachim's lapel started to glow an angry red; the boy hadn't even thought to cover it, so right now the light it was emitting was painting a great big target on them both, which is of course what it was intended to do. Seconds later, Joachim saw a black shape moving at the bottom of the steps and knew that the net was closing in, fast. He thought about throwing Williams down the stairs to land on the enemy and make a run for it himself, but he was too slow; the last thing he saw was a spear of lightning shoot out of the dust and the dark, before they were blown through the door and out of the cellar. Just before curtains of darkness were drawn around them both he heard a thunderclap, followed by a rumble, which made perfect sense to him. Lightning, then thunder, that was just the way it happened.

17 JUNG AND KESSEL

Back in the day when 'Lads Mags' were all the rage, a rather misguided, attention-seeking editor on one of the most popular magazines for young men at the time, decided that it would be cool to compile a list of the top 100 best dressed men of all time. Right at the top, he'd elected to put Johannes Erwin Eugen Rommel, the Desert Fox and Field Marshall in the Wehrmacht of Nazi Germany, because he had real style and a natty wardrobe. Leather trench coats and shiny, knee-high leather boots were in vogue amongst London's 'Artocracy' at the time, so he afforded Rommel a full page, all to himself.

The public backlash was huge, and the editor in question quickly realised that he had scored a home-goal of epic proportions. His readership disappeared overnight and he was thrown to the publishing house's hungriest wolves. Judas had read a few editions of the magazine back then; it was hard to move without seeing one at the Yard, such was its popularity amongst the rank and file of the Met. He thought of the editor and Rommel now, because the Kapitan of the U-boat they were hoping to enlist to their cause had come to the party in his werewolf form and in his number one rig, complete with sword and shiny leather boat cloak.

Captain Conny glided through the crowd and then waited for a natural break in conversation before greeting the Kapitan. Once the required salutes and small talk had been made and each had pointed out his vessel to the other, Conny beckoned to Judas to make the introductions.

"Kapitan Jung, may I introduce you to Detective Chief Inspector Judas Iscariot of the Black Museum at Scotland Yard. We are travelling to Jersey on a matter of some importance, and we were wondering whether we could speak with you for a moment about something that may be of interest to you."

The Kapitan turned slightly towards Judas, made a quick, economic nod of the head and growled slightly.

"Detective Chief Inspector, you are far from land. Are you in pursuit of someone? They must be very wicked if you have chased them across the channel to a meeting of the Ghost Fleet. Are any of my friends here in danger?"

"Kapitan, I have to choose my words carefully as it would be a tragic mistake on my part If I offended you, but I'm afraid that the person I am hoping to find and apprehend is possibly a fellow German officer of yours."

The German stiffened, and he moved the white gloves he had just taken off from one hand to the other. How he got them on and off his claws without tearing them into pieces was a wonder.

"Inspector, the war is over. It was won by the right side. The Allies brought most of those who had fled to South America to justice, so I can't imagine that there are any of those criminals left alive to hang by the heels."

Judas decided to go for broke and appeal to the Kapitan's honour.

"We're trying to locate a man who has stolen a book that could start another World War. He belongs to an order called the Black Sun. Do you know of it?"

The Kapitan's shoulders shot back and up. He turned his full face on Judas and stared into his eyes.

"They were never truly a part of the German Navy or Army! Hitler only surrounded himself with 'soothsayers and charlatans' in his search for miracle weapons and final solutions. Their order died out a long time ago, Detective Chief Inspector. Are you sure that you are looking for the right person?"

"Quite sure, Kapitan. One of my men has been following him these past weeks, and we know for sure that there are members of the Black Order on the island of Jersey, with a ghost army of Hitler Youth children defending them. We also know that these miracle weapons you mention are in fact very real, and hidden on the island. The Black Sun intend to make use of them."

The Kapitan shrugged. He looked around at Evenor and Captain Conny, then out to sea, before he turned back to Judas.

"I heard from another U-boat Kapitan that something unpleasant had happened on Jersey involving the Black Sun and some of the half-German children who were born there. He was making the run up to one of our new secret cities under the Northern Ice with some supplies and a few smuggled scientists, when purely by chance, we ran into each other on the surface. We were ventilating the boat and rewarding the crew with some much–needed fresh air when we saw the other submarine. It was a one in a thousand chance, really. During the war we would have been severely reprimanded for being that close to each other, but the war had just been declared over and my crew and I were trying to figure out where we fitted into the new world order and were laying low – 50 fathoms low most of the time. A submarine crewed by werewolves can't just sail into a neutral port, pop the hatch and ask for asylum.

"We all wanted to return home of course, but we would have caused more problems for the people we knew and loved, and they needed to rebuild their lives, too. So we all decided to stay afloat and out of sight; we run cargo and supplies for the secret cities, and when required we fight for whoever can pay us.

"I knew that there was something wrong the moment Kapitan Kessel came aboard. My crew and I were in our human form, so while they gossiped and exchanged gifts on deck, we went to my cabin and talked. He told me what had happened in the camps in Poland and Germany. The world would never forgive us after that.

"Kapitan Kessel of U-865 was almost in tears when he told me about the death camps, but just when I thought that we could not drop any further into the void of our own destruction, he told me about the rumours he'd heard about the Black City and the tunnels under Jersey. We'd spent most of the war underwater, and when we surfaced, we found out that we weren't the only monsters in Germany's war machine".

The Kapitan growled and Judas saw his hackles rise; when he shifted from foot to foot his tail brushed softly on the deck.

"The Black Sun killed a lot of innocent children, Detective, and you are right to want to bring them to justice. We have talked history and rumour; now, what is it that you would request of me and my boat?"

Judas noticed that the Kapitan's snout was wet; every now and again one of his very sharp looking fangs caught on his lower lip, it made him look sly, and calculating.

"We don't know what we're going to face when we get to the island. My man on the inside said there is a secret entrance to the underground city that only a submarine can navigate. Once there, we'll have to liberate the book and get out alive. We're seriously short-handed, as you can see, and we could do with some muscle on our side."

The Kapitan stopped one of the passing serving apes with a growl, and lifted some glasses of white wine from the tray the monkey was balancing on his head. He passed them around so that everyone had a drink, then slapped his gloves against his muscular leg.

"I wish that I could help you, Detective, but I don't think that I could persuade my crew, I'm afraid. In time, I might convince them that it would be the right thing to do. I might prevail upon them that this is the perfect opportunity for them to show at least some of the world that we still have some idea of what honour really is, and that we were not all animals. But time is something you are very short of, I think. I wish you well, but my sea wolves and I cannot follow you."

With that, the Kapitan gave an immaculate, full salute, and loped off through the crowds of revellers on the deck.

Judas knew that it had been a very long shot, and it seemed now that they were going to have to do it all on their own again, as usual.

They tried to speak to some of the captains from the other ships, but word had spread fast, and no one was willing to help if it meant that the German werewolves might turn on them if they did. So, Judas, Evenor and Captain Conny decided to return to the Gay Hornet and make for Jersey with all the speed that she could muster. Moments later, they were hull up, with white water flying down the Hornet's sides.

Captain Conny had every stitch of sail flying, the cordage was snapped tight to the masts, and all they could hear was the wind roaring in their ears. Judas looked back at the Ghost Fleet and watched it disappear into the endless night at the same speed it had first materialised.

"The sea is on our side!" shouted Conny above the rolling thunder of the wind.

"I'm glad somebody is," said Judas. But the wind stole his words before they could be heard by the captain.

The lights of the Ghost Fleet blinked once and then they were gone. They were all alone with the night and the sea, again.

18 THE DOORS OF DEATH

Stranghold hadn't realised how combustible the robes that the Black Sun wore were, until he burned two of his order to death inside them for returning without completing their mission. They had come back empty-handed and with stuttering, miserable, hollow excuses for their failure, so he had executed them in front of the massed ranks of the Ghost Children army. The next phase of his plan required total obedience, so a little theatre could only help. By his reckoning there were only around 500 of them left, so he had no choice but to act now. He had dissolved the Black Sun's higher council, and now he alone would decide what their course of action was to be. He had consulted the great book and memorised the spell of release. He was ready. He had all the power he would ever need.

The Ghost Children marched three abreast down

the tunnel. Their flags and banners were held aloft, but because there was no wind to bring them to life, they looked more like giant red and black umbrellas that had not been opened. Silence was their marching song, and at that moment they were terrifying to behold. Rank after rank passed into the deep darkness; down and down they went, their ghost forms giving off a faint luminescence that illuminated the way ahead like the flickering of a dying match.

The remainder of the Black Sun followed on behind. Stranghold led the way, of course. His highly polished shoes with their thick leather soles clicked and clacked on the stone floor as he walked proudly on, with the great book held tightly under his arm.

The tunnel sloped down into the bowels of the island. It got colder as they descended, and the haunting boom of the waves reduced in volume until it was just a whisper that called to them through the stone walls that funnelled them down to whatever fate had in store for them.

They finally reached the end of the tunnel and stepped out into a huge, black cavern. The children of the Ghost Army marched in, and with precision and style they formed up in neat lines directly in front of a pair of giant hangar doors.

The doors stretched up into the darkness, and there was no indication as to where they stopped. When Stranghold looked right, then left, he could not make out where they started or ended, either. The only indication that they were actually doors and not just a great grey wall was the huge keyhole directly in front of them. Stranghold opened the book and flicked through it until he found the page he was looking for. He began the incantation that was written there. Then he raised one small, bony hand, and pointed at the lock with a perfectly-manicured finger. The children of the Ghost Army stood incredibly still, just as though they were awaiting inspection on the drill square.

If they had known what was going to happen to them all when the great doors swung open, they would not have waited so patiently.

Stranghold completed his incantation and closed the book with a snap that echoed all around the cavern. The sound made a few, quick circuits of the huge subterranean space and then retired to the silence and the dark. He was tired; the spell had taken more from him than he had expected. The size of the door or opening that you wished to enter dictated the size of the spell, and this opening was the biggest that he had ever attempted. If the remainder of the Order knew how weak he was at that moment, he could find himself in danger of attack, so it was imperative that he projected strength and kept the book with him at all times. If he were separated from it, then the game was truly up, and he would not leave this island again.

Already a few of the more accomplished and ambitious magicians had started posturing, and he could tell from their body language that they would not wait too long before challenging him. He was a small man, slight and unimposing, and an easy target for some. Many people had underestimated him already though, and the world was littered with their dead bodies. Stranghold turned around and looked at what was left of the great Order of the Black Sun. They had once been a force to be reckoned with; they'd had the ear of the High Command and Hitler himself, and they had enjoyed unlimited access to everything and anything that they wanted or needed. The SS and the Gestapo knew where they were in the pecking order, and crossed the Black Sun at their peril. But now they were just a shadow of their former selves. Their belief in magic and the ways of the Old Gods had dwindled, and their appetite for power had been dulled. They were all weak, timid, and small-minded. And they were taking up too much space.

A big, broad smile appeared on his thin face. Many of them were about to fall, and sooner than they realised.

He turned back to the great doors and heard the first, beautiful noise; it came from deep down inside the rock and as it grew louder and louder, a huge wave of relief coursed over him. Somewhere close, just behind the doors, a cog turned, a latch was tripped, and a counterweight began to drop.

The doors shuddered, and a fine shower of dust cascaded down from the darkness like silver rain from the roof of the cavern. The magicians of the Black Sun cheered, and tried to look surprised and even excited. The ranks of the Ghost Children began to stir, because they could see that the doors were creeping outwards and a soft, blue-tinged light was beginning to crawl across the floor towards them. Stranghold could not wait to see what was hidden behind the doors, and he was the first through them. He was impatient and excited. His plan was near to success. London, then the rest of the world would fall to him; he would rebuild the Black Order and they would rule unchallenged, forever.

The Black Robes followed him, and the Ghost Children followed them, and soon they had all passed through the doors and marched in perfect order towards their unknown futures. Death or glory would welcome them inside, but which would it be? The blue light was weak, and the pool it cast was small at first, but it began to grow in intensity; as it grew in size it brightened, and revealed the weapon.

It floated in the air 20 metres above the cavern floor. Hundreds of huge iron chains with links the size of panzer tanks had been thrown over its back in order to keep it anchored to the ground. This was the King of the Air. It was like a Zeppelin in shape, but that was where the similarity ended. It had a great silver body that had to be at least 50 times larger than any other airship to have ever flown before. The skin of the beast was covered with razor-sharp spikes the length of telegraph poles, and magic runes and strange shapes had been painted all over it. Ten huge, black engines hung from its gut, and directly underneath it was a metal stairway that led up from the floor to a black hole in its stomach that resembled a wound.

It radiated fear and death, and it made Stranghold's small, withered heart beat like a field of metronomes in a hurricane. It was clear to him that this machine defied the rules and practicalities of any known human engineering, and that was just from what he could see from the outside.

Stranghold could hardly contain himself, and walked off at a faster pace than normal to inspect his prize more closely. As he passed under the airship's hull, he heard a faint humming sound. At first, he thought it was just the wind passing through the chain links, but the sound was coming from inside the craft. He was impatient to investigate. He wanted to perform the spell that would unchain this leviathan and take it up into the sky, but that could not happen until he had performed the spell. So, rather than running up the stairs and going inside, he turned around and walked slowly back to where his brothers where standing together, underneath one of the airship's sleeping engines. As he grew nearer, he could tell from their faces that they were far from impressed.

Schneider was not one of his supporters within the Order, so it was no great surprise that he had been chosen as the dagger they would use to stab him in the back.

"Is this it, Stranghold? Is this the so called 'Miracle Weapon'? An airship that looks like it hasn't flown since the days of Bismarck! We expected much more than this. You wanted us to follow you to the end, and if this it, we have followed you to your own end. You will surely die, Stranghold, have no doubt of that. Someone else will take your place; someone who will not devote his energies to finding dusty old books of magic and a weapon that the RAF could shoot down with a bow and arrow!"

The rest of them began to shout and wave their fists at him. One of them even started to conjure a containment spell, but decided not to go through with it.

The little man had planned for this. He knew that they expected something magical from the age of wonder, like a giant steampunk, continent-striding robot, sentient homicidal missiles, or the Four Horsemen upgraded for the 2020s. He calmly raised his arm, and waited until their voices had died down enough so that his voice could be heard.

"This airship is much, much more than it first appears. Once it has been brought to life, you will see devastation and power unlike anything else you have ever witnessed before. The H-Bomb would seem like a cough compared to its firepower. And if you think that the RAF could bring it down, you are mistaken. The whole, combined might of NATO, the Russians and the Chinese is nothing compared to the magical force that it can create. Just one spell will bring it to life, and then the world will be ours; nothing can stand against it. One spell, my brothers, that is all. In the Great Book I carry here, liberated from the angel's own library in heaven, is that spell."

Schneider turned to face the remaining members of

the Order of the Black Sun; they formed around him in a tight circle. As the minutes passed, the volume of urgent whispers decreased from inside the ring of robes. Then there was silence, and Stranghold could see that Schneider was being briefed on what to say next.

"Stranghold, what is this spell that you say will turn this mechanical balloon into destruction incarnate?"

Stranghold smiled. He'd opened the door to the trap that would kill them all, and they had unanimously agreed to walk straight into it just like the sheep they were.

"Inside the Great Book is an incredibly powerful creation spell. If we position ourselves at key points around the craft and focus the spell directly through the lens of an imprisoned soul, it will make the weapon's heart start to beat again. If it is done correctly, this old relic, as you call it, will be able to turn the ground our enemies walk upon to ash.

"Many years ago, one of our agents came to me with a story that he had heard during a routine interrogation. They had picked up an old man on the streets of Prague. He was suspected of some magical training, nothing serious, but just before he died, he said something about a strange book that could harness the power of the earth and the elements. It was hidden deep in the catacombs under the city. I knew that this airship, and many of the other weapons that had been constructed in secrecy, could not be powered without an incredible source of energy – magical energy. And I knew when I heard the old man's story that this book was the key, which is why I spent so much time and so much energy in acquiring it.

"So I carried on with my plan in secret. Over the last 30 years I have prepared the ground for an assault, hiding magical beacons in some of London's greatest buildings. Only I know of their whereabouts and how to activate them. And all I need from you is some help to perform the spell. If it fails, you can burn my eyes and consign me to an eternity of wandering the depths of the great tunnels blindly. But if it works, what then?"

There was murmuring from within the ranks of the Black Sun as they debated the offer. On the other side of the hangar, the Ghost Children stood shoulder to shoulder in complete silence, unmoving and unknowing. Schneider turned back to Stranghold and nodded: the plan would go ahead. The Black Sun had agreed to let him put his neck under their axe blade. If he failed then he would die, but if he succeeded, Schneider and the rest would be the ones to burn.

"We must position one of the Ghost Children directly in front of each of the silver stakes; my spell must be directed through them and then on to the ship. Once we have completed the incantation the engines will come to life, and you will see the true potential of the weapon."

There was a low mumble of approval from the Black Robes and then they began to drift away towards the massed ranks of the Ghost Children of Jersey. Positioning the children was easy and achieved swiftly, most of them were just spectral zombies by now and they moved into place quickly and quietly. Stranghold thought it was amusing to see some of them rushing to get into position. They still believed that this was the moment they had all been dreaming of, that they were going to be reunited with their parents, and that they'd be permitted to grow up in some new Aryan utopia where they would be able to feel and act like children again.

How stupid they all were.

Once everybody was in position, Stranghold opened the book and flicked through its ancient pages until he found the spell that he was looking for. He raised his arm to signal to the other magicians that he was ready, and one by one they acknowledged him.

He began to intone the words written on the page in front of him. His tone was soft at the beginning, but as he progressed through the spell, his voice got louder and stronger. The blue light that had illuminated the hanger moments earlier was bleached out of existence by the power of the white light that began to pulse out of the book. Stranghold and the others were now seeing this subterranean world in strobing black and white; there were no colours any more, and no boundaries, just white light, and the occasional shape of the airship or a flag fluttering.

Just as soon as it had appeared, the light flickered,

and went out. All that could be heard was the sobbing of children, and the angry voices of what remained of the Order of the Black Sun.

Stranghold began to laugh. His high–pitched cackle echoed around the walls of the hangar. Every single last one of the Ghost Children had been impaled on to one of the savage silver spikes. They were still alive, just. The Black Robes had been deceived, too. Here and there a black robe hung from another of the spikes; blood spattered onto the floor below them as they bled, the odd shoe lay here and there, shaken off by the force of the spell, and puddles of urine made small silver circles on the stone. In the blue light the weapon looked just like a giant human pincushion; it made Stranghold laugh to see it.

It didn't take him long to find Schneider. The spike he'd been skewered with was sticking out of his chest just where his heart should have been. His eyes were open, and his lips formed a small black hole in his face.

"I'm so relieved that I get to stab you in the chest before you got a chance to stab me in the back, Schneider. You weren't expecting that, were you? You cretin!"

The voice that spoke from Schneider's body was full of rage and anger.

"You little bastard! You traitor, you have betrayed us!"

"Come, come now, Herr Schneider. You surely aren't going to suggest that you would have let me live after I had brought you here, are you?" He waved a manicured hand around in the air.

"What now then, Stranghold? You have taken all our power away from us, now what?"

"It's quite simple, Schneider. Now that the ship can fly, I will take it and set course for London. When I am in position over the city, the magic beacons I hid inside the walls and the foundations of the buildings there will activate, and will act like magnets for the destructive power of the lightning that you will generate for me. The spell I just crafted will draw the electrical energy from out of the air and channel it through you and the Ghost Children. They are the imprisoned souls I needed, and you were an added bonus.

"The beams will be of such concentrated power that they will reduce London to rubble. Anything that tries to engage the weapon or to stop it will be destroyed, of course. The beacons have been planted at specific points throughout the city where they will do the most damage. The banks of the Thames will be breached, and the great river will flow through London's streets, killing thousands. The tunnels of the Underground will fill with the bodies of the dead. I was going to call it a shame that you won't see it, but you will, of course, up close. The lightning will fry your body to a cinder, naturally, and you'll burn for years to come, but it's a sacrifice I'm sure you're willing to make. Goodbye, Schneider."

The wailing and screaming that followed Stranghold around the hull of the airship would have tortured any sane man until the end of his days, but to Stranghold it sounded wonderful. He clasped the book to his heart and ran up the steps two at a time, vanishing inside the black opening of the beast.

19 TWO GREY GHOSTS

The Gay Hornet was flying every stitch of canvas it owned. The triangles of wind catchers fought a running battle with the broad beams of the deck and the hull. Each side pushed the other, and dared it to fail. Rain had started to follow the ship as soon as it had left the Ghost Fleet. It fell from above, then slanted in from both port and starboard, so that there was no hiding place. Captain Conny had issued them all with thick oilskin trousers and a sturdy overcoat with a huge collar that when turned up made them look like vampires at a really bad fancy dress party. Judas, Ray and Evenor kept below decks for most of the time; they had acquired their sea legs, but still had to lunge for something to hold on to when Captain Conny spun the wheel in the cabin above.

The rain finally gave up at some point in the early morning and Judas went on deck. Ray had been mumbling to himself all night, while Evenor still hadn't realised that she had snubbed Ray's advances, which made Ray feel even worse. The sun had risen and had cleared the horizon to reveal the two grey smudges that made up the sky and the sea.

Judas walked back and forth across the woodwork. His mind had mastered the pitch and roll of the sea, and he was able to think clearly and plan for the day ahead. If Captain Conny knew the Gay Hornet as well as he said he did, they would soon start to see a dark grey bump on the horizon. That bump would grow and grow until suddenly, the Island of Jersey would appear.

Shortly after sunrise the angel, Ray, decided to take some air, too. The look on his face showed clearly that he had recovered from his most recent heartbreak, and he was back to normal once again. Evenor, the target of his love, had chosen the Captain instead, but now that his heart had been repaired and his sea legs had shown up, he was back to his annoying self.

The Gay Hornet t-shirt that he had stolen had been returned to its rightful owner, and now he was sporting his 'The Angel of Islington' raglan sweatshirt. Judas smiled; he was glad that Ray had come. He wasn't much use in a fight, but he was willing, and with what probably lay in store for them all ahead, he could use as much 'willing' as possible.

"Land!" shouted Captain Conny, and the Gay Hornet raced towards it.

Jersey has many beaches. Some are just small, picnic rug-sized belts of shingle, and others are larger, sandy versions, jealously guarded by the island's inhabitants who build their houses close by, so they can look down on them in the same way they look down on non-Jersey folk. Captain Conny avoided the big beaches and sailed the Hornet in close to a number of inlets before deciding on one in which to drop anchor.

"I've sailed these waters for a long time, Detective; this landing ground is well used by those who wish to go unnoticed. There are a few pathways up there, just beyond the large grey slash across the cliff face to your left, as I recall. The old gun emplacements don't look down into the little cove; that's why it's favoured by smugglers and the like."

"Looks good," said Judas.

"It's as close as I can get you without upsetting the natives. You're going to get wet feet as well, I'm afraid; the distance to shore is small and an underwater ledge starts not ten feet from the pinnace. A quick dunk, then you'll be able to stand up and walk the rest of the way."

"Wet feet? Not likely," said Ray, and he leapt into the air; with one beat of his wings he glided across the surface of the water and landed on top of one of the rocks that jutted out from the cliff face.

Evenor appeared at the Captain's side and whispered something into his ear. Judas read the signs and made his farewells. After they had shaken hands, Judas made himself absent and walked over to the ladder on the port side of the ship to wait for Evenor to say her own goodbyes in her own special way. He didn't have long to wait and he knew better than to ask her how it went and what had been said. He didn't fancy being karate kicked over to the beach – a freezing cold dip in the sea was much more appealing. It was exactly as the Captain had described, though; one minute they were up to their necks in icy water and the next they felt the hard, stone surface of the rock shelf underfoot. They walked, or rather waded up the excuse for a beach, and once they were fully ashore they both turned to wave goodbye to the Gay Hornet and Captain Conny. The swift vessel had already turned about and was heading out to sea. In a flash, she was gone. Only Ray was happy to see her go.

Judas and Evenor were both soaking, and neither had the equipment to build a fire, so they decided to get moving and get warm and dry at the earliest opportunity. The first pathway was exactly where Conny had indicated. It zig-zagged upwards in short bursts, and was more like a cut than a path, very narrow at the bottom and wider at the top, and so narrow that they spent half the climb walking sideways. Ray had flown up to the top of the cliff and was therefore missing all of the fun. When Judas and Evenor eventually reached the summit Ray was sunning himself on the grass, with the stalk of a dandelion between his teeth.

"Nice climb, was it?"

"Very funny, Ray. Make yourself useful, and scout along the clifftops. Dick Turpin said that Williams was going to make for a secret cave. The opening looks like an eye staring out at the sea. It's a small island so it shouldn't take you too long. We'll wait here and try and get dry."

Ray got up slowly and unfurled his wings.

"Right you are, then" he said, stepping off the edge

off the cliff and dropping out of sight. He appeared seconds later, flying away over the sea and hugging the coastline. Looking for an eye.

Williams woke up on an old military style camp bed. Oil drums with German Army markings stood guard all around him, and the long, steel finger of a spiked field gun pointed out to sea above his head. The boy was sitting with his back against the wall of the cave; his eyes were shut tightly, and his head tilted backwards at a funny angle.

"Joachim! Are you okay?"

"Well, apart from being dead I am fine, Herr Williams." The boy opened his eyes and sat up.

"Gallows humour, I like it. Well done. The last thing I remember is a big, sharp javelin coming up and out of the tunnel, then flying through a white square, which I now realise was the doorway to the cellar."

Williams got up from the camp bed. It took him a few tries; camp-beds are notoriously difficult to rise from if you are not blessed with grace or agility.

"Being a ghost does have its positives doesn't it, Joachim. We could have been killed down there if we hadn't, as you put it so eloquently, been dead already. What happened? How did we get to wherever this is?"

Joachim stood up, and inspected the cave. All of his fail-safes were still in place. He then walked down the passageway that led up to their hiding place and made sure that tripwire that would alert them to anyone approaching was still active. Only after checking that everything was in place did he return. Williams was staring out to sea.

"The Black Sun must have sent two of their most zealous after us, Herr Williams. When they launched the last attack, they must have forgotten where they were for a second, because instead of capturing us, the spell they conjured brought the tunnel roof down on them instead. The blast blew us to safety and sealed up the doorway to the cellar. You're not as heavy as you look, and this is the last place that anyone will look for us, I hope."

"You're a brave lad, Joachim. Now, we sit tight and wait for the cavalry, and hope that our message got through. There can't be that many cave openings that look like an eye."

They had been sitting on the edge of the cave and looking down on the sea for no more than 10 minutes, when they heard the first alarm go off. A soft thump was followed by a crash, then they heard the beating of a solitary drum.

"They have found us!" Joachim was up and had the door locked and rigged to explode before the second alarm was tripped.

"How long do we have?" Williams knew the answer but asked the question anyway.

"Not long, Herr Williams. Whoever it is will be able to get past the last two traps now that they know what to look for."

Ray saw the flash in the cliff face out of the corner of his eye and banked swiftly to investigate. There was the opening he had been looking for; if it hadn't been for the red flare he would have flown right past it.

At the back of the cave, Williams and Joachim had rolled the oil drums across the floor and arranged them into a wall, 2 barrels deep. They were down to their last box of grenades, and once they were gone the enemy would overrun them.

Ray saw an ill-fitting suit jacket trying to make a big, broad Welsh back look good, and knew straight away that he'd found Williams. He didn't know who the young boy was, but they were both on the same side of a barricade, so they definitely weren't enemies. Ray flew into the entrance of the eye; he was surprised by the look of happiness and relief on Williams' face, but less so by the abject horror and disbelief on that of the boy. What's more, he was wearing the uniform of a member of the Hitler Youth. Ray grabbed both of them, then launched himself backwards and into the air. When it was safe to do so he looked back at the cave opening in the cliff and saw another boy standing there. In one hand he held a red flare that the wind was making a mockery of; in the other, he held a drum.

Judas had very nearly dried off. His feet still squelched with every step, and his scar felt tight to the touch. The day had turned warm and the sun was being friendly, though. Evenor sat with her gaze locked onto the horizon. She hadn't said anything since the Gay Hornet had dropped them off at the base of the cliff, and Judas wondered what it was that she and the Captain had talked about. Once this was done, when Stranghold and his bunch of Nazi magic men had been sorted out, and the book had been returned to the angels, she would go looking for Captain Conny. He belonged to the sea and so did she. Hopefully, she'd find him. He was just about to say exactly that when Ray flew around the headland carrying two grey ghosts; one was his Sergeant and friend, while the other looked like a little boy wearing shorts with a red scarf around his neck.

20 THE HIDDEN DOORWAY

Ray was well and truly miffed. No, he was more than that. He was absolutely stung to the core at the lack of praise he felt was due to him for his rescue mission. Judas could read him like a book. If they'd had more time, they would have all patted him on the back and told him what a great job he had done, but they didn't have any. Every second that they spent glad-handing each other and catching up on old times was a second lost. The celebrations, if there were to be any, would have to come much later. Right now, Judas needed Ray on the wing.

"Ray, look, I know you risked a lot to get Williams and the boy back here, and of course I'm grateful, but there is something even more dangerous that I need you to do. The fate of us all rests with you now."

"It would have been nice for someone to say thank you, that's all."

Ray tried to look noble and magnanimous but came

off looking like he had just licked a freshly cut lemon.

"Ray, I need you to go looking for Michael; if you can, bring him back here as quick as you can – we're going to need some back up."

"He could be anywhere, Judas! The dark side of the moon, Arizona, Tooting, anywhere!"

"Try the City of the Heavens first. If you draw a blank there, get back here as soon as possible. That's all you can do, Ray; we've got to try."

Ray shrugged and rotated his shoulder blades in preparation for flight. He was going for heroic, but came off looking like a sub that comes on in the 90th minute with his side already 5-0 up.

"They probably won't let me get near the place, but I'll give it a go."

With that, he turned and jumped off the cliff, unfurling his wings and gliding away in search of a breeze that would take him up into the sky and up into the void that marks the boundary of the greatest city not on earth. Judas watched him go. So did Joachim, who was still in shock at having seen a real angel.

"The first time I saw one of their kind it beat me up so badly that even my eyebrows were fractured. They can be cruel as well as kind. What's your name?"

"Joachim. Joachim Weiss. Until very recently, a troop leader in the Ghost Army of Jersey, Herr…"

"Judas, as in Judas Iscariot, the man who betrayed Jesus and got on the wrong side of God. Detective Chief Inspector Judas Iscariot of the Black Museum Occult Division of Scotland Yard, if you want the full title."

Joachim stuck his chest out and was about to throw up a salute when he saw the man known as Judas smile.

"You don't need to salute like that anymore, Joachim, you're on the side of the angels now. If they turn up."

Judas sat everybody down, and started their final war council meeting with a squelch.

"Whatever it is that the Black Robes and this Stranghold character are about to let loose on London and dear old Blighty, it's got to be big. So, it's either coming up from below the waves or there has to be an opening on the island that hasn't been discovered yet. Any ideas?"

Joachim looked at Williams as if to say. 'Is it alright to talk?' The big man nodded.

"We're all in this together, Joachim."

"There is a place over on the far side of the island. At the bottom of one of the longest tunnels is a space big enough for the whole army to parade on. It was marked as out-of-bounds by the Black Robes shortly after we were first stationed in the citadel below. There is a great door on the far side of that space. You can't see the top of it."

"If it's at the bottom of the longest tunnel, Joachim, how will they get whatever it is out? Joachim took out the small notepad he always carried in his field-shorts; after rummaging around in his chest pocket he produced the stub of a well-used pencil and began to sketch.

"The angle of the tunnel is at 45 degrees, and it goes on for about a mile, like this. Then you step into the great hall, and the doors are on the far side, here. If you were to go through the doors and there was an opening to the sea, it would come out over there, on the eastern side of the island."

Joachim stood up and pointed towards the cliffs, away to their right.

"But if there is a tunnel that runs down to the hall from that side of the island, there could be one that runs back up at the same angle on the other side, which would mean there would be an opening just around the headland from where we are standing now; there was always a rumour of a secret launch pad hidden behind the walls of the cliffs."

Joachim handed his notebook over to Judas. Most of the pages had been filled with tight lines of writing, and here and there were sketches of weapons and people that he took to be his parents. He studied the drawing and wondered how a ghost child that had been living in a cave for the best part of eight decades could draw so neatly and precisely with a stub of a pencil no bigger than a fingernail. The boy had lived, if you could call it living, in the dark of the underground spaces and tunnels of this island and probably knew every inch of tunnel and centimetre of coastline.

There was a chance that he could be a double and that he was leading them into a trap. It had happened before. Judas and Williams had walked into traps more times than they had wished; getting out of the dungeons of the Camden Cabal had been a particular stretch, and they had only got clean away with all of their limbs because a water sprite that lived locally owed Judas for intervening with the local council to stop having the sewage pipes diverted through his front door.

They had to trust this boy, because they had nothing else to go on. Also, Judas was getting really annoyed with his sock now. It wouldn't stop sliding under his foot as walked.

"Lead on, Joachim. Let's go looking for a big invisible door."

21 A FOOL RUSHES IN

Ray was cold. He'd forgotten what space felt like. It's a different sort of cold up there. It flies with you. Down on earth the temperature of the air changes, and cold breezes might cut across a warm air channel and make you shudder for a bit, but up in the inky blackness of the great silver ocean of the stars, the cold attaches itself to you and holds on tightly. It stays at a constant temperature of 'Brass Monkeys Force 10'. Ray felt isolated at first, and vulnerable. The angels flew wherever they wanted to, and he was surprised that he had not been challenged or advised to disappear quickly – or else.

Away to his left, the Sun continued to burn in on itself, insatiable and ever-changing. Occasionally, as if in spite, it spat incredible flumes of fire at anyone who invaded its personal space. Ray had forgotten how vast it was. He'd been flying for about an hour and it was still there, as big as ever. It was time to change course, though. He lifted his chin, angled his wings back and up, and the sun began to drop away to his right. Soon there would be only fragments of rocks the size of Scotland floating by. Once, these had been planets, spherical and whole. Now they were broken, abstract shapes that would one day end up being skimmed across the surface of a calm, flat lake by a child who would never know that what he held in his hand had once been a magical kingdom in the stars. Home to a fantastic race that had long since faded into folklore and memory and become one with the endless void.

Ray was nearing the point of no return. He hoped that Judas had thought about that before sending him up here. He'd been thrown out once and told never to return, on pain of death. When Ray thought of the *point* of no return, he was imagining the *point* of one of those huge spears that the soldiers of the Host flung around. If one of them got angry, he would not be returning, that's for sure.

It was at that moment that two things happened really fast. First, he felt homesick. He couldn't help but think about his lovely two-bedroom flat in Islington, his collection of beautiful art, and the king-sized double that he romped on with whoever the current Mrs Ray happened to be at the time. Next, a great big shadow flew past him at incredible speed, and his wing was expertly taken in a vice-like grip. He started to fall backwards at speed. He couldn't see who or what had snatched him mid-flight; all he knew was that the stars were moving faster than usual and if he went any quicker, he would black out. Which he did, shortly after reprimanding himself for being a bit crap and letting Judas down.

When he woke, he was laying on the polished floor of a guardroom in the City of the Heavens, possibly the West Gate guard room. The points of no return were arranged against the far wall. The spears looked twice as menacing as he'd remembered, and impossibly sharp. The room was empty, save for the weapons and a candle that flickered apologetically on a table by the barred window. Through it, Ray could see the flights of the Host being Host-like and showing off their flying skills and muscles to each other. Ray shivered. At the beginning of the Second Fall there had been a sort of armistice, and the angels that were being booted out were being booted out gently. Then something had happened further up the line, and that's when the fighting started; the real fighting, that is. Ray was far too small to get involved; they would have cut him to pieces without breaking sweat.

Now it looked like he was going to have the lead part in the Third Fall of the Angels. If he survived this, his debt to Judas would be wiped clean, paid in full, and off the books. The door to the guard room opened and an angel that Ray had seen once or twice entered. Ray gulped, and tried to be brave.

"Well then, little one, how come you to be so far from home? You know that you are not granted safe passage if you fly beyond the line of the living stars."

Ray sat up, slowly; he didn't want to appear bolshy, or antagonise the big warrior more than he needed to.

"I am in search of the archangel Michael. He is needed on the earth by one that he calls Judas."

The big angel stirred. He checked his gauntlets and adjusted his tunic.

"You say that the archangel Michael is summoned to earth by the deceiver? Are you sure that you are well in the head, little one? One does not summon God's vengeance!"

Ray had the fear. The slight rise of the timbre in the warrior angel's voice put him on the back wing immediately.

"I was going to say 'don't shoot the messenger' but you might, so please, please don't! A great war is about to start down there on the earth. Millions will die, and one that is under the protection of Michael might just be one of them. It's not going to be fun telling him that, I can tell you. I'm just glad it won't be me."

Ray's point hit hard, and the big angel was already making for the door. He was only gone a short time before returning.

"Get up! Come with me to the South Gate. Now! I've dragged you across the heavens once already today, don't make me do it again!"

Ray was up and out of the door in a flash. His wing sockets were raw and still very painful, and he did feel a bit groggy. But he was lucky that he had made it this far and he really wanted to survive so that he could tell everyone that he had walked the halls in the City of the Heavens again. He'd be dining out on that story for a long time, and if he was part of the brave and outrageously heroic team that had saved the Earth too, well, he might not have to go back to scavenging for antiques. He could set up a gallery! He could launch new artists with swanky party nights and unveil their work to the sound of olives clinking in martini glasses. There would be DJ sets performed by the latest King or Queen of the scene, recently released from prison or the confines of some Reality TV show, and then New York! But he was getting ahead of himself. The big angel was right on his heels and urging him to fly faster.

They weaved through the tips of the great spires that pointed ever upwards from the roofs of the main halls. Then they flew downwards and underneath many of the bridges that linked the realms of the City with the central palace. Ray was feeling weary and he must have eased up a bit without thinking because he suddenly felt a great, muscled arm snake around his waist. All of a sudden he wasn't flying at all, he was being carried, and once again the stars began to smudge into tails of whiteness that got longer and longer and longer. This time he didn't black out.

He was aware of everything that was happening around him. His vision and ability to absorb information had increased ten-fold. The City of the Heavens looked magnificent as they sped through it. It was vast, and he was suddenly homesick and wanted to stay there a while; a century or two, perhaps?

There were six gatehouses in total. The City of the Heavens had never been attacked, for obvious reasons, so they acted like a form of border control. If you wanted to enter the City, you presented yourself at the gate house. Most visitors got in, but that didn't mean that they got out. When they finally arrived at the South Gate someone was waiting for them, and he didn't look happy.

22 FIGHT AND FLIGHT

Judas, Evenor, Williams and Joachim scrambled along the coastal path that was etched into the cliffside. The trails were narrow and filled with small rocks, so they stumbled and staggered along it. At times it felt like that they were trying to run with handcuffs attached to their ankles.

Joachim led the way. The sun had continued to shine, and visibility was good, but the boy was fading before their eyes. His energy levels were great, and he pushed on at a great pace, leading them along secret pathways and through small caves. But it was undeniable; his form was getting less and less solid, his outline was blurring. At first Judas thought that this might just be how he looked in daylight, but Williams, who was just behind him, was still bulky and clearly visible. He wasn't going to mention it, but if the boy did continue to fade he wondered how long it would be until he disappeared altogether. Williams and the boy had obviously been through a lot together and had quickly become friends – adversity does that to people, and the greater the danger, the closer you get to each other. At the first opportunity, Judas was going to have a word with Williams. There might be something they could do for the boy if he was nearing his end.

Joachim came to an abrupt halt up ahead. Williams and the boy whispered to each other. Joachim pointed towards a dark cleft on the cliff face, and beckoned for Judas to come forward.

They were in front of a small opening at the base of the cliff; a pool of grey sea water clogged with seaweed gently rocked back and forth in front of them like a brown, salty jelly. To their left, a series of low flat rocks poked their heads up from beneath the waves. They were all different shapes and sizes, but upon closer inspection it was clear they formed a flat, deck-like pontoon. From the sea they would just look like a series of rocks that had been eroded and shaped by the odd flow of the channel and the power of the rhythmic sea water. If you weren't looking for the anomaly then you would never have found it.

The cleft that Joachim had identified ran diagonally upwards from the base of the cliff on the left. Tufts of grass sprouted from it, and seagulls made their homes in them. Jagged outcrops punctuated the face of the cliff at odd intervals, and the wind sang its song through the grooves and holes in the rock. Everything was as it should be. The cliff looked solid. There was no door. Judas searched the grey wall, but he couldn't see anything out of the ordinary. Time was ebbing away, and there didn't appear to be another path on the opposite side of the clearing. Then suddenly the earth started to shake, and Judas made ready.

The birds were the first to flee. It was every gull for itself. Chicks were left behind and eggs rolled out of their nests, shattering on the ground below. Stones that had sat quite patiently for the best part of forever fidgeted, lost their balance, and started to rain down on the clearing. They fell towards unprotected heads, sending Judas and Evenor scampering for cover. Williams and Joachim stood still, allowing the stone rain to fall all around them. They were in no danger whatsoever. The tide started to race in faster than it had ever done before. The shape of the cliffs below the waterline was being altered and dragged out of position. Massive volumes of water were being rerouted; the waves felt it, and groaned and boomed out their displeasure.

Judas and Evenor climbed up the nearest rock, and stepped over and on to the rocky pontoon. Seawater was filling up the caves all around them, and it wouldn't be long before the only way was up. The pathway they had used to get here had already gone completely. Had they walked into a trap?

Judas got his answer quicker than he expected.

The cliff face began to hum. Judas placed his hand against the rock and there it was, faint at first, but getting stronger; a throbbing sound, like a giant growl of displeasure. Something big was coming up from deep inside the bowels of the island.

The narrow cleft started to widen, and the darkness within it deepened. Dank, fetid air that had stagnated inside the tunnel for decades behind the cliff face seeped out, and turned the air yellow. Birds that had not yet flown away now plucked up the courage to escape. Something that looked like steam puffed out of the widening gap in bursts that sounded like an asthmatic's last breaths.

The ground was vibrating much faster now, and Judas thought he heard the sound of children crying and wailing from the hole in the rock. The sea at the base of the cliff was white and troubled. Huge bubbles of air rolled up from the deep and exploded, sending spray in great arcs across the pontoon where Judas was standing. Then the vibrations suddenly stopped. Judas looked up, and saw that the cliff had been cleaved in two; all that remained was a giant black doorway. It had slowly opened, and now whatever had been hidden inside was coming out.

The seconds passed, and nothing happened. Then, a small green dot of light appeared. It was floating about 100 feet from the ground, right in the centre of the doorway. Then another dot joined it, just to one side. Soon the darkened space was alive with floating pinpoints of green, pulsing light. The scar that ran from Judas' waist up to his neck started to itch and tighten. His early warning system was working well, unfortunately.

The dots were getting closer; as they did, they grew more detailed, and turned into the faces of small children. The faces grew bodies, arms and legs. Judas saw that there were hundreds of them, hanging in the air, screaming to be put out of their collective misery.

The children continued to advance towards them, and Judas saw to his horror that they weren't flying or levitating at all. They had been impaled on enormous silver spikes, and those spikes formed the armoured bristles of a huge silver Zeppelin unlike anything that had ever flown before.

Judas felt impotent. He had to get on board this thing; he was of no use down here. But he had absolutely no chance of getting inside while he paddled around in the surf. He could tell in an instant that the others felt the same.

"We're too late!" shouted Joachim.

Judas looked up into the faces of the children and saw despair and defeat, but then something caught his eye. It was moving across the sky at great speed, and there was fire in the air all around it.

"Oh no we're not!" he said.

23 ABOVE AND BEYOND

Ray was nearly spent. He had never flown so far or so fast in his entire life. Michael was relentless. Each beat of his wings propelled him through the air with such power that the clouds disintegrated in his wake. Ray had been forced to grab hold of the bigger angel's belt and hang on for dear life. His eyes were watering, and his whole arm had gone to sleep, but he dared not let go. He could see the island up ahead clearly now; at first it had been a smudge, but now he could see the waves gathering around the base of the cliffs. He could just make out a ship of silver emerging from the grey rocks. Michael saw it too, and he angled his great wings so that they would come at it from out of the sun.

Judas, Evenor, Williams and Joachim had found a small hollow in the rock face where they could see the airship, and they waited. An irresistible force was about to meet a soon-to-be-moved object. Michael began to slow down, then came to a complete stop. He had positioned himself directly in the path of the eerie airship, with the sun at his back. He hung there like a beautiful statue, perfectly still and focused on the target in front of him. He could see Judas down on the beach and nodded to him. Then, he took his great sword from its scabbard. Its blade erupted with a red flame so intense that it turned the silver skin of the Zeppelin scarlet.

Ray had let go of Michael's belt about a mile from the island. This had given him time to catch his breath. He was still exhausted, but he felt something burn inside him that he had not experienced for a long time. He was proud to be an angel once again. In truth, he'd always felt second rate in London. The humans loved them, of course, angels walking amongst us and all that. But he'd seen the City of the Heavens again, and flying by Michael's side had filled him with hope and positivity. He wanted to show them all that he wasn't just another of the angel drop-outs from Heaven, but something more. So he girded his loins, extended his wings as far as they would go, and flew into battle.

He saw Michael up ahead. His great golden wings were reflecting all the morning's light, and his great sword was flaming. Ahead of him, the silver craft had stopped, and Ray could see a strange green glow beginning to flow across its body. The air directly above it was beginning to darken, and Ray could see tiny spider's webs of lightning beginning to form in the clouds. Michael was not in the least bit intimidated; instead, he seemed to swell in size right in front them. Destruction was coming.

Ray was nearly at his target. The sea and the sky had become a tunnel for him. Nothing else existed outside of that moment. All his muscles and sinews were strained to their limits, and his body felt more alive than ever. A strange calmness had come over him. He clenched his fists tightly, banked around Michael, and went in for the kill.

The lightning grew in intensity inside the clouds then, just as if some great switch had been pulled, they emptied their payloads into the Zeppelin. The silver craft throbbed with blue energy, then the children pointed at Michael; the lightning surged through them, and out of their mouths like beams of living destruction. Michael was ready, of course, and had already raised his sword to deflect the lightning strike. But just before it reached him, Ray flew directly into its path.

The severity of the blast was enormous. It passed straight through Ray, and he dropped like a stone into the surf. Michael saw the brave little angel fall and hesitated; in that split-second he took the full force of the blast on his chest. The silver ship fired again, and the air all around Michael exploded.

Judas was stunned. He'd never seen such power before. The blast had shaken the earth they were standing on, and all was lost if even the great Archangel Michael was defeated. He started to climb the rock face, determined not to give in. If he could stop this evil then maybe, just maybe, he would have repaid his debts. He could go and live in Cornwall – if they'd have him.

He was half way up the cliff when he became aware that Evenor was beside him. They heard the engines of the airship throb, and turned to watch as it began to glide out to sea. It was now or never, and it looked like never was in the driving seat.

The first of the shells hit the craft head-on. The airship was knocked out of its stride and rocked backwards. Another shell exploded on its hull, and the blast removed several of the spikes from its starboard side.

Judas hadn't spotted the U-boat surfacing. It lay in the water, about 100 metres from the shore, having performed an emergency rise, blowing all tanks and then hanging on for dear life. As soon as the boat had surfaced, all of its hatches had been popped, and the crew had raced on deck to fire the field gun. Werewolves were fearsome hand-to-hand fighters and had no equal on land, but it seemed they were no slouches when it came to firing guns, large or small, either. Those that weren't involved in sighting and loading the gun had already dived into the water and had nearly made it to the beach. Judas looked down at them, amazed.

They had arrived in the nick-of-time, clearly having chosen to attack the real enemy and regain their honour. If you'd told him a week ago that he'd be happy to see a crew of seven-foot tall, sopping wet werewolves in German naval uniform storming a beach, then leaping up cliffs onto a magically super-powered Zeppelin in order to destroy it and save the world, he'd have called you barmy. But today? Well today, as long as they brought the aircraft down, anything would go.

Michael picked Ray's body up from the beach. He was barely alive. The blast he had taken for Michael had burned his entire body, and all that was left of his wings was two brown stumps that twitched and spasmed.

"You will live, little angel, with me and the Host in the City of the Heavens, where you belong. Sleep now, little one, and when you wake, all things will be well."

Michael placed one huge fingertip on Ray's forehead, whispered something into his ear, and then his body went limp. The battle was raging all around him, but Michael paid it no heed.

The look on his face at the moment would have brought an army to its knees; if whoever was flying the silver ship had seen it, they would have turned about and fled. There was little hope for them now. The Enforcer of the Heavens was angry, and when he was angry, war and God's judgement followed swiftly after.

The airship had not yet made its escape. It was being attacked and held by strange-looking wolves, but they looked as if they were nearly finished, too. The flying craft had continued to fire off its lightning bolts and blasts in all directions, and huge sections of the cliffs were disintegrating and falling into the sea. Michael looked down at his hands. One single, solitary feather rested on his palm. The little angel would return to the City of the Heavens and he would be made whole again, he would see to it. He tucked the feather carefully inside his armour and reached for his sword.

The Archangel was angry now and he was in world crushing mood. He was just about to leap into the air, when the whole side of the cliff face above him detached from the rest of the island and dropped right on top of him.

Judas and Evenor had reached the top of the cliff by now, and had raced around the headland to where the Zeppelin had been pinned to the cliffs by the firepower of the U-boat and the commando attack of the werewolves. It was close enough to the land that they could both leap onto it. But then they discovered the booby traps that Stranghold had set for them. As they searched for the hatch that would lead them inside the ship, they came face-to-face with the children on the spikes, literally. It had never occurred to either of them that the ghost children would be conscious of them, or that they would or could act independently, both had presumed that they would only be activated when they were near their intended target. Some of them had been primed to go off much sooner than the rest.

Evenor looked at one of them, and thought to herself that there was not enough pity in all the world for it. But she looked for too long, and the child simply raised an arm in a Nazi salute before a short burst of energy burst from his hand and nearly killed her where she stood. If she hadn't been trained since childhood to always remain ready and anticipate an attack, she would have been just another scorched silhouette on the surface of the silk membrane of the airship. She saw the attack coming just in time, and rolled away to her left. The eyes of the dead boy searched for her, manically, but they closed forever when she chopped his head from his shoulders with one savage blow. Judas had seen the Saints in action many times. They'd fought side by side in some of London's darkest places and he'd always been glad that they were able to move between the worlds of the dead and the living whenever it was needed most. He'd tried to quiz Thornton about it but all the old man would say was that their power come from across the sea and across the ages.

Judas looked down on the face of the child, knowing immediately that it was yet another image that would speak to him in the dark of night. His memories were full of the sorry stories of the innocents. Here, at his feet, was the head of a child that had been poisoned with the evils of the world, instead of being educated with the good and the bright. Judas and Evenor raced onwards, running and dodging the blasts that came from every angle. When they finally found the hatch, they leaped before they looked. and walked straight into a trap.

24 ALL HANDS

Lindelhoff and the rest of the crew were panting hard. The steam from their bodies filled the air of the U-boat's cabin, and they could not see from one end of the compartment to the other. Their claws were clogged with dead flesh that crackled, and their fur was matted with black blood that tasted of the underworld. The Ghost Children that were wrapped around the airship were too many in number, and the Kapitan had signalled for them to return to the ship. The deck of the U-boat was covered in black blast marks where the lightning from the airship had struck it, and the field gun was completely destroyed. The barrel was bent in two, while the loading platform had been melted so that it looked like a giant candle that had seen out the night before someone had blown its flame out. The wolves that had been firing it were gone; nothing remained of them save an odd scrap of uniform that had been blown away from the platform and had snagged in the deck gratings.

They had done as much as they could. The airship was still flying, although badly damaged, but if they had continued the attack they would have all been killed and their boat would have been sunk. They could do no more, so they retreated to their floating home and closed the hatches, diving as quickly as the boat would allow. From an original crew of 25, only 15 remained; the Black Forest and the low plains of their homeland would never hear the howling of the Moon's Children again.

Lindelhoff hoped that someone would tell their story, a story of honest men who had fought for what they believed in, and still went on and fought with honour at the end, when they had learned that they had been betrayed. Maybe they would have time to think about it, or maybe the airship that had brought the cliffs down on them was about to reach down into the deep water and crush them. The Kapitan had made the right choice, and if Lindelhoff and the remaining Werewolves were going to die right now, it would be a good death. They were animals, but at least they had fought like real men, unlike the monsters that had and started this war.

Ahead, at the ship's bridge, the Kapitan wiped the blood from his wounds on a signal flag and switched the lights to red. The boat dropped into the deep and disappeared. All that was left to mark its passing was a flight of bubbles that raced towards the freedom of the surface. It was time to for this U-boat to go back to the sea and wait for the next full moon.

In a steel-lined room 1000 feet above Lindelhoff and the quietly retreating submarine, Judas sat up and tried to get both of his eyes to look in the same direction at once. His head was throbbing, and his scar had decided to hold its own rave. He could just make out the body of Evenor on the floor opposite. She looked like he felt. Her sunglasses were gone, and there was a nasty gash that leaked dark brown blood down the side of her beautiful face. He was about to ask her if she was okay, but she beat him to it.

"Not so bad, Evenor. I might be a bit groggy, but I'll mend."

"I've heard that from Thornton; he says that you heal quickly, and that it's because you have a gift. He often says that you have someone watching over you and that he wouldn't be surprised to find that you are immortal. He also says that if you're ever in a fight, make sure you stand next to Judas, because he has a way of getting out of the trouble that he gets everyone else into."

"I've always got on well with Thornton, but he does have a tendency to wax lyrical and go a bit Drury Lane, doesn't he?"

"Are we talking about the same Thornton, Judas?"

Evenor stood up and picked her sunglasses up from the corner of the room. She put them on like she had done a million times before, and then slowly removed them because one of the lenses had been shattered.

"Wear them – you look great," said Judas.

Evenor gave Judas one of those smiles that told him he'd be single forever.

Judas got to his feet and looked around. They were in a steel box; there was no other way to describe it. There were no vents or spy holes on any of the walls or floors. They had jumped down a hatch to escape the lightning spewing children of destruction that were trying to incinerate them, and had lucked out by leaping straight into a prison cell on an airship heading to London, with a mad WWII magician at the wheel and no way out. Brilliant.

Judas and Evenor examined every single centimetre of their cell, and both came to the conclusion that they were in a bind. So, they talked and waited for the little man to make his move.

"What is it with you and the sea, Evenor? It calls to you, doesn't it? I could see it in your eyes as soon as we set sail."

Judas had regained full 20/20 vision by now and his scar had calmed down to a mild itch. He'd straightened his tie and checked his Frahm jacket for holes and tears. He was relieved to find that the coat was intact, so he sat down with his back against the cold flat wall of his prison cell and listened to Evenor's reply.

"They all think that Atlantis is a fable, a myth and a story for graphic novels to dredge up whenever the storyline needs a destination or a full stop. They're making films about the place now. Billions of dollars spent on talking crustaceans and submarines that fly using dolphin technology! In the early days it was all tunics and clever whales, but now, they seem to have worked it out. Atlantis was a place for science and the arts, engineering and magic, a place for the willing to find enlightenment and possibly a new faith to follow. The best and the brightest from all of the races of the Earth were summoned there a long, long time ago. I was one of them.

"Atlantis was a place for the exchange of intelligence and knowledge that would make the whole world a better place, not just some parts of it. Unfortunately, there are always thieves amongst agents of peace, and many of the most precious secrets were stolen from us. The words of the history books and the legends of the magical councils will tell you that Atlantis was destroyed by a tidal wave or by some murderous race of legendary creatures, but it is not so.

"Atlantis still thrives and endures. It cannot be found on any map and no human will ever be able to chart a course for it. It is well hidden, believe me. I was one of a small group of inhabitants who were tasked with retrieving the secrets that were stolen from us. We thought that we would not be gone for long, but it has been a hard task and still some of the knowledge we seek is in the hands of people that would use it for the wrong purpose. Thornton is one of us – a mighty warrior, well-respected among our people, and he volunteered to lead the search for the stolen secrets. It was only natural that we would follow him. Thornton decided long ago to remain in Albion. He saw that there was a need for our people there – the streets were full of demons and Fey folk that prayed on the humans. There was a lot of interaction between the races, too, and a lot of that was good. We learned a lot from the Forest People and the spirits of the land about Albion and its connection to the old magic.

"Thornton wanted to help bring order to the young streets of London; I guess he may even have wanted to turn it into another Atlantis. All of us Saints of Clapham are bound to him, but he has always said that he is no jailer, and if any of us wishes to return to the sea, the way will not be barred. And that, Judas is why I was chosen to accompany you. My time with the land is done. If we get through this, I shall seek out the Gay Hornet and Captain Conny, and make for Atlantis."

Evenor had talked more in that few minutes than she had in the whole of their journey so far, so Judas welcomed her words. Thornton and the rest of the Saints had been fighting crime and keeping the borders of their borough safe from the occult and the enemies of humans for hundreds of years, and it had never occurred to him that they did so voluntarily.

Their conversation lapsed into silence.

The vibrations of the engines continued, but every now and again there came a skip and missed beat from one of their pumping mechanical hearts. The ship was limping along rather than cruising at full speed, and that sound gave Judas hope.

Evenor got up and walked around the room. She sat down beside him again and he realised how badly hurt she was; he had forgotten that she had been injured on their way to their present incarceration. Judas turned to look at her. The blood from her wound had run from her temple down her face in one beautifully straight line, then on down her neck to disappear underneath her white collar. Judas listened to her ragged breathing and knew that she was running on empty.

"Evenor, I'm going to take a look at your wounds. I'm going to have to remove your jacket and shirt, are you okay with that?"

Evenor rolled over onto her side and closed her eyes.

"If I get into bed with Captain Conny and he decides not to go ahead with the deed because I have some hideous new scar, Judas, you had better be ready for my wrath."

Judas hoped she was joking, as she drifted away into the welcoming clouds of comforting unconsciousness.

Judas ripped Evenor's shirt open at the neck and saw that she had been hit twice. Once on the head, with another blow that had hit her just above her right breast. There was blood everywhere, but this was the sort of wound that always made him smile. Whether it had been a blast, a shot, or a stab, whatever it was that the Ghost Child had hit her with had passed straight through her body, fortunately missing any of her bones or vital organs. Evenor grumbled as he wiped away as much of the blood as he could with what remained of her shirt. Then he placed the palm of his hand flat against the wound, and waited for the 'thing' to begin.

He had lost count of the number of times that he had performed this action. It wasn't a spell or a charm, and he hadn't studied any medicine or anything remotely like healing, but he could save a life if he needed to. There was often wonder and gratitude in his patients' eyes as they reawakened, and realised that they had just been saved after being hurled through a 10th floor window, or having an arm ripped off by some ghoul in the sewer.

But there were other times when they came to and the shock and the memory of what had just happened to them was too vivid and awful for them to comprehend, and they died, again, in his arms.

As he waited for Evenor to heal and to come back to him, his thoughts drifted to a young woman that he had saved 500 years ago in the small town of Tavistock, on the edge of Dartmoor. It was a bad time back then, and many innocent young women were being tried as witches.

The general population had no idea what magic really was, and how good it could be for them, if they allowed it to just happen. The fields would yield a good crop as long as the spirits and the sprites were kept happy with small offerings. Harmony was all that the countryside and the forests wanted. And giving thanks to the Old Gods at the right solstice was all that was needed. But there was a new terror afoot, consuming the innocents and drowning them in suspicion and religion. Judas had been walking for days across the moors, with no particular destination in mind, when by chance he had stumbled across the pond where the young woman had just been drowned.

Her helpful neighbours and erstwhile denouncers had at least pulled her body out of the water and dumped her corpse on the bank. She had been a really pretty girl, which was possibly why she had been accused of witchcraft; maybe a jealous friend had set her cap at one of the boys and found out that he had eyes only for this girl instead. Judas wasn't sure why he did it – perhaps it was God working through him – but he had brought her back to life.

The girl had woken with a start, coughing up half a pond's worth of muddy water. Once he had explained to her that she had been resurrected because she was innocent, she was happy and full of hope. He warned her not to return to Tavistock, and as he walked away from her, he hoped that she had taken heed, or she would have been back in the pool before nightfall.

Evenor began to shake, then she sat bolt-upright so quickly that she knocked Judas over. In the time it took him to get up again she had snatched her jacket from the floor and dressed herself.

"What happened?" she demanded.

"We can talk about this another time, Evenor. Right now we have to get out of here and stop this airship!"

Evenor put her hand inside her jacket and felt her wound.

"Whatever you did, Inspector, I thank you. I am in your debt now, and you must allow me to repay it."

"Fine. Afterwards, okay?"

Evenor nodded, and Judas was both surprised and grateful when she did something that she didn't do very often – she smiled. Then it was back to business, and she went back to checking the walls and the floor for some sort of entrance or way out.

Seconds later their way out found them instead, as the floor beneath them suddenly disappeared. Gravity pulled them out of their prison with unusual gusto, and they fell.

Judas tumbled through the air like rag doll in a washing machine and was lucky to spot a steel girder flying towards him with unnecessary haste just in time. He would have smashed straight into it, and although the impact would not have killed him, it would have seriously ruined his day and stolen valuable time from his mission to kill the little man and take back the book. He managed to angle his fall, but still landed flat on what looked like some machine housing instead. The landing was dramatic, and ripped all of the breath from his lungs, but he was up and ready to go within seconds. He looked around for Evenor, and was pleasantly surprised, and not a little jealous, to see that she had performed some sort of acrobatic twist, coming to rest with the grace and balance of a ballerina on one of the steel supports above him. She waved, and casually dropped down from the steel beam, landing like a cat next to him.

Their cell had been built high up in the web of steel girders that criss-crossed the interior of the aircraft in a latticework that strengthened the hull and stopped the ship from imploding. Looking up, they could see that the airship had sustained some damage to this skeleton of steel, and a couple of girders had snapped, ripping the floor from their cell.

They were just orientating themselves when the engines started to roar incredibly loudly. They could tell from the slant of the deck that the ship was listing badly, and Judas quickly realised that the engines on the starboard side must have failed, or were failing fast, at least. In response, someone, somewhere, was taking drastic action, and they heard the port-side engines working to level the craft again. A couple of seconds passed, then the breathing of the metal beast they were inside started to regulate itself and sound more comfortable. They were back on course and underway again, but the odd little skip in the sound of the engines had returned, and this time it had brought a friend. The ship shuddered once again, and from close by they heard a dull snapping sound. The sounds grew louder; Judas unhappily realised that he had a good idea about what was snapping, and which way it was heading. The structural supports that kept the big bag of helium and air from tearing itself to pieces were giving out, and the aircraft was going to be landing much more quickly than normal.

25 THE SEA CALLS

The air inside the airship was dank and fetid. Rows of small blue lights ran fore and aft down the length of the craft, so Judas and Evenor were able to see where they needed to go. But there were no crew on board. The engines were running by themselves, and the only sound they could hear was the wind rushing along the skin of the ship outside, and the wailing of the Ghost Children as they crackled with lightning.

Evenor had regained all her strength and mobility quickly, and Judas had to move fast to keep up with her as she raced forwards. She leapt from gangway to gangway, vaulting over the machine turbines with ease. Judas took the long way around, but managed not to slip too far behind. The ship was huge, but it had a very simple floorplan and there was only one control room. Zeppelins were always steered from a cabin that was slung under the belly of the beast, exactly midway between the nose and the tail. So, once they had made it halfway down the length of the craft, they looked downwards. The steering cabin and the main controls would be located directly under where they were standing right now. A set of iron steps lead down from the platform they were on. They followed them down, but when they reached the bottom of the steps they realised that this walkway didn't seem to go anywhere.

They couldn't see a hatch or a doorway leading off it at either end, but something inside Judas told him that they were in the right place. It was just a hunch, but he could sense that there was something wrong about the dark space ahead and he listened to his hunch, because it had saved him from danger many times in the past.

"He's in there, Evenor. But he must have cast a glamour over the door so that we can't see it. Watch my back – I'm going to try to get through it."

It was because the magic hit Judas first that Evenor survived. He'd walked into the darkness first, moments before it erupted with an intense light flare that blinded them both. They were thrown back against the stairs, then everything went black.

"There you are, Inspector! And you have brought a friend along – how lovely."

When the light returned, Judas could see the little man in his sharp suit and highly polished shoes standing directly in front of him, The Book clamped firmly under one little arm. He held it like a rugby ball, and Judas could see that his knuckles had gone blue because he held it so tightly.

"The Book is what you are seeking, Inspector, isn't it? But it's too late for that, Inspector. Surely you know that now? We passed Finisterre long ago, and the wind is blowing us to London like an extra jet engine. The dark clouds are beginning to gather over the capital, and the End Days are coming on swift wings."

Judas stood up, and was relieved to see that Evenor had not been injured again. She stood to his side, and he could tell from her body language that she was about to go in for the kill. He was just about to reply to Stranghold, but he was too slow, because it swiftly became clear that the little man certainly wasn't waiting for anything. He moved faster than Judas would have thought possible, perhaps due to the power of the book. He lifted it up, and rapidly spoke some indecipherable words, then Judas found himself being lifted over the metal rails of the walkway and into the air.

Evenor saw the next blast coming, and realised that she could repay her debt to Judas by barging him out of the way and taking the main force of the spell on herself. Maybe it would give Judas time to fight back, or to find a way to disable this evil floating torture chamber. All she knew was that she had to give the Inspector a chance to prevent this horrible little dwarf in pin stripes from killing millions of innocents.

The force of the spell was meant for Judas, but she took it in his place. The pain entered her body through her eyes, like being punctured by millions of shards of ice that caught fire once they'd made their way inside. She was lifted from the ground and blown straight through the skin of the airship, and into the sky. Her blood surrounded her like a cloud of red mist that was sucked away by the wind. She was still conscious, at least, despite the cold of the sky trying to turn all of her senses off. She was falling now, at great speed, and the silver airship was getting smaller and smaller in the air above her. She turned over, and there below her was the sea. It rose to meet her, and she welcomed it with open arms. The force of the impact was brutal, and she went down deep. What was left of her strength was fading fast, but she remembered to follow the bubbles of her breath and kicked for the surface. Her head was ringing, and her body was broken, but the sea held her up.

She wanted to go home. She wanted to sail the seas. She wanted to do so many things. She drifted in and out of consciousness with the waves. The cold call of the welcoming deep was sounding in her ears, and she was taking in more water than air now; she knew that it wouldn't be long. The sea takes us all in the end. Life begins there, and ends there. Evenor looked up at the sky for the last time. The sun was a steel disc, white against the grey of the clouds. One more look to the horizon, and then she would sleep. She wanted to live, and most of all, she wanted the small white triangle on the horizon to be the sail of a ship. She hoped it was. She wanted it to be real. It got closer and closer, but the sea was winning the race for her soul.

26 FIRE AND WATER

The small fishing boat rounded the headland, fighting valiantly against the outgoing tide to take up its favoured position in the inlet before dropping the battered pink buoy that used to be red. The skipper of the boat and his nephew emerged from the warmth of the cabin and began to prepare the nets. A battered radio that had been made good against the window with gaffer tape and an ingenious combination of a child's cricket bat and a spare door hinge hummed with angry, insect-like static. Every now and then a man's voice slipped past the droning and crackling, to inform his listeners that 'the High Street was closed to HGV's for the foreseeable'. The boy went about his business, but the Skipper took one look at the water and knew that there was something wrong with it. The cliffs looked different, and where were the gulls?

They should be knee deep in the little buggers.

They'd be perching on the roof of the cabin waiting for the bait buckets to come up from below, screeching and squawking, and painting the deck with yesterday's dinner. But the sky was empty, and the water that should've been blue was brown. The boy lifted the nets up to make sure that the cork floats were on the top, and waddled to the stern. He hadn't registered that the Skipper wasn't helping, and casually waited for the swell to drop the stern a bit before throwing the nets as far away from the boat as he could. He made sure that the end line was still attached to the nets, and secured them to the winch that would gradually pull them back into the boat when they had completed a full circuit of the bay.

The Skipper was still perplexed, and stood looking towards the shore. He was trying to remember if the cliff face had always had a big crack running through it. Was that great big opening always there as well?

His nephew came to stand by his side. They were both staring at the shoreline when the water began to bubble and froth all around them. It was as if a giant invisible whisk was being pushed into the shallows and turned up to full power. Suddenly, a great plume of steam escaped from the new hole in the cliff face, and the rocks screamed.

Their boat started to rock and buck in the swell. It skittered on top of the waves, and lurched around like a drunken uncle at a village wedding. The Skipper and his nephew raced to the stern, quickly released the drag nets, then dived inside the cabin, pulling on every lever and pushing on every button, hoping that their panic would spread to the engines and jolt them into life. The engine puttered, giving false hope, and then died.

The boat was forced around by the pull of the erratic tide, and their eyes were drawn to the water not 20 feet from the port side of the vessel. Even though the water was the colour of weak gravy, they could see a light in the depths, and it was getting brighter. Later, down at the pub, after his eighth pint and fifteenth retelling of his tale, the Skipper would say it was the sword that scared him the most.

"It came up from under the water like some monstrous version of King Arthur's sword. As soon as the blade met the air, it was engulfed in a blue fire that singed my eyebrows clean away. When I looked again, there he was, the biggest, angriest looking angel I have ever seen. Bigger than that angel they got over at Penzance by a long way. This one looked like one of them King angels.

"He hovered in the air above the boat. Didn't even see us to begin with, and looked mightily peeved about something. His wings came out, grey and silver they were, and then loads of water cascaded out of his armour – showered me and the boy proper. Then it looked around for something, spotted us, ignored us just as quick, and then beat its wings once, nearly capsizing us. Then he was gone; he shot up, and the last thing we saw was a great big hole in the clouds."

27 THE NEW BLITZ

Judas was alone in the dark. Again. Evenor had shoulder charged him with great force. He had gone over the handrail and landed here, wedged between two big steel boxes that hummed and rattled. He was also covered in grease and some sort of metal powder, and had ripped a hole in his new Frahm City coat. He was already going to kill the little magician, but now he wanted to do it twice. He'd watched as Evenor had been blasted through the side of the ship, and he wanted to get up there and wring the little man's neck. The blast from that bloody book wouldn't kill him, but it could clearly stop him in his tracks, so he needed to think and act smart from now on. It was just him and Stranghold now, and by the diminishing sound of the engines, they were nearly at the end of their journey.

Judas had been thinking while he had been locked

up in Stranghold's metal prison cell. Where were the RAF? Where were the ground to air missile batteries that the PM had hidden away in underground car parks all across the city, just for situations like this one?

He was going to have to think and act like they were gone. Stranghold must have planned for an attack from the ground and the air, and had probably also made sure that the aircraft would not pop up on any sort of radar. Williams and Joachim had probably fallen and been destroyed back on the beach in Jersey. Evenor had just been blasted to pieces, and it was going to be a watery grave for the bits that weren't evaporated by the blast. As for Michael and Ray, he hadn't seen them since the initial contact with the Zeppelin. If they weren't here now, then they must have fallen already. The werewolves had fought well and Judas really wanted to return to the Ghost Fleet one day and thank the Kapitan and his crew, if any of them had survived. Captain Conny and his Gay Hornet would be miles away by now, sailing happily along and bickering at each other, good naturedly of course, like two old women. Thornton was not going to best pleased with him either; if he ever made it back to Clapham Common and the church, he would be sure to pay his respects and make amends, if he was able.

Judas readied himself and managed to get to his feet without making a noise. He could see the little man watching and waiting on the walkway above him. He was scanning the deck of the airship for movement; fortunately for Judas he was looking in the other direction, but his gaze would soon land on his hiding place, so Judas crouched down and edged back into the darkness between the metal monoliths. Judas was good at waiting, and it wasn't long before he heard those little feet tap, tap, tap their way back to his secret room. The magician must have thought that Judas had been sucked out of the same hole as Evenor and perished along with her. Big mistake. Colossal. Judas closed his eyes, counted to eleven, and planned his next move. The engines of the great craft started to slow still further, and the noise abated until only the wind and the air could be heard.

The thunder clouds had rolled in with such great speed that they had caught London's café owners and waiters with their trays down. Umbrellas were going up all over the capital. But they were going to be useless, because the rain that was about to fall would be accompanied by thousands of bolts of lightning. Helicopters from the Heliport in Battersea had been grounded due to incredibly high winds, and record levels of airborne static. Planes were being rerouted from London City airport to Luton, and all flights that normally used the Thames corridor were now going the long way around the city. It was only 14.00hrs, but it looked and felt like night had already fallen. Possibly for the last time.

Londoners looked up at the sky and reached for their umbrellas or their hoods in order to prepare for the unscheduled downpour, but instead of rain, all they saw was a vast shadow hidden deep inside the grey clouds overhead.

The angels were the first to realise that something was wrong. They could feel the sudden change in air pressure, while the unusual formation of the clouds themselves reeked of danger. They called out to each other in their ancient tongue, and pointed up to the heavens. Something large was hiding up there, and no angel could – or would – fly any closer. They could all feel the dark energy emanating from inside the clouds above, and even the bravest knew that they were no match for whatever it was on their own. So they dropped out of the sky, landing on the tops of the tallest buildings, and readied themselves. They would not run away a second time.

Stranghold was on the aircraft's bridge. He was wearing a smile that would have made coffee nervous. His eyes had practically disappeared because his cheekbones had been pushed up his face by the intensity of his grin. Banks of lights and switches worked themselves all around him. They flipped up and down, and winked at each other. Meanwhile the wheel spun left and right, countering the speed of the wind, and keeping the airship flying and level. He pictured the ship in his mind's eye, and willed it to stop. The Book gave an excited little shudder, and the sound of the Zeppelin's engines faded away altogether. Then, with a wave of one small, well-manicured hand, the steel shutters that had been raised to protect the windows from shattering during the earlier battle came down, and grey light edged its way inside the cabin.

Stranghold shuffled over to the window and looked down on the maelstrom he had created. Little threads of lightning were jumping from cloud bank to cloud bank. They were increasing in size all the time – it wouldn't be long before he could conjure the final spell and make the Ghost Children sing once again. Victory was near, and a new age was about to begin. He was going to lead the forces of the darkness and bring the world to its knees. England would be gone, wiped clean from the surface of the earth with all its people burned to ash. He closed the steel shutters once more, and made his way across the cabin to the small door. Behind it were the steps that climbed all the way to the top of the airship and the miracle weapons.

Away to the west of London, the orchids of Kew Gardens fluttered, and the glass panes that made up the walls of its glasshouse started to vibrate at such a pitch that a number of them failed and shattered into millions of small pieces. The sonic boom that followed soon after sent everyone racing for cover. Something was flying in low and fast, cutting a long wide channel into the clouds as it went.

Stranghold popped the hatch and stepped out into the wind. His tie flicked out from his neck like an angry snake, then flopped over his shoulder and died there. The nearest Ghost Children shrieked at him, but he just giggled as they pointed accusing fingers at him Their eyes told the same story they always had. A story of deception and pain. Their mouths opened and closed, but instead of words only cries escaped, and soon they seemed to give up, drifting back into the twilight places of their existence, and dreams of lightning and death.

At the very centre of the top of the aircraft was a spike. It was longer than the ones used to skewer the children. It was made of marble and black in colour, apart from a thin white vein that wound through it from top to bottom. Half-way up this evil totem was a symbol. The symbol of the Order of the Black Sun. Stranghold placed the palm of his hand against it and in hundreds of secret hiding places across London, the black rods that would direct the lightning came to life.

Judas had followed the small man at a safe distance up the inner stairwell and on to the roof of the craft. He had previously only seen the Ghost Children from afar, when the airship had first edged out of its hangar like a great, blind worm. Up here, he could see them more closely, and when he did so he despaired, because there was no way he could save any of them. He'd seen the look in their eyes many times before, in the faces of others who had been eaten up from the inside up by evil spirits. The damage done to the human mind and body was far too severe in such circumstances, and even if you could save one, the other would quickly perish. He tried not to make eye contact, and crept through the forest of electric children without causing any of them to react to his presence.

When he was only a few metres from the little man, he stopped. Stranghold had taken up position by a big, black spike, and was busy conjuring up some sort of spell, so he didn't see Judas approaching. Judas was very close, and was making ready to leap when the air all around him suddenly filled with lightning. The Ghost Children screamed, then they started to glow and crackle. Their eyes melted before his own, and their eye sockets turned to holes that were filled with an unnatural fire. Then their hair turned white, and stood on end. The sudden shockwave that followed hit Judas hard, and he was thrown to the floor.

Stranghold hadn't noticed what was going on behind him. He was far too busy chanting and motioning this way and that with his skinny little hand. The Book lay at his feet, and as he got back to his knees, for the first time since he had encountered Stranghold in Ray's flat in Islington, Judas saw a chance to get it, and stop this nightmare from succeeding. He crawled across the floor, being sure to avoid contact with the Ghost Children and the spikes they were impaled upon. He was getting closer – the book was nearly within reach. He shot one arm out, his fingers brushed the leather spine, then he felt a judder, before hearing a boom that rocked the airship.

People standing on the viewing platform of the Shard and sitting in the rooftop gardens of London's pricier drinking holes saw the huge, living spear of lightning issue forth from the dark rain clouds that had just showed up out of the blue. Everything stopped. The lightning was very real now, alive and sentient, and searching for St Paul's Cathedral. It shot across the sky, turning the clouds it touched to vapour.

The fork of the lightning tickled the great dome, and sheets of steel and stone that had stood for centuries exploded, and melted. The full force of the blast was catching up with the light, destined to flatten the building like a crisp packet. The watchers hid their eyes and covered their ears. When the blast hit, it shook London to its foundations. But St Paul's still stood,

Floating in the air between the Zeppelin and the cathedral was Michael the Archangel. In the centre of his breastplate was a black hole that steamed and hissed. One of his wings had taken part of the blast, and there were a few small holes puncturing that, too. His great sword still burned with the energy of the heavens, and the look on his face was frightening to behold.

Stranghold snatched up the book and opened it, barely noticing Judas' presence in the mayhem. He searched frantically for some spell that would defeat the angel, and found one, muttering a few words and tracing a strange shape in the air. The Ghost Children sang once more. This time the lightning was not focused on one building or one place, but began to set off in a hundred different directions.

Michael saw this, and so did Judas. The great angel leapt forwards and flew straight at the airship. He lifted his great sword above his head as he did so, and shouted something. It was not a shout of anger, but something else. He closed with the great airship, and with one murderous great overhead cleave he sliced it open. He'd put all of his strength and skill into the blow, and the fire from his sword searched its way through the ship, burning it from within.

All over London, bolts of lightning still flew towards their targets but none of them hit, because the call that the Archangel Michael had made had been answered by every angel present. They put themselves between the lightning and the buildings, and the people trapped inside them, and many died so that many more mortals would live.

The Zeppelin was now in flames, exploding wherever Michael's sword had struck it, and it was dropping like a great, silken leaf. The water of the Thames would douse its evil flames. The Ghost Children had disappeared. Nothing remained of them. Only Judas and Stranghold were left alive. Judas was hurt badly, one of his arms was broken and bending back the wrong way, he'd lost half of his hair, and there was a deep gash in his side that oozed when he breathed. He staunched the flow with pages from the book with his undamaged arm.

On a nearby spike, Stranghold looked out on the world he had tried to destroy in silence. Judas had caught up with him seconds after Michael had struck. In the confusion, Stranghold had dropped the book, and as he tried to pick it up, Judas had casually lifted him off the ground, pushing him down on to the spike with all of his remaining strength. He had wanted to say something witty to the little man, but the airship was going down, and he wanted to get off before he got wet again.

London was growing in front of his eyes; it seemed as though the buildings all around were getting taller by the second. They were climbing into the sky like abnormally straight concrete weeds – up they went, and through an eye covered in his own blood it looked like they would only stop when they had pierced the clouds and punctured the sky. He was drifting in and out of consciousness, and his mind was performing tricks on him. But the undeniable truth was that he was laying on his back with the book clutched to his chest. It was in his possession once more, and there was no power on Earth that he would allow to take it from him again. It had caused too many problems.

He looked up into the sky again, and realised that the buildings weren't growing upwards, he was just going downwards. He could feel something strange happening to him, though. The light was diminishing. It was getting darker, and a fierce wind was blowing directly into his face.

Before he drifted into the deep sleep of the wounded, he heard a familiar voice telling him that he would be okay. He talked quickly then, knowing that he might not have the chance later, asking a favour of the voice and hoping that he was not too late.

28 A GHOST DIES

Williams watched the string of small brown beads of seaweed float towards him. It never ever made it to the shore. Every time it came just within reach, the sea pulled it back on an invisible cord. He was in a reflective mood. He'd never been in a battle, save for a few skirmishes with the odd football firm at a service station.

Joachim was standing in the opening to the small cave they had retreated to when the fighting between the werewolves and the silver airship had reached its bloody apex. The tide had gone out, and the song of the sea was just a whisper now. Everything was quiet and flat. The birds had flown away, possibly for good, and the rocks had stopped talking in their grating, hollow tones. The battle was over for them. And it had been a battle; a real, proper, no-holds-barred, to the death scrap. They had been there, right in the middle of the action. They had climbed aboard the ship and made it to the top of the craft, and doing everything they could to bring it down, but the ship had flown away, and now their fates were entirely in someone else's hands. Joachim had showed Williams how a ghost was able to kill another ghost before things had gone truly south. It was simple, really; it just required a clear focus, the ability to channel your anger, and the technique to be able to reach inside another ghost's chest and pull its soul out as quickly as possible. Although in this case, there was also a slight additional complication, caused by the other ghost potentially burning your life essence to dust with its lightning bolt-shooting eyes while you were attempting to extinguish its own.

The boy had changed so much since they had first met back in the citadel in the depths of the island. It was impossible to guess or imagine what he'd seen and done since he'd been turned into a ghost, but Williams didn't need to be a Detective to know that it couldn't have been good. During the fighting he caught sight of Joachim pleading and crying with someone he had recognised, whilst ripping their chest open and destroying them at the same time. The boy's mind would be a turbulent place for however long he lived. Williams watched him in silence,

The night fell quickly and Williams, sick of sitting in one sort of darkness, exchanged it for another, with fresher air. The boy followed him, and they sat on the small shingle beach watching the moon rise together.

The sea was impatient, and it fidgeted so that the moon's reflection could not find anywhere to rest.

They sat there together for hours. It must have been close to midnight when Joachim sat up with a start. He'd seen something moving on the horizon. At first, he'd thought it was just another shooting star, but this object did not fly from left to right or vice-versa, it was flying straight towards them. He tapped Williams on the shoulder and pointed at the horizon. They couldn't make out what it was, and then fear, always clever and creative, began to play tricks with their eyes.

Had the silver Zeppelin returned?

Williams looked at the boy, and then they turned and ran for the safety of the cave. They were almost there when Williams felt a downdraft so powerful it whipped up the pebbles on the beach all around him, and blew them away.

Michael landed without making a sound. His huge, armoured frame blocked out the moonlight. Joachim, who had not seen the Archangel before, was afraid, and tried, unsuccessfully, to push himself through the cliff face. Williams, who *had* seen him before, felt like doing the same but instead laid a reassuring arm on the boy's shoulder. Michael did not say a word. He just reached down, took each of them by the hand, and gently lifted them off the ground as though they were feathers. He placed them both on his back, in the space between his wings, turned around to look the moon in the eye, then jumped into its glow.

They had only been in the air for what seemed like

minutes before they were angling down through the clouds and heading for the patchwork quilt of a billion lights that is London at night. Michael landed on the roof of Scotland Yard, and set them both down safely on the gravel in front of the door that led down the stairs and along the corridor to the Black Museum.

"I shall wait for you on the other side," he said, jumping off the edge of the building and disappearing.

Williams walked straight through the closed door; Joachim followed, and was admitted to the secret realms of the Black Museum. Williams took the stairs two at a time and Joachim followed him as quickly as he could. For so many years the boy had dreamed of leaving the island and the Black Sun behind, and now he had escaped that place. He was now free to go wherever he wanted.

Williams made his way down the corridor. The sensors built into the plasterboard panels overhead thought about flickering on automatically, but the sensor just couldn't be sure that there was something in the corridor at all. Williams stopped outside the door to the office he shared with Judas; he felt like he was finally home.

Nothing had changed; everything was where it should be. Williams smiled as he saw his old brown coat hanging on the coat hook by the filing cabinets. He'd hidden his escape letter in the front pocket, and thankfully Judas had found it. The metal cases that lined the walls rattled and twitched, the files inside them were alive, and eager to talk. On one wall hung the familiar giant map of London, with hundreds of blue pins puncturing it, marking the places where many of the Black Museum's stories had been made. East London had its vampires and its ghouls. South London had its witches and Fey folk. West London? Well, anything went out there. It was all so reassuring and familiar that Williams had to tear himself away from the warming sense of the normal when Michael tapped on the window and asked to come inside. The only way that Archangel could get inside was through the special, custom-made windows that the Superintendent had allowed to be fitted – at great expense, of course. Joachim helped Williams to lift the catches, and the window swung outwards. Michael clasped the window frame in one great hand and levered himself in. Once he had removed his scabbard and laid his great sword down on the nearest table he spoke.

"Listen to me now, ghosts. Your Judas is badly wounded, and a decision will be made soon, to either heal him again, or to let him go. But that is not for us to concern ourselves about right now. I have left him somewhere safe, where he will be cared for, and if it is the will of the one who commands me, you will see him again there. For now, I have been tasked with ensuring that you two are safe, and because of your actions, I have been told to tell you that you may ask one thing of me in return; a reward for your service, if you like. Do you understand me?"

Williams sat down, and Joachim followed suit.

"Can you grant me *anything*?" Joachim looked straight at the Archangel for the first time since he had met him. The boy's face was alive with hope, and Williams felt for him. He knew exactly what the boy was going to ask. He also knew that the angel could not bring his parents back.

"Before you ask me, boy, you must understand that there are some things that even I am not allowed to grant. I am God's vengeance, after all." Michael folded his wings back tightly, stared down at Joachim and waited.

"This ghostly form, this fading body, can it ever be whole again? Can I live and breathe and have a life again?"

Michael smiled. It was a small smile, of course, and a very unexpected one at that, but it was still a show of emotion that Williams had never seen before. He bet that Judas had likely never witnessed it, either.

"No, child. I cannot give you back that gift. There is something that I can do for you that will be as near to life as you could wish for, though."

Joachim stood up. Tiny tears that looked like small pips of steam rolled down his cheeks, and Williams had to look away.

"If you cannot bring my parents back, or rewind the clock of ages so that I can take back the years that were stolen from me, then what is left?"

Michael took one giant step forward. He towered over the small boy, but the defiance and anger in Joachim's face lent him such height that he was not afraid.

"Do you wish to fight at my side, Joachim? Do you wish to be able to fly across the void and through the ages of man? Eternal, seeking only to do good and the will of the one who commands me? It is not an easy task, believe me, but if you ever wanted to be a warrior, a true warrior, on the side of all that is right, then cast off those rags and that insignia of evil, and I will show you the far-off lands, the kingdoms of the ancients and the secrets realms."

Joachim reached up to the badge on his lapel. It had always been impossible to remove but this time, when he snatched at it, it came away in his hand easily. He clenched his fist around the small disc and willed it to disappear, but when he turned his hand over and opened it, the badge was still there in his upturned palm. Michael waved his great hand slowly over the small metal disc, and the badge turned to dust right in front of Joachim's eyes.

"There is no real power in the trinkets of the dead and the petty symbols of the dark path, Joachim."

Joachim looked into the lattice of lines that ran across his palm, and began to see the roads that lay ahead for him clearly drawn there. He looked up into the giant angel's eyes, and for the first time in his life, he felt alive. He considered the rest of his uniform. It seemed so comical to him, now. He remembered the first day that he had worn it, how proud he had felt, how strong and grown up and indestructible, even. Nothing could have stood in his way, because his father had told him so. The uniform was the extension of the man; it was the symbol of his faith and the lens through which his soul and his honour would be noted.

On that day, Joachim had swallowed the words greedily and stored them away deep down inside him. He believed that they would nourish him for the rest of his days.

His father had never spoken to him much – perhaps that was the reason that he hung on his every word back then. Here, today, knowing what his Father had allowed to happen to him, and after seeing what the Black Sun had done, he knew that he had made the right decision back there in the cave. He smiled, and ripped open his brown shirt, sending the buttons flying through the air like little drops of confused rain that didn't know whether to fall or fly. He tore off his breeches and threw away the armband that had disgusted and tortured him for so long. Finally, he was naked; his uniform was gone, it lay on the floor like a collection of rags. His clothes and everything that they signified were dead, and he felt pure for the first time.

Michael nodded, and laid one heavy hand on the top of the boy's head.

The air all round them began to crackle with an unseen energy. The boy's hair stood on end, his eyes turned white, then his face took on a look of such calm and peacefulness that for a second he could have been mistaken for a marble sculpture. Williams watched the soldier leave and the little boy inside him return to the world of the living. The decades of darkness that had threatened to consume him were being burned away.

Then a pinpoint of light appeared in the middle of the boy's forehead. It was small, but the beam of light that it projected outwards was so intense that it appeared to cut the room in two. Williams was unable to look at the its brightness directly, and turned away; as soon as he did so, he stepped out of the present moment and into a space without time. He could have been standing there for a second or it could have been a century, he was unsure of where he was, and it was only when he saw the familiar raincoat on the peg and the chair that only squeaked when you spun it anti-clockwise that he relaxed, knowing he was back again.

The boy was gone, and in his place stood something beautiful and terrifying all at the same time. The new Joachim was far taller now, more muscular, and two perfectly formed, symmetrical, white wings flexed from broad, powerful shoulders. Michael looked from him to Williams.

"And you, Williams; what would you have as your reward?"

Williams did not have to think for too long.

"The Black Museum needs a new custodian doesn't it, Michael? Malzo is gone, returned to the City of the Heavens. Judas is wounded, and Joachim here doesn't look like he'd be a good fit for a desk job. I can't go back to my old life, rubbish as it was, and I've seen things that I neither can nor particularly want to forget." He nodded to Joachim's wings. "I'd quite like a pair of those too, if it's not too much to ask?"

"Step forth then, Williams. If we are to add to the ranks of the Host, then we must kill a ghost tonight."

Michael raised his hand once again, then placed it gently down on the top of William's head; the ghost of Williams died – but in a good way.

Later that week, a member of the Neighbourhood Watch in Marylebone reported seeing a white light that shone from Scotland Yard with such intensity that it could have lit up a yard in Scotland. It was so bright that it woke her and her cat 'Frisky Pants' up. She went on to say in her statement to PC Thomas James of the Met, that she also saw three rockets being launched from the roof of the building. They all had wings on them too.

The report was never circulated.

29 CALLEVA

The ancient walled town of Silchester in Hampshire is visited by thousands of tourists each year. They come to walk in the footsteps of the Iron Age tribes that built the settlement and the Romans that moved them out to replace them. The visitors touch the ancient walls and try and feel a connection to the memories locked inside. The majority leave empty-handed. Their digital cameras have done all the remembering for them. Some do maintain that they have seen 'things' moving along the tracks in the twilight and the penumbra. But none are ever really believed, and their sightings are put down to a little over-indulgence on the barley wine. But on Pagan high-days and long forgotten holidays that don't feature on any normal calendar, Silchester occasionally drops her defences and allows 'the knowing ones' to enter the hidden parts of the town.

This secret place is called 'Calleva' and it is a place of learning, ancient lore, and medicine. It is also a hospital for monsters.

Judas woke to find that he was not in fact skewered on a steel spike, with lightning jetting out of every single one of his orifices. Nor was he laying on the seabed, drowning for all time, next to his old friend and enemy John the Baptist. His body was sore. Every single centimetre of it. He could still feel the cold, sharp fire that the ghost children had hit him with. The little man had nearly broken him, too. But it seemed his side had won the day, stopping the miracle weapon from destroying London and destroying the Order of the Black Sun instead. Its banner would never rise again. Once the dust had settled, someone was going to have to go back into those tunnels under Jersey and make sure that there was nothing left behind. That was a job for another time, though. Judas rolled over on his side and drifted off again; the days danced with the nights, and produced weeks of quiet and solitude.

The healers that attended to him went about their business quietly. Although he was aware that they were passing their hands over him, they spoke words that he had absolutely no memory of. He ate well, taking plenty of fruit and vegetables, and drinking the clearest and coldest water he had ever tasted. Unsurprisingly, no 'Get Well Soon' cards arrived.

Judas came to know his room like all patients do. He knew how many stone tiles there were on the floor, how many strips of wood had been used to make the door to his room, and how many sunflowers stood in the garden below. He had a large window on the wall opposite his bed. Through it, he could see that this garden was tended by a large, shadowy figure that never came close enough to the hospital for him to identify properly. The walls of his room were constructed with huge blocks of a material that looked very much like flint, although it could equally have been made from melted down suits of armour. Separating the blocks from each other were row upon row of impossibly straight rivers of white mortar that smelt of old forests and young trees.

He was sitting on the end of his bed, dressed in a linen gown that would not have looked out of place in a Texan death cult, when there was a soft rap at the door.

"Come in," said Judas.

The door opened a few inches, then it was pushed open. Evenor stood in the doorway. She looked around the room, and upon seeing that she was not intruding she stepped in.

"It's good to see you up and about" she said.

"It's good to see you up and alive" replied Judas.

Evenor stood in the centre of the room. The doorway was directly behind her, which meant that Judas did not see Captain Conny of the Gay Hornet until he was by her side.

"It's good to see you too, Captain."

"Our paths were always going to cross again, Detective. I'm just glad that I could bring this young lady to see you when they did. In truth it was the Hornet that found her, really; the ship heard Evenor dreaming as she floated on the waves. She called out to her, and told her to hang on. We got to her just in time."

Judas asked them both to sit, and listened intently to Evenor's story. After she had stepped in front of the spell that Stranghold had intended for Judas, she had been blown straight out of the airship; it was her good fortune that they were still over the sea at the time. The sea held her up, and kept her alive. She felt as though she had let Judas down, though, and she was racked with guilt for days after the battle. Later, the angel had sought her out, and told her where she could find him.

"Stranghold would have succeeded if hadn't been for you. It took all of us and an Archangel to bring him down. So please, Evenor, no guilt."

They spent the rest of the afternoon talking about the angels and the Black Museum, and about the Ghost Fleet and where Evenor and the Gay Hornet were heading. She was heading home first, then she would take to the sea again. And from there, who could know? He thanked her, and when there was nothing left to say she kissed him on the top of the head and left with the Captain, just as quickly as they had arrived. For the remainder of that day and the whole of the next, the room smelt of the sea, and Judas was able to fall asleep to the soft rumblings of the waves.

Judas was feeling well rested and mended. He was told to walk in the gardens, but was also warned by the Healers not to annoy any of the gardeners unless he wanted to be bitten or eaten. So he wandered through the trees and made sure not to tread on any of the plants.

He was sitting comfortably with his back to the trunk of a large tree some days later, combing the grass with the flat of his hand, when he felt, rather than noticed, that something was not quite right. The birds had disappeared, and a handbrake had been applied to the wind. There was something at once both strange and familiar about the sensation. Then a humming started, and he knew who was coming. He stood up, and pressed himself back against the tree. He pushed so hard, he could feel the patterns of the bark through his shirt. The hum got louder, then a noose appeared right in front of his face. It slipped over his head, and the knot tightened.

He tried to pull it off and cry for help, but his windpipe was being crushed. He was jerked off his feet, yanked into the air, and he went home to the branch that held the rope that held the betrayer up for all to see, and for all to hate, for all time. He hung there for days, twisting in the soft breeze; then he passed out, and the world died.

When he woke, he found that he was back in the olive garden again. The town of Silchester and the hospital in Calleva were gone, they were thousands of miles away. The air was warm, and the smell of the olives unlocked memories that he had filed away long ago. He looked down, expecting to see his guts and entrails still decorating the ground underneath him. But there was nothing there. The ground was smooth and dry, the rain had not yet come. Judas hung there, wondering why he was alive.

This was the moment he had been hoping for – the chance to die knowing that he had done the right thing and been a good man after all. He had paid his debt in full, and now it was time to go wherever it is that decent souls go. They certainly didn't go to slave pits in Colliers Wood, that's for sure. Judas wondered what would become of Williams and Jack the Ripper and Dick Turpin and the rest of them. But that was someone else's problem now, because he was on his way.

Then the sky filled with rain, just as it had done before, and the lightning appeared in the sky like fractals in slow motion. The green and brown leaves started to swirl, and the air shattered into a million pieces.

Light flooded through his eyelids, as if the most intense white flare had just exploded an inch from his face. His eye sockets started to hurt. The pain scampered around inside his head like panicked bees. Water in his mouth pushed his tongue forwards and made his lips feel heavy and swollen. Black and white squares made sheets of geometrically perfect patterns in his mind's eye, and he felt like someone was pushing their thumbs into his pupils, forcing them wider to accept more light. He felt like his thoughts were being forced into the mists of some far off and forgotten time. Then suddenly the pain was switched off; he opened his eyes and saw an outline drawn in the heavens with stars and his heart stopped beating, again.

He felt odd. He felt heavy and his extremities were numb. He was ascending now. Spinning slowly, falling further and further upwards. His hair was streaming out in all directions, and his scar was pulsing and beating ten to the dozen. Then he stopped. There was no gradual reduction in speed, his sudden arrest defied all the laws of earthly physics. But, he was no longer anywhere near the earth or any of its stars. He was far away, between time and the conventions of reality. Cold flooded across his inert body, and he waited.

He must have slept or passed out, because the voice shocked him, jump-starting his heart once again. The words the voice uttered were big, stampeding, savage words that said far too much for a mere mortal to understand all at once. They punched and bludgeoned him like construction site wrecking balls, over and over again. They entered through his ears and eyes, and blew him up like a human balloon, forcing the air back into his lungs.

The voice told Judas of his past and of his future. Judas began to cry, because he had wanted to hear these words for such a long time and now here they were, falling on ears that were wide open and hungry. But there was no full stop at the end of the final sentence. There was no forgiveness, yet. His road stretched on ahead. It led onwards, into fire and fury.

Judas heard the words come to an end, and the

silence engulfed him. The form that filled the horizon and crackled with universal energy faded and disappeared. He stopped crying and looked into the void that was left before him, leaping into it and screaming all the way down. In a moment of lucidity, he understood how Lucifer had felt when the Morningstar had been cast out and thrown down.

God had told him to wait until His other child sought him out. Jesus had a brother or a sister out there, and Judas had to wait until that person appeared to know whether or not his punishment would go on. He didn't know whether redemption or revenge would follow.

30 THE LEY LINE EXPRESS

Judas sat in his first-class compartment on the Ley Line Express and moved a piece of lemon around his gin and tonic with a very smart silver stirrer. Even the bubbles in the tonic were acting professionally, taking it in turns to pop and fizz. The carpet in the compartment was thicker than any of the rugs Judas had at home, and he had spent a lot of time and money choosing those floor coverings. He had his own W.C. and shower, a pull-down double bed, and a brass panel with at least 20 buttons on it that enabled him to order any food he wanted, reserve a table for dinner, or simply to annoy one of the hard-working train staff who had pulled the night shift. The train had been scheduled to leave the station at Winchester Under at 13.00hrs exactly, but it had departed at 13.25hrs. Judas was in no hurry, though. He had placed his leather weekend bag in the compartment overhead and settled down to read the newspaper. He took his silver coin from his pocket and rubbed it gently between forefinger and thumb. His thoughts had been jumbled and anarchic of late, but now they were orderly and serene. He had time to drift, and to lose himself in the world. The Order of the Black Sun was no more. London had been spared, and he was alive and mostly free.

He was still DCI Judas Iscariot of the Black Museum Occult Division of Scotland Yard. He was still immortal, and he could still call on a certain muscular angel and his new sidekick whenever the chips were down. Back to business as unusual.

"You'll know that you will have reached the end, when it is the end of all things, Judas," the Almighty had said.

Judas smiled and rubbed at the face of the coin even harder than usual.

His reward for services rendered by the Chief Superintendent had been a short break from London; some time away from the trials and terrible occurrences of the Underworld below the Underground. This was it. Ten days of leafy green countryside, and small towns with no Vampires or Witches to contend with. The Black Museum was in safe hands, and the Clapham Saints had agreed to keep an eye on South London for him. Apparently there was another, very different organisation in North London, who looked after their patch. They had been contacted, and had agreed to keep a watch over their side of the river, too.

This was just the rest Judas needed. He put the silver coin back in his pocket, laid his head back against his well-padded seat, and started to doze off. The smooth, rhythmic bump of the tracks sang to him in soft tones of miles travelled, and he was soon asleep. The train had departed later than scheduled, and the driver and the rest of the onboard staff were eager to make up time, upholding the honour and prestige of the Ley Line Express.

Judas slept soundly as the train wound its way through the rolling hills and downs that had once upon a time welcomed the people from across the sea and become home to the tribes of the forgotten ones. It followed the paths of uncrossable streams, and disappeared into deep unknown tunnels, hewn from the rock in ages past by the old giants. The Ley Line Express travelled along ancient Albion's power lines, and called at the country's 'Mirror Stations', which is why the station at Winchester they had left hours earlier was actually 'Winchester Under' if you were travelling this way. These 'Mirror Stations' were used by the magical creature and entities that preferred to travel through the land using the old paths and ways.

Judas woke, poured himself another G&T, and kicked off his brown leather Trickers brogues; he picked up a book from the marble topped table at his elbow and started reading.

In his peaceful bubble of calm and contentment, Judas stretched his arms and back, and decided to stretch his legs, too. He opened the sliding door to his compartment, and stepped out into the corridor. The thick carpet underfoot gave ever so slightly, and he heard a soft click as the door crept back into place behind him. Night had fallen while he slept, and the lights inside the train had come on. The dining compartment was located towards the rear of the train and Judas had been warned by his stomach that it needed filling already with two hungry rumbles. He passed through three carriages, nodding politely to other passengers whenever he caught their eye, or they caught his.

The dining car was practically empty. The waiter, a lower order angel, was very attentive and took his order quickly. The meal was incredible, the wine was even better, and the relative silence and lack of disturbance made him feel very happy indeed. The coffee was served with a selection of mints in a variety of coloured foils, and milk in a porcelain jug designed to look like a small white milk churn. He poured its contents into his coffee cup, and watched as the small white stream of cow juice slowly spiralled inwards to the centre of the dark liquid. The dining cabin filled up around him. The noise began to rise. More angels appeared in the train's livery, serving dishes and collecting glasses. Everyone aboard seemed happy, and Judas found it hard not to notice the small crimes that they couldn't help committing. One couple was trying hard not to be noticed; both parties kept covering one hand with the other as nerves and guilt kept prompting them to cover the space where their wedding rings should be. They were having an affair, and the Wood Sprite that sat across from them was keeping a record of their movements. The Sprite was clearly a private detective, and a very good one at that, because the naughty couple hadn't noticed him.

Three tables down on the right, directly in Judas' eyeline, sat a beautiful woman. She kept checking that the small leather pouch she wore around her neck was still exactly where it had been five minutes before. Judas didn't need to guess at its contents. Inside that pouch were the secrets of forests, hedgerows and fields, and all of the spells that the witch had learned from her teacher. The locking twine that had been tied around the neck of the pouch gave it away. She was in no danger, though. Anyone or anything that tried to separate the witch from her spells would wind up longing for the return of its hands, memory, eyes, or all three.

Here was life. Some of it was good, and some of it was bad. When he got back to London he was sure that there would be plenty of the bad for him to investigate.

THE CHILDREN OF THE LIGHTNING

If you've enjoyed this book please do consider leaving a brief review of it on the Amazon website. Even a few positive words make a huge difference to independent authors like me, so I'd be both delighted and grateful if you were to share your appreciation.

Many thanks, Martin